Red Sky

Red Sky

A Michael Tanner and Mary Whitney Mystery

Carl Brookins

Brookins Books

1

"Wow. Look at that sky, will you!" Michael Tanner raised a hand in the soft morning sea haze to shade his eyes against the warm brightening light. Great streaming expanses of pink-tinged clouds poured toward him pulling long ragged tails. They extended from the horizon in white and flaming yellow streaks as though flung against the sky by an angry God. Bronze and orange flames flared and dropped from the thin cloud bank that lay against the edge of the horizon where sky and ocean met. It was as if the whole eastern sky was ablaze. The streamers shifted and the distant light flickered.

A nearly naked Mary Whitney scampered to the cockpit to see what her companion was exclaiming over. Tanner was standing on the cabin roof beside the mast above her, one hand lightly resting on the boom of the sailboat. He shifted his gaze to admire the way the morning light lent a fiery glow to the outlines of her body. She stretched and smiled as the sun rose above the cloud line and molded more of its warming light to her curves. She turned and smiled again, this time directly at her husband.

"Nice morning, don't you think? I slept the sleep of the just, which is unusual for the first night out." She stretched again and yawned. "Unfamiliar boat and all."

"Nice morning indeed, and do you remember that old sailor's rhyme?"

"Which one is that? Oh yes, 'Red sky at night, sailors delight, red sky in the morning, sailors take warning.' Is that the one?"

"That's it. What's your pleasure? Shall we breakfast before getting under way?"

"I'm in favor of that, I think," Mary said. "It's calm, I can have a swim while you make us Bloody Marys and then we'll get under way." She unhooked the gate in the safety lines at the side of the cockpit and winked at Tanner. Then in a single lithe motion she dropped her silk panties, the only garment she was wearing at the moment, and dove cleanly over the side of their sailboat into the warm Caribbean Sea. She made hardly a splash slicing into the water.

Tanner grinned, breathed deeply and considered again how fortunate a man he was. He watched her progress as Mary gracefully swam a full circle around their chartered Beneteau. He had no intention of going below while she was alone in the water, even if they were securely anchored in this calm and protected cove on the southeast side of Ginger Island.

"This is great," she shouted. "You better come in here." She treaded water, one hand resting on the gunwale of the dinghy floating at the stern of the sloop. Then she started another circuit, slower, this time, backstroking rhythmically along.

Tanner grinned, admiring the way the clear water caressed Mary's naked body. He dropped below, grabbed a big soft beach towel from the counter beside the companionway and shed his shorts. Without a pause he stepped out of his shoes and stormed back up the ladder topside. He dropped the towel and cannonballed into the water a few feet from Mary with a great holler and an even greater splash.

"Whoee! You are so right." Tanner surfaced with a rush. "This is really a paradise. How come we've never done this before?"

Mary laughed and swam closer. She treaded water again and slid her arms around his neck. His hands touched her slick sides and slid to her waist, drawing her closer into an intimate embrace. She kissed him, three quick pecks on cheek and chin, feeling his body sliding along the length of her. Then she hooked her heels around his calves and pressed her body completely against him, trapping his legs. When they both stopped treading water they slid smiling, beneath the serene surface. Tanner barely had time to grab a breath before the water rose over his head. A moment later he opened his eyes to see Mary smirking at him through bubbles rising from her mouth as she pursed her lips. Her auburn hair floated around and above her head as together they sank deeper. She flexed her hips against him, freed his legs and shoved away toward the surface.

Tanner felt the hunger building urgently in his lungs for fresh air and he stroked hard for the surface. His head broke free and he sucked in a big breath. When his vision cleared he saw Mary grabbing the rails of the swim ladder hooked to the side of their yacht. He stopped swimming briefly to admire the swell of her hips switching side to side as she pulled herself up the ladder. When Tanner clambered aboard she tossed him a towel. He wiped himself down and dropped to the galley to build a pair of tall Bloody Marys. Breakfast followed and soon their sloop, *Passions Messenger*, was creaming through the building waves against the constant trade winds that blew all the way across the south Atlantic from Africa. The peaceful anchorage and their passion of the previous night was already a fading memory. The big Beneteau slid through the waves, racing the couple toward their next planned anchorage. Mary stood at the wheel, comparing the feel of the boat with her own Hunter, now resting securely on the hard at a shipyard in upper Puget Sound where it was suffering through an extensive refit.

"Trim that jib, Michael," she called, adjusting their course slightly to spill a little more wind from the straining sails. "I don't understand why neither of us has ever been down here before. This is great sailing! And the other benefits." She grinned wickedly at her husband, her meaning clear. She shook out her hair, already almost dry in the sun and wind. She glanced around, scanning her horizon. Several white sails were visible at a distance this fine June day, but the seaway wasn't crowded. They'd deliberately chosen summer for their first trip to the

Caribbean to, avoid the huge cruising crowds of the high season.

Hours later Tanner maneuvered the sloop into position directly downwind from a big plastic buoy bobbing in the restless water. At the bow, leaning precariously over the water and swinging a boat hook, Mary Whitney pointed down at her target. She waggled the hook, reaching for the thick loop that protruded from the top of the buoy. "Ahead," she hollered, voice almost lost in the space below the prow. Tanner nudged the throttle trying to get closer slowly enough so Mary could snag the mooring buoy. The boat lost way and began to drift back and to one side.

"Rats! I'm not gonna reach it. My arm isn't long enough. You come and try. Just swing it aboard as we go by." Tanner let the boat fall off the wind and began to drive the sloop in a sweeping circle. Mary swung herself back inside the safety line and carried the boat hook to the stern. Tanner smiled and took the shaft as they changed places. He shook his head and went to the bow.

"I'm going to take the buoy on the port side. Be ready." She spun the wheel, nudged the throttle and drove the boat toward the target. As they slid by, pushing the buoy to one side, Tanner leaned over the safety line and hooked on, using the momentum of the sloop to help him swing it aboard. With deft movements he coupled a pigtail from the anchor line to the buoy and dropped the whole rig back over the side. Mary reversed the propeller for a moment and then killed the engine.

Except for the sound of small waves sloshing against the hull, it was quiet. They had chosen an anchorage closest to the huge rock cliff just past the entrance to the cove. Outside the cove, the almost cease-less trades sent big rollers across the mouth. The crashing surf could be heard as a pulsing, rhythmic roar that could stir one's passion. The path through the coral reef had been the trickiest of all the Virgins, accord-ing to their charts, and it gave them the advantage of privacy. Only the most experienced would choose to join them, preferring the group of anchoring positions in the larger cove of Ginger Island where boats had a straight-in approach. There were already four boats at anchor there and Tanner and Mary could hear the faint sound of music from deck-level speakers and shouts of participants on the boats who appeared to be well-acquainted.

"I'm ready for a G & T, how about you?" asked Tanner.

"Umm, not just yet. I'm going to slather on some more sun screen and take my ease on the foredeck for a while. I'll make due with a bottle of water, if you don't mind." Mary took her little mesh bag of tubes and the water Tanner handed her through the forward hatch. She put down the small futon and looked over the quiet anchorage. Her tee-shirt came off quickly and she stripped to her ruby thong, then laid back, totally relaxed. She slathered on sun screen, stretched out and her eyes soon closed as her pulse flattened. In the aft cockpit, Tanner sipped a drink and likewise drowsed in the afternoon heat. The trade winds blew ceaselessly around the cliff, and rocked them gently in nature's embrace. It was a perfect afternoon end to an exhilarating sail that day.

2

The sun had barely cleared the swaying palms on nearby Ginger Island when Tanner was awakened by the sound of a splash and a fine spray of water on his face. He quickly determined that the source of the noise and of the water was the open porthole next to where his head lay on the pillow.

"Hey," he grumbled. "I'll have you pumping the bilge by hand, you keep that up."

"Up, up! Sleepyhead" Mary called. 'It's another beautiful day and you're wasting it in that bunk."

Mary heard Tanner's answer, he firmly shut the porthole against a repeat of the artificial wave. Then she heard him gallop the entire length of the boat from the forward cabin, up the ladder and out over the stern in a long flat dive into the warm and placid Caribbean Sea. He narrowly missed the dinghy that was tied off the stern. Mary smiled at his antics, treading water near the boarding ladder. She noted with a smile of approval that her husband hadn't taken the time to don swimming trunks before he dove over the side. She grinned and turned toward him at the stern. But Tanner surfaced, threw the water out of his eyes and began a distance-eating crawl around the stern away from her. Mary stopped. She knew she could never catch him. She swam back to the boarding ladder, content to wait for his return along the port side of their boat to where she waited.

He didn't turn up when she thought he should have. Minutes passed. She listened and couldn't hear the sounds of him swimming toward her. After another minute she began to ease her way along the port side, listening intently. Her concern grew.

"Michael?" She called. "Are you all right?"

"Hang on." His voice from close by at the bow startled her. "I'm here." Almost at the same instant Tanner's head appeared beside the anchor chain where it clove the surface. He was holding on with his left hand and slowly treading water. He stared at something in his other hand. Mary swam nearer.

"What have you got there?" she asked.

"Money. Currency, bills."

"A windfall perhaps?" Intrigued, she swam to her husband and grasped the anchor chain beside him. He handed her a damp bill. She looked at it and her eyes widened. "Wow, this would buy a few drinks at the Soggy Dollar Bar, wouldn't it?"

"I'll say. Hundred dollar bills don't turn up very often anywhere, I'll wager."

Mary said, "You would, huh? Wager, I mean. Where did this come from?"

"These, my dear. The proper question is where did these come from?" Tanner swung his right leg up in the water until his foot rested in the crook of her elbow. Clenched between his toes were two more dripping hundreds. Mary plucked them out.

"Goodness, three hundred dollars. Are there more? Maybe we can pay for our vacation this way."

"I only found these three floating submerged just below the surface. They were right over there, between the boat and the shore. That is, the cliff." He pointed.

Mary glanced at the cliff, twenty yards away. It was an ordinary looking cliff of black rock, not smooth, but with no evident cracks or caves. In fact there were only a few hardy lichen growths. Overhead a brown pelican squawked once as it soared by on outstretched wings.

"Where do you suppose they came from? Buried treasure? This isn't Treasure Island, is it?"

"Nope, that's farther west." He was referring to Norman Island, popularly thought to have been the model for Robert Louis Stevenson's tale of pirates and treasure by the same name. No actual treasure had ever been found there.

"I don't see any caves on that cliff face that might hold pirate treasure. Besides, I doubt these bills had been printed in Blackbeard's time."

Tanner had been looking out into the wider cove and then he looked at Mary and said, "I think we ought to get aboard and get dressed."

The couple swam to the boarding ladder near the stern and climbed up and into the cockpit. A bit of unfortunate timing put them both naked on the ladder, Mary above Tanner, just as a large ketch was leaving the cove. A long hoot from the ketch, together with faint whistles and applause, acknowledged they'd been noticed and appreciated.

Tanner took the three wet hundreds and placed them between the folds of a towel on the galley counter and then hurriedly dressed.

Mary handed Tanner a cup of hot coffee as they passed each other between their forward cabin and the galley. She joined him in the cockpit a few minutes later, her hair tightly wrapped in a big fluffy towel. "So what do you think? And what do we do with the money?"

"I don't know. Maybe we should just forget about it."

"We could throw it back," Mary said. "Then just erase the whole incident from our memories."

"Yes, or we could just consider it a nice windfall and stick it in our wallets and spend it somewhere."

"Hmm, or we could call the authorities," said Mary.

Tanner grimaced. "That'll ruin our vacation for sure. We'll be stuck for hours trying to answer a bunch of questions and in the end there won't be any answers. Let's face it, if somebody dropped the bills and they even discovered it already, they've probably just written them off as gone."

The pair took their coffee to the cockpit where Mary unwrapped the towel from her head and said, "How about we just set the money aside and tell the authorities when we get to Road Town, if we decide that's the best idea."

"Good. We'll think about it for the day. I don't really believe we should keep the money without saying anything to somebody," Tanner agreed, "so if we wait until we get back to Tortola at the end of this trip we won't screw up our vacation. We can explain to the authorities exactly where we found the bills and if it turns out there's something about them that's special, we'll be out of it."

Mary stopped rubbing her hair with the towel and looked at Tanner. "Do you suppose they could be counterfeit?"

"That had occurred to me. If they are, that's a really good reason to dump them in the lap of authority, sooner rather than later."

"We can't claim to be anonymous," Mary said. "All manner of boat crews, and there goes another one." She waved to the fat Morgan Offshore that went slowly by, the crew leisurely working her sails up the mast. "All manner of boats have gone by and some of them have noticed us enough to remember *Passions Messenger* if asked." A woman at the stern of the Morgan waved back.

"So it looks like we better report this find. And soon."

Mary rose and started down the companion ladder to the cabin. "Listen, bud, I agree we need to report that we found the bills when we were here at anchor, but I don't believe there's any rush. I'll bring a chart and we'll plot our course for the next planned landfall."

Tanner agreed and turned to sorting out their routine to get under way. He untied the roller-furled jib lines and rearranged the main, taking out the reef points they'd tied in the day before when they'd still been less than fully comfortable with their charter in a blow.

Mary reappeared with a rolled up navigation chart in one hand and a cup of strong Arabica coffee in her other hand. Tanner stepped down from the foredeck and reached for the chart. Simultaneously Mary extended the coffee to him. They smiled at each other. He took the coffee and she sat down and unrolled the chart.

"Lots of smiling on this boat, have you noticed?" he said.

Nodding Mary pointed. "Look, here we are. The trade winds are constantly from the East in this region."

Tanner nodded. "O.K., what about the currents?"

Mary looked at him. "Oh, you're wondering where those bills might have come from, right?'

"Something like that," he admitted. "I've been thinking about it. There are a couple of possibilities. First, this could be just a purely innocent circumstance. Somebody dropped three hundreds into the water by mistake."

"But you don't think so."

"No," Tanner said. "Put it down to my naturally cynical nature, if you want, but...."

"Did you look really closely at those bills?" Mary interrupted.

"I guess not."

"I just did. Their serial numbers aren't sequential."

"And they aren't brand new bills. Curioser and curioser. It might mean the money is from a bank vault. Maybe from a robbery?"

"Let's think about that later. Right now I have the feeling we'll be more comfortable if we leave the scene of whatever this is behind us."

"Okay. I've got the engine, you get the anchor and we'll split."

It took longer than they hoped. Mary Whitney, an experienced deepwater sailor who grew up aboard sailboats in the Northwest United States, realized faster than her less experienced husband that now that it was morning, the twisting path through the coral heads to get to this anchorage was lit by the sun from a vastly different angle than when they had made their cautious late afternoon passage to their chosen spot. To return safely to open water and avoid hitting or going aground on the submerged coral heads required careful and deliberate maneuvering of their boat to leave the small protected cove.

Finally they made the last turn away from the island and sailed right into a covey of power boats intent on making their way to the principal anchorage on Ginger Island. Tanner waved to several skippers as they passed while he raised the mainsail. "So much for getting out of there unnoticed except by a few," he called to his comely skipper who was concentrating on coming around to head away from the island and directly into the Sir Francis Drake channel. The main slid smartly up the mast, bellied out and the sloop leaned from the wind pressure, surging ahead. For a brief time the couple paid all their attention to serving the needs of their boat and thoughts of hundred dollar bills and dealing with the authorities fled. Sun, sea and wind occupied the totality of their existence. For the time being.

3

Late that same afternoon the forty-two foot Beneteau *Passions Messenger* slipped through the narrow entrance to Gorda Sound. Tanner and Mary had bypassed the obvious choices of turning north to the commercial and residential community of Road Town, or to Maya Cove, where they'd chartered their boat. Instead, with hardly any conversation, they'd elected to continue their planned sail to The Bitter End, a resort community at the southern side of Gorda Sound on the east end of Virgin Gorda. Reporting the finding of the three hundred dollars would wait until it was a more convenient time for them.

"I'm ready with the anchor," called Mary. She'd loosened the ties that secured the anchor to its cradle at the bow and was holding the control for the electric windlass in her right hand. They'd already dropped the main and furled the jib coming through the entrance to the sound between jagged Colquhoun Reef just off Mosquito Island and Prickly Pear Island on their left side. The water was calm and the winds had subsided a little as they passed into the protection of the small islands that sheltered the sound from open water.

"Let's take it closer to the resort. That way we'll have less fuss getting in and out from the gas dock."

Mary nodded her assent and sat down on the foredeck, content to relax for a few minutes more. But now her thoughts turned again to the bank notes lying under a towel in the galley below. Dammit, she thought. *That money is going to be a complication. I just know it.*

Behind her, Tanner leaned over and picked up his favorite pair of binoculars. They were too powerful to be of much use on a rocking sailboat in a turbulent seaway, but at times like this, they came in handy. Hooking one foot in the steering wheel, he twisted and stared through the glasses back toward the entrance to the sound, now half a mile distant. He was looking north and the sun reflecting off the water made it difficult to tell for sure, but then he saw the long dark shape of a boat. The shape seemed to tease him, slipping in and out of the sparkling reflections. It was the same power boat, he was sure of it.

He'd made no mention of it to Mary, but he'd been aware of the vessel that seemed to be shadowing them. It had been there almost all day and now he was more sure than ever. They were being watched. But why? In such a peaceful and benign setting, why would another craft follow them to the Bitter End? The other craft, a power launch, was maintaining its distance. There was nothing threatening about any of its actions and Tanner admitted to himself that he might be overly sensitive to the boat's presence since he had found the money floating just under the surface beside their boat at Ginger Island, but it just didn't seem right. The other could easily have overtaken them as other powered craft had done, but this one hung back, a couple of miles distant, throughout the long hot and windy day. Elusive, almost a wraith, the power boat cut occasionally through the distant flickering horizon only to reappear again. He had to tell Mary but maybe he'd wait until they'd gone to dinner ashore.

His ruminations were abruptly terminated when Mary called "Yo, Captain. My Captain!"

He glanced forward. He'd gone a few points off course, aiming closer to Gnat Point in the moments he'd seen their shadow and been thinking about the implications. Correcting his track, he glanced at Mary who was staring at him.

"You all right?" she asked.

"Yes, sure. You betcha. Stand by to drop anchor."

Crisply Tanner maneuvered them into their chosen spot. The anchor went down and it grabbed immediately. He shut down the engine and had a quick look at the cruising guide, a manual that provided a wealth of information about the islands, anchorages and other useful information for chartering boaters in the Virgin Islands. Unlike Sir Francis Drake who'd had to rely on the sharp eyes of his crew, careful reconnoitering and years of experience reading water color, shorelines and weather, as he explored uncharted regions of the world, charterers in these islands had the benefit of many people's experiences and detailed marine charts, beginning with those of Sir Francis himself.

"I say we go ashore and find a bar," said Mary. "There'll be somebody around to ask about fuel, fresh water and off-loading our garbage."

"Works for me," Tanner agreed.

A few minutes later Mary shipped the oars and they grounded on the hot sand. They dragged their dinghy to the long narrow dock and tied it off. The resort had a large number of tables shaded by big parasol-like umbrellas scattered around the flagstone patio. It was hot in the tropical sun, but the almost constant breeze ameliorated the temperature somewhat and kept pesky flies that inhabited the islands from becoming too intrusive. The temperature was in the mid-eighties and the humidity was high enough that there seemed to be a perpetual haze in the air over the islands. Both Tanner and Mary were dressed in Island Casual; loose knee-length shorts, deck shoes with no socks, loose light-weight cotton shirts and lots of sun screen on exposed skin.

Mary led the way to a table shaded by a fully extended umbrella. A slim young waiter appeared and took their orders. "I guess we should call the island police," Mary said softly, squinting up at Tanner.

Tanner fished money from his pocket as he watched the waiter return. He paid the boy, sat and smiled. He sipped his gin and tonic. "I've pretty much come to the same conclusion. I didn't say anything earlier because I thought you preferred to leave it to the end of our trip."

"I had, mostly because I sensed your reluctance to get engaged with island bureaucracy. But since we're of common mind, as they say, I'll go inside to the desk and see what I can find out," said Mary.

"I found the damn money, would you rather I did it?" Tanner said.

Mary sighed, smiled and started to shake her head. For a second she hesitated and Tanner saw a shadow pass across her face. It was, he knew, a fleeting reaction to the trauma of her kidnapping and abuse by her ex-husband the previous year on Lake Superior, as well as its horrifying aftermath. The doctors had warned them that certain kinds of stress might trigger recollections of that experience. They'd also said that for Mary, it probably wouldn't take much to trigger a reaction.

Mary shrugged and reached for her glass. Tanner stretched across the little table and squeezed her fingers as he rose. He walked through the slanting sun to the entrance to the resort office, sorting through his mind possible approaches. He decided on a minimalist position.

Inside the cool dim room he strolled to the desk and smiled at the woman standing there. She was rapidly entering data on her computer, fingers flying over the keyboard. "Excuse me," he said. "I wonder if you can tell me how to reach someone in authority in your local police force."

She looked up. "Is there a problem, sir?"

"Not at all. I'm doing some research and I'd like to ask a policeman some questions."

If she thought it odd that this lanky American wanted to speak with an island policeman, her smooth expression gave no hint. "There is the main station in Road Town, of course, and a patrol boat comes by occasionally. There is also the Coast Guard and we do have an island constable. But he is sometimes difficult to locate. I will get some numbers for you." She shrugged as if this were a normal circumstance.

Tanner nodded his understanding. "Thank you. I assume I can just call for the information I want. Whom do I talk to about topping up our water and fuel?"

"I will have our service get in touch. The name of your boat, please?"

Tanner gave her the necessary information and then he strolled into the adjoining small barroom to replenish his Boodles and tonic. The native bartender gave him a friendly wave and walked toward him, breaking off a murmured conversation with the only other person in the place a large, casually dressed, white man in rumpled sun-bleached slacks, the ubiquitous island sandals and a loud, loose, short-sleeved shirt. He held a tall amber drink that looked a lot like dark rum of some kind with ice cubes floating in the liquid, and a twist on the rim. He gave Tanner a friendly wave. Tanner returned the wave and asked for a gin and tonic, specifying Boodles Gin.

He rested his elbow on the bar and watched the barman's practiced moves as he skillfully built the drink and placed it gently on a napkin before him. Tanner took a sip and nodded. There was a touch on his arm and the woman from the front desk was there.

"Excuse me, Mr. Tanner? Here is the number for the British Consulate, as well as for the constable in Spanish City. You can reach the Coast Guard on your radio."

"Thank you." Tanner pocketed the slip of paper and turned back to his drink. A moment passed and he felt a presence at his side. A hand slid forward and placed a white card embossed with black lettering and in one corner, the crest of something called British Criminal Investigation Division. Tanner stared at the card, then slowly turned his head to look at the large sandy-haired man who had been lounging at the other end of the bar, apparently without a concern in the world.

"Excuse me," Tanner said quietly. "Is there something I can do for you?"

"I think it's more likely the reverse," said the other man. "I am always intrigued when one of you chaps comes in and asks for our local constabulary. "What's the difficulty? Did someone violate the rules of the road out there?"

Tanner looked the man straight in the eye. In spite of his light tone and the frivolous nature of his query, there was little doubt the man was serious. "I'm afraid it's more than that. I'm in a bit of a quandary."

"Well young man, Her Majesty's Government is always interested in helping people, especially visitors who find themselves in quandaries.

I have a certain influence in official circles. Perhaps I can be of some assistance?"

Tanner hesitated, then he mentally shrugged. "Maybe you should come and meet my wife." Together they went back into the lobby and headed toward the door. A burly white man in grimy yachting garb, brushed abruptly by them. Tanner and his new companion stepped into the heat. They walked to the table occupied by the lone woman sitting relaxed, her legs crossed at the ankles beneath her table, staring out to sea. The gentle breeze off the water ruffled her auburn hair. There was a tall frosty drink glass within reach of her slender fingers. She looked up at the two men as they approached.

"Mary, this is a man I met in the bar. He's with…"

"Ian McGwean, ma'am, with the British Government. I'm so very pleased to make your acquaintance. May I have the pleasure of your name?" He leaned forward in a way that might have been a formal bow, had he been more elegantly dressed. He offered Mary his hand.

Mary took off her dark glasses and responded by offering her own hand. "Won't you sit down? I'm Mary Whitney." McGwean slid into a chair beside her before relinquishing her fingers. He looked at Tanner who stood across from McGwean. "I don't believe I caught your name, sir."

"It's Tanner. Michael Tanner. From Seattle."

McGwean turned his head. "Whitney? Hmm, I say, are you related to Lord Whitney, by chance?"

"Excuse me? Lord Whitney, did you say? I believe we are of English heritage, but there is nothing of which I am aware to suggest we're related to any Lord, past or present Whitney. We hail from the state of Washington. Seattle, to be specific." She smiled and reached out to her husband, and drew him into the chair on her right. "Is Lord Whitney an important individual in the UK?"

McGwean shrugged elaborately. "I'd rather talk about your…quandary…if you don't mind." He offered her a business card. Mary glanced at it and then at Tanner. Her expression was unreadable.

"He overheard me getting some phone numbers from the woman at the reception desk," Tanner explained squinting into the sun. McGwean had seated himself with the setting sun at his back.

"Anyone can acquire a business card. Do you have other identification, Mr. McGwean?" Mary demanded, although in a most pleasant tone of voice.

"I do, but please, let's keep this as confidential as possible. If you don't mind." Tanner frowned and Mary leveled a piercing look at the man. He reached into his pocket and produced a scuffed leather case. He didn't exactly look around to see if anybody was paying attention, but Tanner had the feeling McGwean knew who was where on that sandy strip of land.

Inside he revealed an embossed card that identified Ian McGwean as an investigator employed by the British Criminal Investigation Division. Mary looked at it closely.

"Are you working undercover, Mr. McGwean?"

McGwean looked for a long silent minute into Mary's face. Apparently, thought Tanner, he was satisfied by what he saw there because he said, "Not exactly. On the other hand we're not advertising my presence here in the islands. I'll trust you to keep my little confidence." He hesitated and then went on, "I'm working on a complex case. I can't go into detail, of course. I had a hunch when I heard your Mr. Tanner here inquiring about contacting local law enforcement. I often follow my hunches. That sometimes puts me at odds with my superiors in the Home Office. It is, in fact, one of the reasons I'm here in this sailing paradise, even though I have little experience or interest in the sea faring life.

"Of course, there may be no connection whatsoever between your, er, quandary and my inquiry. I won't know whether there is until you explain your interest in contacting local law enforcement." McGwean smiled disarmingly and spread his hands. "Even should there be no connection, if I can be of assistance, I'd be happy to oblige."

Tanner said, "Would you mind showing me your credentials again?"

McGwean shrugged and fished his wallet from a hip pocket. This time, instead of showing it to Tanner and Mary, he handed it over. Tanner looked at the identification card carefully. He ran a finger over its surface. As near as he could tell, it was either legitimate or a very sophisticated forgery. "Okay, Mr. McGwean, here's our story. We were anchored overnight at Ginger Island. While swimming early this morning I chanced to find some US currency floating near our boat. Specifically, I found three hundred dollar bills."

McGwean's eyebrows shot up. "Nothing else, just the bills? No packaging or bank bands or anything? Just the three bills?

"That's correct."

"Did you examine them? Are they real d'you think?"

"Yes, I did look at them but I don't have any expertise in counterfeit money," Tanner said. "They seemed real. Nothing stood out that would say otherwise. But I didn't examine them closely. What would I look for?"

"I wonder if you'd allow me to examine these bills?" McGwean looked back and forth between Mary and Tanner. The couple glanced at each other. In spite of the man's identification cards, they really didn't have much basis on which to trust McGwean. On the other hand, what could happen? He was a charming, smiling man. There were two of them, there didn't seem to be any reason not to show him the money.

"They're on our boat. We'll take you aboard, if you'll come." So saying, Mary rose and took McGwean's arm. The trio strolled to the end of the dock and boarded *Passion Messenger*'s dinghy. Three was just about the limit for the tiny inflatable and the waves lapped at the top of the gunwales, McGwean seemed a little tense seated on one of the thwarts in the small dinghy. As they reached their yacht, resting quietly at anchor, a larger red dinghy propelled by a small outboard motor puttered by on the opposite side of their hull, headed into the wider harbor. McGwean, in spite of his professed ignorance of sailing, went up the ladder with agility and bounced into the cockpit. When Tanner arrived on deck behind Mary, McGwean was standing easily, hands on hips eyeballing the sloop.

"Very nice," he said. His eyes roamed over the bagged sails lashed to the rails, the lines neatly coiled and the clean brightwork. "Shipshape. Very very nice."

Tanner smiled and went to the hatch. He hesitated when he discovered it was not locked as he thought he'd left it. He gestured to the cabin below. Once there, to the muffled sounds of the big motor launch thirty yards behind them as it got under way, Mary and McGwean seated themselves in the main salon. Tanner stood at the counter and slowly unwrapped the towel. He stared aghast.

"They're gone! I put them in this towel to dry and just left them on the counter. But they're gone. My God, I don't know what to say."

For a long moment McGwean looked back at Tanner with no expression. Then he reached into a pocket and extracted a small notebook and a pen. "Describe them please. The bills, in as much detail as you can. Did you suspect they might be counterfeit? No? Did you happen to write down the serial numbers?"

"I did," said Mary suddenly. She got up and went across the salon and into the forward cabin. In a small cabinet beside the bunk she pulled out a notebook she used to record events on an almost daily basis while they sailed. "This isn't the ship's log," she explained, "just random notes I make about whatever interests me."

Tanner abruptly turned and raced up the steps to the cockpit. He stopped on the top step and stared aft. Bathed in the golden afternoon light a large motor launch fifty yards away was making steady progress through the water toward the entrance to the sound. Mist and turbulent air from the ship's exhaust prevented him from reading the name painted on the transom, but the shape of the craft seemed familiar to Tanner. He felt certain it was the same motor vessel that had anchored behind them and he was pretty sure it was the one he'd seen had that had shadowed them down the long passage through the day. He returned to the salon, gnawing on a knuckle. He said nothing to Mary's enquiring look, except to give a small shake of his head.

When McGwean had finished copying the serial numbers into his notebook, he said, "They aren't sequential or identical, which is often the case with counterfeit. The numbers may help trace their origins. You're sure the bills were wrapped in that towel." He picked up the towel and peered at it, then shook his head in frustration. "Too bad, too bad. Let me ask you. Are you on some sort of schedule? I ask because it would be helpful if you could remain here at the resort until I get a response to my inquiry."

"How long would we have to wait?" asked Mary.

"I expect an answer by mid-morning tomorrow, I should think."

"Of course," said Mary. "We're happy to oblige. It'll take us that long to top up our tanks and off load our garbage." She and Tanner locked gazes. He knew what she was thinking in spite of her nonchalance; the same as he. More involvement. Possibly more time away from their own pursuits.

4

"You're hiding something, my dear," said Mary a half hour later. She handed him a tall frosty glass of tonic topped with a thin slice of fresh lime and sank onto the portside settee in the cockpit. Tanner smiled his thanks and took a long sip to organize his thinking. He watched Mary arrange her brilliant orange skirt while holding her own drink. The light material of her skirt rippled over her thighs as she settled. She too sipped her drink and stared at him over the rim of her glass. "Hmmm?" She said.

"Perceptive, as usual. Is that a new sarong?"

Mary laughed her full-throated rich, from-the-diaphragm laugh. The strapless top slipped, revealing a little more of her elegant sun-bronzed cleavage. "Certainly it's new, you goof. It's the first sarong I've ever owned." She stuck her fingers between her breasts and yanked the bodice a little higher.

"Oh, don't hide anything for my benefit."

Mary grinned. "I'm not. This thing doesn't conceal much, unlike you, I might point out."

"I admit, I have certain suspicions I concealed from our Mr. McGwean."

"Such as?"

Tanner shifted on his cushion. "Do you recall, after we went ashore, a boat that anchored behind us? A big motor yacht? Bronze hull I think."

Mary frowned in thought and shook her head. "I don't think so."

"What about after, when you were sitting out on the veranda? While I went inside in search of a police contact. Did you see a man come up from the beach, heavy-set, not too tall, wearing grungy sailing whites?"

"Oh, of course. He had a short beard. No hat, blondish I think. Somebody was with him."

Tanner nodded. "That's the one. I have a strong suspicion he came from the boat anchored behind us. What's more, I think that boat shadowed us all day."

"Since when?"

"Since we left the anchorage on Ginger this morning."

"You mean they knew you found those bills?"

"They certainly do now. At least I suspect so. I have a strong suspicion they may have been watching us from the time we anchored there, because we were outside the main anchorage on Ginger."

"Then they followed us all day?"

"And when we came ashore, snatched back those three bills. By stealing the bills from us there's only our word that they ever existed."

"But what if we'd spent one? Oh, wait. So what. The chances of just one being traced if we'd cashed it, even a hundred, would have been remote to almost impossible."

"Exactly," said Tanner.

"You said 'snatched back.' Interesting choice of words. Hmm. And if we'd radioed the Coast Guard, say, they'd have known by monitoring Channel 16." Mary made a face, thinking back to their idyllic morning cavorting naked in the sea, but under the watchful eyes of…who? Now she took a long drink from her glass and reclined onto the cushions until she was nearly prone. Tanner claimed she did her best thinking, and made the most outrageous proposals from a prone position. Now she was silent for several minutes and Tanner did nothing to disturb her.

"Okay. I think we better do something about this."

"Such as?"

"Weren't we going to sail to Road Town tomorrow?"

Tanner agreed that had been the plan. "Since I don't propose to tell our policeman friend about our mysterious shadow until we have a chance to check him out a little more, there's nothing more to be done tonight."

"Except dinner ashore, eh?"

"Yes," Tanner said. "You radio for a reservation while I prepare the dinghy." By the time they reached shore, the tropical light was fading fast and the resort patio was lit by the soft glow of tall Tiki lamps and a few judiciously placed electric lights. The rental huts scattered as by a giant hand up the steep hillside behind the main lodge, were mostly occupied, and contributed warm golden glows from their windows. The temperature had fallen a little. Their dinner reservation was for an hour hence, so Tanner and Mary had a drink at a table oin the beach. The small crowd was mixed, from couples like themselves dressed more or less in the kind of hot-weather evening wear one expected to find on a tropical shore, to a number of more casually dressed visitors, some wearing the most abbreviated swim suits and cutoffs either of them had ever seen. Mary watched with amusement as her companion tracked the acres of exposed flesh on the beach and at surrounding tables.

* * *

By seven in the morning Mary was up on deck, preparing to move their yacht to the dock for the servicing Tanner had arranged the previous afternoon. After their water tanks had been topped up and fuel replenished, Tanner backed the sloop away from the dock, reversed and, re-anchored, waiting for some word from McGwean who had not yet appeared.

At ten, Mary muttered an imprecation to herself, slathered on some sun screen and took herself to the hot foredeck, clad in her favorite bikini.

"You'll give McGwean a heart attack if he sees you in that," smirked Tanner.

"Hah, this is for you, sweetie. I see you eyeing those sweet young things at the beach bar over there." Mary waved toward the cluster of umbrellas raised over a small bar-like apparatus and tended by a bronzed smiling native. He in turn was attended by a covey of young nubile girls barely dressed in the smallest bikinis imaginable.

Noon came and went and McGwean did not appear, nor was there any radio call.

"We need at least four hours sailing time to get to Road Town," pointed out Mary. "If we delay much longer we'll be stuck here for another night."

"I'm not sure I'd call it stuck," said Tanner. "It's pretty nice here. But you have a point. I'm going to radio the resort office."

A few minutes later he leaned over Mary still lolling on her air mattress in the shade of the loose jib she'd raised part way up the forestay. "Interesting. According to the desk, there is no such gentleman, either by name or from my description registered at this place. Alarms are going off in my head. This place is as isolated as these islands get. Let's go somewhere more crowded."

"I'm with you," Mary exclaimed. She rose and tossed her towel and air mattress through the forward hatch into the cabin below. "Let me get shoes and a shirt."

Within minutes with practiced efficiency the couple had raised their anchor and headed out to the entrance to Gorda Sound.

* * *

They cleared the reef, rounded the entrance and met the trade winds on their quarter. Tanner said, "Okay, that's enough lollygagging about. Let's make some time."

"You think we fooled anybody?" Mary began hand over hand hauling on the jib sheet, unfurling the big sail to its maximum size. The sail luffed and cracked once and then filled, heeling the boat. Their increase in speed was instantly apparent. She turned to the main and cranked the winch hard. In moments, with full sails set, Tanner adjusted their course and aimed directly across the wind toward the western end of Tortola and the entrance to Road Harbor.

"I don't know, but we gave a pretty good impression of not having a care in this world. If whoever was watching us, and I didn't detect any surveillance, didn't know our guest is a cop, we may just have slipped away." Tanner spoke with satisfaction. He scanned the rapidly diminishing entrance to the sound behind them and then settled down to getting maximum trim and speed from their ride. Last night they'd agreed that immediate but private contact with the authorities in Road Town was the first order of business after they reached port.

There weren't many boats out this mid-week day. Through the day and their hourly watch changes, Tanner and Mary kept an eye peeled for other vessels that might have been on a parallel course, or making a stern chase. They checked the radio messaging service periodically. There were no alarm-raising messages. The trade winds blew steadily from the east and they made good time along their twenty mile track. They smiled a lot and drank plenty of water. The atmosphere was relaxed, in spite of their concerns about the missing McGwean. Tanner was sure when they'd reached Road Town and talked with someone from the island police department, they'd be able to get back to their reason for coming to the Virgin Islands, a long relaxing and romantic time under sunny skies and gentle breezes where the water temperature was almost the same as the rain that occasionally fell, and both were about the same as the air around them.

Mary had reverted to her hedonistic impulses and was sunning herself in the cockpit in just the briefest of red bikini bottoms and no top. "No lines, this way," she grinned impishly.

"Sunscreen, my dear," Tanner scowled at her. "Melanoma would not be pretty on that fine pelt you're wearing."

"No worries. Look, I'm using so much of this forty, I'm gonna be out here in the sun for hours with no tanning at all." She was slathering on the stuff on her chest as she talked, a further distracting sight to her husband. "I can't go into the harbor topless, I'll just grab my long tee."

By four that afternoon they were entering Road Town Harbor and turning directly for Wickham Cay and the transient boat dock. Radio hailing had given them directions to a visitor's slip on the outer edge of the marina. General rules of dress in the islands were casual except the wearing of swimming costumes on the town streets was frowned on. Shorts and cover-ups were the rule. Tanner donned a clean white short-sleeved shirt and a pair of new topsiders he was breaking in.

They acquired directions to municipal offices from a smiling native island woman at one of the shops after they docked. Tanner took a close look around and didn't detect any untoward attention from among the tourists and native islanders. They walked casually along the sun-blasted streets, admiring the bright clothing and other wares. Mary turned into a place called The Shirt Shack which sported what appeared to Tanner to be hundreds of different kinds of Tee shirts hanging on huge round racks. It was cool and pleasant in the store. Tanner positioned himself where he could see the wide entrance to the store and a large section of the street outside while Mary examined and then selected two new shirts with spectacular abstract tropical designs.

The black woman who assisted Mary admitted that she was the designer as well as the store owner. "Those are among my favorite designs," she said. "I did them just this past spring."

"Silk screened here in the BVI?" Mary asked.

"Oh yes, mon," a tenor voice from the back of the store. "By these very hands." The grinning man held up his two slender arms and wiggled his fingers suggestively.

"My husband does all my silk screening," laughed the woman. They seemed to be enjoying themselves in their shared enterprise.

"This silent fellow over here is my husband, Michael Tanner," said Mary. Tanner who had been staring out at the street turned and shook hands with the man and nodded, smiling. Mary paid for the shirts and they strolled out of the shop arm in arm.

"Anything?" Mary murmured, leaning on Tanner's arm.

"Nope. Isn't it a little warm for this cuddling?" Tanner responded turning and grabbing a nibble of Mary's ear lobe.

"Oh sigh, all the romance has fled," groused Mary, pulling away.

They strolled on up the street, climbing the hill behind the harbor toward the city offices. Once on the steps of the building, they both turned to admire the view, and to see if they were followed. Beneath them spread a busy harbor with several power boats spreading white wakes behind them. On their right a white cruise ship was tied up to the long wharf, accounting, Tanner supposed, for the crowds of pale tourists who thronged the streets. Whereas a little earlier the town had been relatively quiet, now the street was crowded with open taxis, bicycles and crowds of walkers.

"Look at the variation in this human race," Tanner commented. "I can see a lot of black people, of course, but their color variation is amazing. And I see a number of Asians, Europeans and lots of other white folks like us. Well, let's find a cop." They went through the glass doors into a quiet air conditioned lobby.

The young receptionist said, "Good afternoon. How may we help you?"

Tanner had considered what approach to use and decided that playing it straight would be best. "We'd like to see one of your detectives, a Mr. McGwean?"

Tanner saw what might have been a flicker of concern pass over her smooth face. "May I ask what this is about?"

"We met Mr. McGwean yesterday at the Bitter End resort. Something has happened since then that we think he should know about."

"I see. Won't you be seated?" she gestured to a row of chairs along one wall of the room. "Someone will be with you shortly."

"Did you notice," Mary murmured, "she said someone would be with us, not that she'd find your Mr. McGwean?"

"I did notice. What do you mean my Mr. McGwean?"

Mary grinned and tucked her arm under his. "You found him, sailor."

"Mr. and Mrs. Tanner?" The tall well-built black man had approached so swiftly and softly they'd not taken notice. He stood before them smiling easily, white teeth in his dark skin flashing at them.

Tanner rose and offered his hand. "Good afternoon. This is Mary

Whitney, to whom I have the pleasure of being married, although she retains her birth name."

"My name is Archambault, Detective Lieutenant Lionel Archambault. Won't you come this way." He gestured down a wide hallway and they went a short distance to a tiny office just large enough for a small desk and two side chairs. Archambault gestured the couple to the side chairs and folded his lean form into his own desk chair.

"Now. I understand you wish to speak with a man named McGwean, employed as a detective by this department?" The man's careful diction was leavened by the natural rhythms of the native islander. "The problem is we have no such individual working here."

"You're kidding!" exclaimed Mary. She clapped a hand over her mouth, quickly regained her composure and glanced at Tanner.

"You have no one on your roster named McGwean. Is that what you're telling us?"

"That's correct. No one. Not on the uniformed staff, not part of our small detective staff, not undercover. No one by that name." Archambault delivered his statement in a flat, unemotional but firm voice.

"I take it," Tanner remarked, "You've made that statement before."

"Quite correct. In the past month we've had other inquiries about your Mr. McGwean. In the previous cases no one actually showed up here claiming to have met the man. Now, here you are. I must say, I'm a bit impressed that you sailed all the way here from Gorda Sound to bring this to our attention. Whilst on your vacation, I take it. Unfortunately, I have no information to give you."

"Is it possible this Mr. McGwean is working for some agency not affiliated with your department?"

Archambault looked at Tanner for a long moment. "You are perhaps thinking of your CIA or DEA or one of those other Homeland Security operations."

"Yes," Tanner said. " But first I was thinking about MI5 or MI6 of Her Majesty's Government."

"MI5," smiled Archambault. "MI5 is strictly domestic."

Mary said, "Of course. But do we always know everything our governments are doing?"

Archambault appeared to agree, offering a nod and a slight smile. "We do have drug traffic through the islands, though not a great deal and boat hijacking is really quite rare. However, because you are not the first, perhaps you would enlighten me as to the nature of your encounter with the gentleman you call McGwean?"

"He certainly was a gentleman," Mary said.

"He overheard me asking about contacting the authorities at the reception desk at the Bitter End." Tanner took up his narrative again. "You see, that morning while swimming in the cove where we were anchored off Ginger Island, I found three one hundred dollar U.S. bills floating in the water." Archambault's level of interest became palpably higher.

Tanner continued. "Eventually we decided that our discovery ought to be reported so since Gorda Sound was our next planned stop, that's where I inquired. This man introduced himself in the bar. He showed us what I considered adequate identification so we took him aboard to show him the bills. But they were missing. I had noticed a big cruiser following us from Ginger Island. They always stayed a good way off so I couldn't be positive of that. And frankly, I didn't pay too much attention. Obviously I should have paid more. I hadn't hidden the bills, so while Mary and I were ashore, having a drink and relaxing…"

"And chatting with the charming and now mysterious Mr. McGwean," Mary chimed in, "it looks like the men on the cruiser went aboard and filched our three hundred dollars. Fortunately, I wrote down the serial numbers." She produced a piece of paper torn from her journal and slid it across the desk.

Archambault looked at the paper. "I see the numbers are not sequential. What was the condition of the bills? Did they look new?"

Tanner shook his head. "Mr. McGwean asked the same thing. I'd say they were not new, but not old either. You wouldn't expect bills of such high denomination to be heavily used. I couldn't tell if they were real. They certainly looked authentic." Tanner watched as Archambault wrote down the numbers of the bills. "Is it possible there has been a bank robbery or perhaps a payroll gone missing?"

Archambault shook his head. "Not here in the islands and I would know. There has been nothing like that for years. For ever, in fact. However, we are aware of certain, shall we say, passages of people and questionable goods through the islands. There is nothing official, nor is there any arrangement, such as existed in that place in the United States. In a state called Minnesota. St. Paul in the early thirties, I believe. When the Chief of Police required gangsters to register and promise not to commit crimes in the city. In exchange they would not be arrested or investigated. There is nothing like that here in the Islands. On the other hand," Archambault shrugged.

"Yes, there are always people who are ready to look the other way for some easy money. Except it turns out not to be so easy, every time." Mary rose and extended her hand. "We will be here in the Virgin Islands for another eleven days, and we'd appreciate it if you'd let us know what you learn about those bills."

"We'd also be interested in what you learn about our mysterious Mr. McGwean, if you can tell us," said Tanner, taking the officer's extended hand as well.

"If anything at all," murmured Mary as she and Tanner left city hall. "Why didn't he ask for a description of McGwean?"

"Probably because he already has it, regardless of whether they'll admit to knowing McGwean."

5

The couple walked back down the hill past the busy grocery store and produce market to the dock where their yacht was tied up. "You have some doubts, my dear?"

"Not exactly. Not about Mr. Archambault. I just think this is shaping up to be something."

"Now what?" asked Tanner as they stepped back aboard.

"You know it'll take a few days at least for any information to arrive. Let's do what we came here for. Go sailing."

"Good idea. You get out of that skirt and I'll start the process."

Mary disappeared below to change into more casual clothes. Tanner started the engine and re-routed the bow and stern lines as was their habit so they could get out of their slip from the deck of the cruiser. The lines snaked from cleat to dockside bollard and back, making the job of leaving easier. Mary reappeared and took the helm waving at Tanner she was ready to go. Tanner nodded and they backed efficiently out of the slip, turned about and headed toward the open end of the harbor. Stowing the bumpers and the mooring lines, Tanner kept a wary eye behind them. He didn't see anything that suggested they might be under observation, or that anyone was following them.

They cleared Burt Point and headed southeast across the Sir Francis Drake channel. Their destination was Manchioneel Bay on Cooper Island where they expected to anchor for the night. The short tropical dusk was just descending as Tanner dropped the anchor in just under twenty feet of water. He glanced around doubtfully. "Doesn't this seem a little exposed to you, weather wise?"

"Yes, but things are really quiet and expected to be for about twenty-four hours. Tomorrow, early, we can dinghy around the point to a really nice secluded cove I know about." She waggled her eyebrows suggestively at him.

Smoked oysters and fresh sea bass they'd obtained earlier in Road Town provided a satisfying meal and they turned in, both hoping they'd heard the last of McGwean and three soggy hundreds.

Early the next morning in swim suits with ample supplies of sunscreen, towels and a couple of air mattresses, along with several bottles of fresh water, Tanner and Mary Whitney set out for Mary's cove. The sea was still benign, only gentle swells disturbed their tranquil run around the point. The cove was well protected from most points and while the narrow strip of sand showed signs of human intrusion, there was no one about and the thick green jungle growth at their backs seemed to isolate them entirely.

Two hours later, after a third application of sunscreen to replace what had been lost by his dip in the warm ocean, Tanner sleepily considered his dozing wife's near-naked body and opened his mouth to suggest it was getting on toward lunch when there was a giggle and a smothered grunt from inland. He sat up and looked behind him at the edge of the jungle where a young couple stood staring at them. Mary grimaced, sat up and leisurely covered herself with an old shirt of Tanners she had brought along.

"Sorry, mate," called the boy. "We didn't expect to find anyone here at this time. We're staying at the resort over on Manchioneel Bay." The girl holding his hand giggled.

" 'Sall right," Tanner said, "we were just about to go back to our boat, anyway."

"Are you off that nifty sloop anchored around the point?"

"Yes," answered Mary.

"There was a motor boat out there earlier. Someone looking for you, I guess," said the girl.

Tanner and Mary glanced at each other and made the same decision. It was past time to get back to their boat.

Tanner watched the young man's gaze follow Mary as she bent to retrieve their belongings. The boy's eyes were riveted on her bra-less bosom. They walked to their dinghy and stowed their gear. Mary waded into the water with her back to the beach. She stripped off the shirt, grinning at Tanner, then she rinsed the sand out of the shirt and put it back on. Tanner shoved the dinghy into deeper water and they scrambled aboard.

"You enjoy displaying yourself like that to strangers?" Tanner said as he turned and pressed the starter button on the little outboard. Mary's smiling response was lost as the engine caught immediately and Tanner swung around in a tight circle and aimed back toward the point.

When they rounded the point, their yacht rode serenely at anchor in the gentle swells exactly where they had left her. "Looks all right, would you say," said Mary. She grabbed the ladder rails and swarmed up, carrying the dinghy painter in her teeth. She quickly tied it off and ran below. Tanner swept a leisurely gaze over the hull on both sides from stem to stern, checking for anything that might seem unusual. Then he took hold of the ladder and eased his body into the water. With slow measured strokes he swam to the bow and then back along the other side. Everything looked as it should. When he reached amidships on the starboard side, he took a deep breath and sank deeper, following the centerboard five more feet down into the water. Below him he noticed the dark shadow of a large fish sliding across the sandy ocean bottom. The water was remarkably clear and he could make out the anchor line leading away from the bow.

Tanner reached the front of the craft and continued his slow inspection of their boat's hull, coming up for air a couple of times. The hull was mostly clean of the performance-robbing detritus and barnacles often found on the hulls of ocean vessels. Still, nothing unusual came to his questing inspection. There was a splash and he heard and felt Mary as she closed the distance between them and paddled alongside. At the very stern he went under again to examine the place where the engine's shaft came out through the hull and connected to the propeller just in front of the rudder. Then he surfaced to find Mary clinging to the ladder watching him.

"Oh dear," she said, reading the expression on his face. "What did you find?"

"A radio transmitter of some sort, I think. It's like one of those tracking devices they use on animals. This one has a short flexible antenna sticking out of one side. And of course it's a waterproof container."

"Could it have been put there by the charter company?"

"Possible but doubtful. I left it there. Not sure what to do about it, if anything."

Tanner sat down in the cockpit and toweled off. The boat was equipped with a freshwater shower at the stern ladder. The water tank held an ample supply of fresh water, so long as they weren't wasteful. The snorkel gear had been replaced in the locker and Mary had brought a chart of the area to the cockpit to consider where they might go to anchor for the night.

"I'm inclined to stay right here," Tanner said after a cursory glance at the chart Mary offered.

"Isn't it just a bit isolated? Given the time, I'm surprised we haven't been joined by anybody else."

"Let's just check the weather and if there's no compelling reason, we can stay here. The lack of any other boats is actually an advantage. It would be harder for anyone to get close without our noticing, and," Tanner grinned, "you can continue to indulge your penchant for running around naked."

Mary tried pouting, but couldn't quite bring it off. "Do I detect a note of disapproval here, my Lord and Master?"

"Hey, I'm just saying, all this tropical weather seems to have brought out the self-indulgent hedonist in you. I never said I don't enjoy feasting my eyes on your lissome form."

"Well, how about feasting on this?" With a quick glance around the empty bay, Mary stood and dropped her shirt to the deck. Tanner reached for her and in moments they had forgotten about the mystery of the wet Benjamins and began to explore more immediate mysteries of the flesh.

Much later, after the sun had set, they had a light supper in the cockpit, aided by the light of a couple of battery powered lanterns hung from the standing rigging. It had been a long day with rigorous exercise and plenty of wind and sun; fresh air in abundance. Sailing is fun and exhilarating. It is also work. Maintaining balance on the deck of a sleek sailboat lunging through the water in a brisk wind can wear you down. In minutes after they doused lights aboard *Passions Messenger*, the couple was asleep.

* * *

The sound of the tiny electric motor attached to the rear of the four-man inflatable boat was lost to any but the most acute listening ears. The trade wind blew, surf along the shore of the bay could be heard in the near distance, and water gurgled under the hull of the darkened sailboat. The man at the helm of the tiny boat expertly brought his craft close to the hull midway down the length of the sloop. Anxious gloved hands reached out to keep the dinghy from touching the hull and sending unusual vibrations through the hull that could awaken those on board.

At the bow a single hand signal sent the third member of the team sliding over the side into the water. Soundlessly, he took a deep breath and slid beneath the surface. Almost immediately the two men remaining in the dinghy saw a glow as the swimmer activated a special underwater battery powered flashlight. The light moved slowly under the hull as the swimmer groped his way to the place where the small transmitter Tanner had found was still attached.

With a single violent motion the swimmer ripped the small tracking transmitter from its nesting place against the hull and dropped it. It slowly disappeared toward the seabed. From a small mesh fanny pack secured around his waist he extracted a small black similar-appearing box. He smeared a dollop of a special adhesive on one side of the box and held it against the hull in the same place where the other box had been. A minute passed while the intruder hung motionless under the hull, only inches away from the sleeping Tanner and Mary Whitney. At last he gently wiggled the box to be sure the box was securely adhered to the hull. He pushed gently away from the hull and swam back to the bow and reached the surface where the dark inflatable waited.

The dinghy operator dragged his man away from the side of the sloop and its sleeping occupants. As soon as they had put several yards between them, the two men in the dinghy pulled the third man over the gunwale and into the boat. Gradually the inflatable seemed to fade almost silently into the thin mist of the night that hung over the restless sea.

6

"Look at that sky," called Mary. "Wow. It's like the whole universe is burning. Talk about red sky in the morning. Whee!"

"Don't forget the old rhyme," responded Tanner from the galley below where he was preparing breakfast.

After a light breakfast Tanner spread out the charts and they planned a route to their next anchorage. It wasn't far.

"I think I'll take a swim," Tanner said, rolling the charts back in to a thin metal tube.

"Mmmm," Mary responded, already deep into her novel. She lifted her head a moment later, hearing a large splash when Tanner cannonballed off the stern. It was some minutes later when she realized he hadn't come back aboard and she marked her place and stood to locate her husband. "Michael?" She called. There was only the plaintive sound of gulls overhead in response.

She leaned over the fantail and saw her husband lying motionless on the surface, one hand resting on the hull to keep him in place. He was staring down, apparently examining the sea bed fifteen feet below. As she watched, he bent at the waist and thrust strongly with his flipper-clad feet. The water was clear and calm so Mary could easily follow his progress. He swam to the bottom, took hold of something and stroked hard with his legs. What Mary saw when he reached the surface and took a big breath, was Michael's fingers wrapped around a small yellow rectangle.

"When I went swimming I looked again at the transmitter or track-ing thing or whatever it is on the hull and realized it was a different color." He climbed aboard and laid the yellow box on the cockpit floor.

"This is the thing that was attached?"

"Yeah, the box I told you about." Tanner peered at it.

"You mean there's another one still on our hull?"

Tanner nodded. "Yes. I just happened to see this lying on the bot-tom. Somebody must have come by last night, or anyway, sometime after we anchored and replaced this box with a different one."

They both peered down, heads together. Mary poked it with one finger. "It has writing on it. I'll get the camera."

They photographed the box and the strange writing of letters and numbers on two sides. "What should we do with it?"

Mary pursed her lips. "Let's leave it in the water. Maybe it quit working and somebody replaced it and they'll come looking for it. If we leave it here, whoever dropped it may not realize we know about the new one."

"Good idea," Tanner said. He dropped the box back over the side. In just a few minutes they weighed anchor and began a southeast run out of Manchioneel Bay. They were headed toward Anegada, a low piece of coral and sand surrounded by something called a drying reef, meaning a piece of real estate that literally lay right at the surface that sometimes dried in the tropical sun when the water was quiet.

Mary stood at the wheel as the big sloop raced across the waves. Her hair rippled in the wind. Tanner grinned at her obvious enjoyment. They'd long planned this trip and even though they enjoyed frequent sailing in Puget Sound and north into Canadian waters, those were fa-miliar places they could almost see from their big living room windows in Seattle. He glanced aloft at the sails, assessing the tell-tails attached to the main sail. They streamed straight back, parallel to the deck, as they should. He surveyed their horizon, seeing only a small dot almost direct-ly behind them, appearing out of the gap between Beef Island at the end of Tortola and Scrub Island. He put the binoculars on the dot, difficult to do from a surging sailboat and he gave up after a few minutes. Ahead there was nothing to see but the rolling, often white-topped seas, all the way to the horizon, some thirty hazy miles distant. He settled down to tending to the needs of the boat and his helmsperson. He pushed his worries about the missing hundreds and the mysterious Mr. McGwean almost out of his mind for several hours.

Around two that afternoon they turned more off the wind and slowed the boat. They were approaching the reefs of Anegada. They knew more than a few boats had come to grief and ruin on the sharp coral that lay too near the surface and guarded the entrances to the few safe anchorages. There were no completely secure anchorages on this reef and the charterer had been reluctant to give Tanner and Mary Whitney permission even to visit the place. He relented after reviewing their extensive sailing credentials and they posted an additional insurance bond.

"According to the sailing guide, we can anchor right in here if we want to go ashore," said Mary. By now they'd luffed up into the wind and were lying to in the waves, a gentle rocking motion the only disturbance. The winds were light, pushing *Passions Messenger* away from danger, toward deeper water.

"I guess I'm not really interested in maybe ruining a pair of beach shoes on those rocks and coral outcroppings," Tanner said, staring at the reef through his binoculars. Why don't we do a run around the reef. Then we can heave to out here and have lunch."

"Sounds like a plan," Mary agreed.

Engine sounds reached them. A dark reddish-bronze-hulled power boat drew near. With its shallower draft, it was able to get closer to Anegada and it moved inside the indentation in the visible rocks. Tanner studied the boat as it rumbled by, no more than fifty yards away. He couldn't swear to it, but he was sure it was the same boat that had been briefly anchored behind them at the Bitter End. Only the driver was visible. The 80-foot boat had wide smoked glass windows at deck level. Mary waved, but the driver on the flying bridge ignored her. The whole thing reminded Tanner uncomfortably of another yacht he had unhappily encountered halfway around the world on another ocean.

Above the craft, a varied array of antennae swayed in the wind. Tanner, who knew little about modern radio electronics, realized he'd be unable to identify a radio direction finder, even if one was there. He could see nothing that even suggested this boat carried the people who had placed the tracking device on their boat. He closed his eyes briefly, trying to blot out memories of his troubles on the water of the Inside Passage, and concerns about what they might have stumbled into, here in the Caribbean. He wished he'd never noticed the half-submerged hundreds. When he returned to the present, he glanced behind him to see Mary, hands grasping the wheel, watching him with concern on her face.

"Hey, are you all right?"

Tanner smiled and shrugged. Nodded. "Sure, sweetie. I'm betting that's the same boat we saw at the Bitter End."

"The one that parked behind us and then left suddenly?"

"Well, it seemed sudden to us. Look at the stern. Notice how the dinghy slung from the davits is canted a little, and it isn't drawn up quite right."

Mary looked and nodded. "Cover's the name on the transom in an innocent-appearing way, don't you think?

Tanner nodded his agreement.

"I don't get why, if they have a tracking device on us, they're here now. I also don't get why they came so close. Now we can surely identify them."

"Well, the boat we can, almost. But I couldn't pick the driver out of a crowd, could you? I wonder if the tracking thingy maybe has a limited range, and maybe they want to see if we're going to run south to the leeward islands."

"Oh, that's right. We'd be doing just what we have done this morning if we'd decided to sail to St. Martin."

"Since with our usual foresight, we already have some sandwiches ready, I'll open a couple of beers and we'll have a tasty, relaxing lunch.

Why don't you just get us a little farther off from the reef and we'll heave to."

Rocking gently in the waves, Mary and Tanner ate their a light lunch of sandwiches, a small cup of hot soup for each, some locally grown bananas, and hot tea.

"Switch on the radio and let's hear the news," said Mary.

Tanner tuned in the broadcast receiver and they listened to the noontime news. It mostly concerned local events in the islands, with frequent mention of places they had no knowledge of. The last item was something not normally carried by the local station. "Police," the announcer reported, had been called to a warehouse in the industrial part of the Road Town waterfront by reports of a body. The body was described to be a white male in his early forties with light sandy hair. He was wearing a soiled white linen suit. He was unidentified at the moment.

"That description sounds something like your Mr. McGwean," remarked Mary. She poured them each a second cup of tea.

"I wish you'd stop calling him my McGwean. We are not attached at the hip, nor is there any blood between us, good, bad or indifferent. He approached me, remember?"

"What do you think we should do now?" Mary said. "This sailing vacation is sliding into the dumper. I vote we head back to Road Town, maybe to Maya Cove. From there we can contact the police."

"O.K. I agree we need to get unwrapped from this thing before we can concentrate on relaxing the rest of the week. But because of the tracking device, let's go either to Road Town or Beef Island. Then we can dinghy in and maybe lose the people who are following us."

"We could just rip the box off, couldn't we, and drop it in the ocean as we sail back?"

"We could. I'm hesitant to do that because then they'd know we're on to them. It wouldn't be all that difficult to find us again in these islands. Although I guess it could take a couple of days for them to relocate us if we made it harder."

"Unless we sailed away," Mary said. She stood up in the cockpit and scanned the horizon. Other than the evil-looking reefs of nearby Anegada, and the low-lying, misty profiles of Virgin Gorda and Tortola, their world was empty of all but sky and ocean.

Tanner unhooked the boom from its restraints and repositioned the jib. *Passions Messenger* heeled under the pressure of the wind and the boat gradually gathered speed until they were slashing through the rolling waves at exhilarating speed. They retraced their course toward the northern end of Tortola and before long had eased into a sheltered spot lying just off Beef Island. One other sailboat was already at anchor and soon two more arrived and found themselves quiet anchorages.

"Let's go ashore and find a telephone," Mary said. "I think a radio call would be too public."

The dinghy soon brought them to shore only a few steps from a small bodega with a battered public telephone, fastened precariously to the wall beside the open air display counter. They tried to be unobtrusive and keep their voices down, but it was difficult not to reveal that they were talking to the police station in Road Town.

"If you can get to the terminal at the airport, we'll send a car directly," said Lieutenant Archambault.

"We'll need to go back and secure our boat but we can be there in an hour," Tanner responded. "I'm not sure about the dinghy, though."

"I'll have someone at the airport take charge. Thank you for your willingness to come in."

A large black policeman in a uniform was waiting at the terminal manager's office when they arrived. The terminal manager explained that a man would keep an eye on their dinghy while they were gone.

The constable drove well and fast back across the island to town. None of the three had much to say to each other on the short ride. The driver passed the municipal hall where the police department was located. He noticed Mary's raised eyebrows and said," Hospital. Lieutenant Archambault will meet you there."

The hospital was a small one-story pale-yellow painted concrete-block building with a lot of smoked glass across the front. Their driver swung into the driveway and stopped. "Ask for the morgue," he said. Tanner and Mary stepped from the air-conditioned car, walked through the heat and into the air-conditioned atmosphere of the small clinic and hospital. At the desk the pretty receptionist directed them down a long hall that appeared to bisect the building. At the other end they turned left as directed and found themselves before a heavy white-painted door. Tanner put his hand on the door and it swung slowly inward, revealing an open space with three doors, several hard-looking chairs and a small desk shoved against one wall.

Lieutenant Archambault stubbed out his cigarette in the ashtray at his elbow and rose from his chair to greet them. The white-coated attendant, after a glance from Archambault, disappeared through one of the doors.

"Good morning," Archambault said. "I'm sorry to bring you into town from your boat, but I thought you ought to see this." His dark eyes switched back and forth between the two. He seemed to be assessing them in a different way from their first encounter.

"I assume," Tanner said, "since we're meeting in the morgue, that you want us to look at a body."

Archambault inclined his head and then turned and ushered them through the same door through which the attendant had vanished. "I don't think both of you need to view the body, if you wish to remain here, Mrs. Tanner."

Mary nodded her understanding and kept pace with the two men. The room they entered was only slightly larger than the office they had just left, with white painted walls, like everywhere else they'd been. There were several hard chairs in a row against one wall, a small sofa against another wall and a window in the wall opposite the door, next to a second door. This door, Mary noticed, had no knob or handle, only a brass escutcheon with a dark slot for a key. The window was covered by a white curtain that hung on the other side. The ceiling lighting was somewhat more subdued than in the previous space. The room smelled. It smelled of death, with that peculiar odor of chemicals used in morgues everywhere to unsuccessfully mask the odor of death.

Archambault gestured them wordlessly to places close to the window. His gaze flowed over them once more as if assessing whether they were up to the experience. Then he reached up and pressed a small white button beside the window. Tanner and Mary heard a faint buzz from the other side of the wall. The curtain parted and they saw what was obviously a body on a gurney, covered with a white sheet. After a momentary pause the disembodied arms of the attendant appeared and he drew the sheet down below the chin of the body on display.

Tanner and Mary looked down though the harsh, direct illumination of the overhead light at the man they had met and briefly known at the Bitter End Resort on Virgin Gorda. Simultaneously, they nodded and Tanner spoke. "That's him. That's the man we knew as Ian McGwean."

"How did he die? " Mary asked.

"Shot. Two bullets in the chest from close range," replied Archambault. He pressed the buzzer again and said, "Come, we'll go to the office and talk." He led the way back to the first space near the exterior doors to the morgue. Here the smell of death was only a lingering memory under the sterile odor of the hospital.

They sat together around the desk, quiet for the moment, each with personal thoughts about the dead man and his abrupt and violent death and what it might mean to each of them in the coming days.

Tanner finally said, "Where was he found?"

"In Fish Bay. It appears he may have been shot somewhere else and then dragged behind a boat to the bay where he was dropped." Archambault paused and tugged on his lower lip. Then he shook his head and said, "it also appears he was dragged some distance through the water before he died."

"Tortured?" asked Mary.

Another silence. "Possibly. We can't be sure. It's a great puzzle."

"Was he carrying identification?" asked Tanner.

"Yes. His identification tells us he was George Simeon, a French national who seems to have worked for a large British firm that specializes in security for banks. The firm has been contacted and is sending someone here to Road Town." Archambault sighed. "This is going to be a complicated, multi-national mess," he murmured. To Tanner, "Why do you think he approached you?"

"I really have no idea. I suspect he overheard me calling your department. But I didn't say anything about the money we found when I enquired for a police contact at the Bitter End. We did tell him later that day about the money and he came aboard to inspect it."

"I liked him," Mary said. "He seemed cultured, not rude. Nothing off kilter, you see, and I thought we'd get along, in a casual, social sort of way." She waved her long fingers in the air. Tanner looked askance at his wife for a moment, wondering why she was acting this way. Then he looked down, hoping Archambault hadn't caught the look. "So we invited him aboard and I can tell you it was unsettling to discover that the currency we had found was gone."

Tanner picked up the narrative. "I can't prove it but there are some other things that tie to this. After we left the anchorage where we found the currency, through the whole day, I had a feeling that somebody was watching us."

"You never mentioned it," Mary said.

"I know. Now I wish I had. No particular reason, I guess I just didn't want to worry you."

Mary lowered her chin and gave him one of her "looks" that said he should know better.

"Anyway, later, I got bumped by a man in the lobby of the resort after I met McGwean, or whoever he is. I think he lifted the keys to the cabin from my side pocket. I'd locked the hatch when we went ashore, and it was open when we came back aboard with McGwean. The keys were on the counter. I also think the boat that anchored behind us was the one that had been shadowing us all day. I think the people aboard that boat stole the three bills while we were ashore. The keys were on the—" Tanner stopped for a minute and made an abrupt decision.

"Lieutenant, I also think the people on that boat put a tracking device on our hull so they can keep track of us without having to maintain visual surveillance."

The lieutenant had straightened in his chair at this new revelation. "You people are full of surprises. Did it ever occur to you we might have gone at this quite differently had we known all this sooner?"

"Yes, I'm sorry, but the first time we came to you—"

"The first time," Mary drawled, "you just didn't seem all that interested."

"I see. Well, that's all behind us now. I wonder if you'd mind staying ashore for a few days while we sort this out?"

"Actually, Lieutenant Archambault, I would mind a good deal," Mary responded before Tanner could get his mouth open. "I've been wanting to sail these waters for quite a few years, and we only have so much time, you see. If you can get rid of that signaling thing attached to our hull, perhaps we can get on with our vacation and avoid any more trouble altogether. We are involved only by chance and since our time here is limited and we know nothing else, I'd very much appreciate being left to go about our vacation as planned." Mary smiled sweetly and fluttered her eyelashes at the lieutenant.

"Quite a performance," Tanner muttered as he handed Mary into the back of a waiting police car outside the morgue.

The same constable who had picked them up chauffeured them back to Beef Island. They went aboard and occupied themselves with routine maintenance chores and soon the soft put-put of a tiny outboard motor announced the arrival of a police scuba diver. He was towing an old fiberglass rowboat that had clearly seen better days.

"The lieutenant has instructed me to reattach the tracker to this derelict and anchor it in that small mangrove site across the bay. It should provide at least some temporary confusion, and we may be able to figure out who is listening." The diver flashed a huge white grin in his brown face.

"Do you know it is a tracking device?" asked Mary.

A momentary look of confusion passed over the man's face, then he smiled again and said, "Well, no matter. I will know for sure what it is when I have it in hand." He tied up to the stern ladder, slipped his feet into large blue fins and flipped over the side of his yellow dinghy with hardly a splash.

It took him only moments to remove the small box from the hull. Holding it just below the surface he popped back up and dashed the water from his face. "This is a professional device, not something we would find in a retail store, even one that caters to the conspiracy and undercover spying crowd. Quite sophisticated. And expensive." He slipped straight down and while Tanner and Mary watched through the clear water, attached the small box to the rear of the ancient dinghy just below the water line. He crawled back into the yellow police boat and smiled at his audience. In moments he was halfway across the bay heading for the mangrove trees.

"I think this calls for a drink," said Mary. "Besides, it must be cocktail hour somewhere in the world, don't you think so?"

"I do, I do. I think we should spend the night right here. Since we can assume our unfriendly trackers know where we are now, they may not be so alert to movement early tomorrow morning. As a further inducement, there is, I'm told, this fine little restaurant just across the bay there with an excellent reputation for drinks, fine cuisine and a rowdy atmosphere."

"Outstanding," responded Mary. "I'll just change while you get the dinghy ready. What's the place called?"

"The Last Resort," smiled Tanner. "Sometimes they have a show."

"Certainly a small island," remarked Mary as they nimbly disembarked from their dinghy at the long dock that meandered out from the rocky shore, "more like a large collection of boulders." Trellis Bay was shallow enough that yachters anxious to sample the hearty fare at the Last Resort always rode in on shallow draft inflatables or small dinghies.

"The story is that this rock is named for a pirate named Bellamy. Back in the eighteenth century He would sit here on the Cay and lie in wait for the ships of the Royal Navy, or of some of the other European countries that were exploiting the Caribbean. Sometimes he needed a replacement ship but mostly he plundered the cargoes."

"Mary grinned. "Maybe we should start diving for doubloons."

"I never heard of any buried treasure hereabouts, but you never know." Tanner held the door for Mary and they stepped into the heavy heat of a boisterous restaurant, already crowded with boaters and island vacationers. Their hostess found them seats at a big table shared with a New England group of charterers off a big Swan ketch they'd admired in the bay.

"It might have been interesting to transfer that tracker to another charter," murmured Tanner.

"Yes, except we have no idea what kind of reaction might occur when they, whoever it is, found out about the trick."

"True enough, but it would have been nice if they'd followed the box all the way south, say, to St. Vincent."

"Do you want to explain your air-head act back at Road Town?" asked Tanner.

"I just thought it might be useful if the good lieutenant felt he could discount my presence even more than he was already doing."

"Ah," Tanner responded.

Their quiet conversation became more difficult as the minutes flew by, due to the constant flow of interesting rum concoctions, the drink of choice, and more and more people crowding into the spaces. Even the donkey that occasionally stuck its nose through a hole in one wall seemed to have retreated for the night.

Their food came and Tanner and Mary tucked into tender broiled shrimp and succulent lobster surrounded by rice and various local vegetables.

The dense Caribbean night had come to Trellis Bay as Tanner and Mary walked slowly arm in arm down the uneven planks of the narrow dock. Mary stumbled.

"Whoops, more rum than I usually drink at one sitting," she laughed. She clutched Tanner's arm more tightly. "But you won't let me fall, right, sailor?" She giggled and snugged his arm against her breasts. "You won't let me be a fallen, woman, will you?" More giggles.

Tanner grinned in the night air and turned her gently toward their dinghy. "Watch your step here, lady. No dunking allowed."

He helped Mary into the dinghy then cast off and stepped into the center where he unshipped the stubby oars. They'd elected to row in instead of using the small outboard that was supplied by the charter company.

"So, Mr. Navigator," Mary giggled again. "Think you can find our boat? I'd hate to have you rowing around out here all night."

"I thought to bring a flashlight, which will help if things become uncertain." Things were already a little uncertain, he was discovering. The potent combination of a single rum drink, the dark night and an unwieldy rubber boat that seemed to have a mind of its own, made things dicey. He found it difficult to row a straight line.

Mary was sitting in the stern so she could point the way to her companion who was rowing with his back to the direction they wanted to go. After a few minutes she said, "Where's the flashlight, my love?"

"In the bag at your feet, precious."

"Thank you, darling."

It was so dark that Tanner could barely make out the pale oval of her face. There was no moon. She waggled her hand, giving no consistent direction. He figured he had just about reached the halfway point, if his direction was anywhere close. He glanced over his shoulder looking for the masthead light and single cabin light he thought he would recognize. He had memorized the relative positions of the two lights so he thought he could find their boat. After a moment he picked out a clear path to their sloop.

When he turned back Mary was sitting primly on the stern thwart, knees together and the flashlight lying on the floor of the dinghy so it cast a faint light over her. She had untied the strings of her sleeveless top. Tanner was confronted with a lovely vision of half-lit naked female flesh. He spluttered and caught a crab with one oar which almost put him over backwards in the dinghy.

Mary giggled again and leaned toward him.

"Whoa, don't stand up!" Tanner exclaimed under his breath, trying to avoid making too much noise as they passed another yacht, dark except for a single dim light at the mast. Every boat at anchor displayed such a light to warn approaching craft of their position and condition.

Mary was still giggling at Tanner's reaction to her semi-nakedness. "Hmm. I won't stand up but maybe I'll just get rid of the rest of this rig." Then she glanced beyond him and said, "A little more right oar, sailor. We're almost there."

Tanner risked another quick glance behind him to see that she was right. He rested a moment, then turned the boat around so Mary could step out onto the transom step carrying the dinghy painter in one hand. Tanner secured the oars, handed Mary the small mesh ditty bag they'd carried along in lieu of a purse. When he stepped up beside her she whispered, "There was a man in the restaurant who watched us almost the whole evening."

"An admirer?"

"Perhaps, but he was a dead ringer for the guy you described to Lieutenant Archambault."

7

In the morning, after a restless night, Tanner stood in the cockpit staring at Trellis Bay. Nothing suspicious disturbed the tranquil scene. He sipped his strong black coffee. There didn't seem to be anything they could do about the possible threat from a man Mary had noticed watching them last evening. Since she wasn't absolutely sure it was the same man who had bumped into Tanner at the Bitter End, it didn't seem useful to call the incident to the attention of Lieutenant Archambault. Besides, Tanner agreed, he might have just been ogling Mary. At the same time, they recognized that their growing unease over the whole affair was beginning to put stress on what had started as a relaxing sailing vacation in the Caribbean Sea.

Mary popped her head above the companionway hatch. "Breakfast is ready, my liege."

"Excuse me?"

Mary shrugged. "I just thought you looked a little kingly, or lordly, gazing out over your royal holdings. Anyway, sausages and scrambled eggs, with a piece of toast. On the table. Now."

"Coming," Tanner smiled and dropped down the ladder behind his mate. She didn't seem to harbor any after effects from the rum she'd ingested the previous night. "Have you come to any conclusions about our next move?" he said, slipping into a seat at the table.

Mary shoveled a mound of steaming scrambled eggs garnished

with sliced green peppers onto a plate and handed the serving across the table to his waiting hands. Tanner reached and plucked the salt and pepper shakers from their nest above the table, but when he upended the salt shaker, only a few grains came out.

"Looks like we better add some rice to that thing before the humidity locks it up permanently."

"Hmm, it may be too late already." He banged the shaker on the heel of his hand and then screwed off the top.

"How 'bout you?" Mary said. "Any thoughts on what we should do next?"

Tanner shook a few grains of salt into his palm. "We have what, four days left? I say let's go visit the Spanish Town and the Baths. As I recall that was one of the places you specially wanted to see. It's a straight shot from here with this wind almost dead on the beam. And the strait is wide open with not much traffic. If our friends are following closely, we should be able to pick them out."

Mary nodded, wiping up her plate with a piece of bread. "Good idea. We have to try to make as much of this vacation as we can, in spite of whatever this is all about. Since the Baths are pretty popular, we'll be among folks and less vulnerable, I should think."

Mary conned the sailboat out of its anchorage and pointed it toward Spanish Town on Virgin Gorda, not much more than a half hour sailing from the bay where they had spent the morning. It was an exhilarating sail under a deep blue Caribbean sky. Only a few scattered white clouds marred the canopy overhead. Blue-green salt water creamed off the sharp prow, splashed onto the big jib and ran in small rivulets down the scuppers. The waves added a rhythmic pulse as they sliced their way east toward the huge boulders that lay tumbled along the shore of the island. The boulders were a favorite visiting place for cruisers in the BVI. The huge rocks thrust up out of the ground, formed mysterious sun-dappled grottoes and winding tunnels in the waist-deep water. Underfoot, the bright sand was soft and inviting. Around a bend in the rock, one might find a secret pool in the cool shadows, punctuated by the sounds of happy children, echoing off the smoothly eroded rock walls.

They anchored twenty yards off shore. Their dinghy was big enough so they sat separately, facing each other on the bouncy thwarts, each wielding an oar. They quickly mastered the flat-bottomed dinghy so their path to shore was almost straight, if punctuated with an erratic rowing rhythm and much splashing of the warm sea water. Nearly drenched from the waist down, and clad in swim suits and loose white shirts for protection from the sun, they paused to smear each other with sunscreen, grinning and waving at other boaters. Worry-free enjoyment of the day and each other was firmly in mind. They ventured along the sandy beach onto the winding paths beneath the tumbled boulders. Some of the caverns they encountered were streaked with sunbeams from overhead that made the restless water sparkle. Others were nearly completely enclosed, lending a dark coolness to the atmosphere. Since there are no significant tides in the Virgin Islands, they had no worries about the time or the sea conditions. For the time being, their concerns about the death of the agent Ian McGwean aka George Simeon and the mysterious money Tanner had happened upon, faded from their thoughts.

Perched on a rock in the middle of one two-story high cave, Mary smiled at Tanner, admiring his smooth skin and sleek form. "I notice you are staying in pretty good shape, my friend."

Tanner grinned back. "I have to, if I'm going to keep up with you." They were alone in the cave and no one appeared to be nearby. The sounds of frolicking children and other vacationers was distant for the moment. Tanner moved closer and kissed Mary's cool shoulder, sliding one hand up her side to her breast as he did so. She turned her head and put her lips to his ear, leaning in slightly. The couple, unobserved for the moment, stayed still, leaning into each other for a long romantic moment, totally wrapped in each other's presence and the moment itself. Concerns about murder, money and tracking devices seemed far away.

Mary raised her head and whispered. "I guess we'd better be getting on to Spanish Town, don't you think?"

Tanner slowly pulled away and nodded agreement. "You're right, as usual."

They wandered hand and hand along the sandy paths beneath the boulders to their dinghy. Back aboard, a cursory examination of the craft showed no indication there'd been any unwarranted visitors. Mary waved at the woman seated on the bow of a nearby sloop. She'd been there when they went ashore.

"I don't suppose our friends showed up?" Mary called while Tanner maneuvered their boat over the anchor.

"Haven't seen a soul nearby," the woman responded.

Tanner started the engine and Mary took up the slack on the anchor chain with the electric windlass. They turned away amid friendly waves and headed up the coast toward the harbor at Spanish Town.

Soon they were tied to the dock in a visitor's slot, there being no room to anchor in the harbor when they arrived.

"That's got it," Mary called, threading the bow line back from the wharf cleat and under the lifelines to the deck. The arrangement would allow them to cast off from the deck rather than from the dock, should that be necessary.

Tanner shut off the idling engine and tied the wheel to the pedestal so the rudder wouldn't swing back and forth from the wake of passing boats. It was quiet but hot in the sheltered harbor. Tanner mopped his damp forehead.

"I'll lock up and we'll go explore, what say?"

Mary nodded and disappeared below to change into something more discreet. The dress code in the islands ran more to pants or skirts and blouses for the women. Shorts were frowned on and some shop owners refused to sell to tourists who came to their stores in brief swim suits.

She reappeared a moment later in a one-piece silk sun dress with narrow straps and a high curved neckline that showed off her shoulders and neck to good advantage. Tanner was decked out in tan Topsiders, mid-calf beige cotton shorts and a loose madras shirt with short tails that flapped about his waist. Mary handed him his tan straw boater and, smiling at the world, the handsome couple stepped through the narrow gate of the lifelines and strolled down the wharf toward the marina building and the small gaggle of shops drowsing in the tropical afternoon sun.

* * *

Unbeknownst to the couple, they were being watched as they strolled along, by two pairs of eyes, one set friendly and approving, the other expressionless under a heavy brow in a dark-seamed and weather-beaten face.

The owner of the second pair of eyes was seated behind a large flowering bougainvillea in a tiny shop offering exotic spices and a variety of teas. He was careful to keep his facial expression neutral. He didn't want his second cousin worrying, or even wondering what he was doing or who he might be observing. He held his position and a cup of warm tea as long as Tanner and Mary Whitney were visible strolling, sometimes hand in hand, in and out of the shops along the dusty street where children ran laughing. It was a school holiday, and mothers went leisurely about their afternoon tasks.

From everything he could observe, the old man with the seamed face and the watchful dark eyes, began to think the couple was in a holiday mood. A shrewd and long-time observer of his fellow humans, the old man became confident that Tanner and Mary Whitney were exactly who his employers said they were. They were a wealthy American couple, experienced sailors both, on a long vacation in the British Virgin Islands. That they had found some floating hundred dollar bills in the warm sea in a remote anchorage was pure happenstance. That they later encountered an alcoholic agent of Her Majesty's Internal Revenue Service was odd, but more than likely, merely a coincidental happenstance. It was just unfortunate that the agent had later been found murdered.

Neither the old man now making his slow arthritic way down the street in the same general direction as Tanner and Mary, nor the old man's present employers, careful and cynical as they were toward those honest folk they encountered in their various illegal activities, would spend any more effort or treasure tracking the couple's movements. It was their mistake.

The other, more benign eyes tracking the pair also made note of the old man when he rose from his perch on the veranda of the tiny coffee shop. These eyes, also dark and watchful, recognized the old man and with a tiny frown, processed his image in her mental data bank. She would contact her superiors in far away Saint Croix as soon as she was able to determine the Tanners' next stop. Why was the old man, a legend among island smugglers, following Tanner and his wife, an heiress of some significance? That he had been watching the Tanners she had no doubt. She would have had his place on the restaurant porch had he not got there first.

8

Oblivious to the rival observers, Tanner and Mary ambled alomg the street, kicking up small puffs of dust in the hot still air of Spanish Town, and admiring the goods on display in some of the shops. "I have an idea," Tanner said, watching Mary eyeball a bright red and blue long silk dress. The straps would nicely complement her deepening tan, he thought, but she shook her head and moved on to the next crowded rack of light-weight cotton tees and blouses.

"I have an idea," he said again.

"An idea? You have an idea?"

He grinned at her. "You don't have to say as though it's maybe only my second idea since you've known me."

Mary turned her bright smile on her lover husband to say, "Oh, phoo. You know that isn't so. What's the idea?"

"How 'bout we leave the boat in the harbor and get a room at one of these nice-looking hotels or B'n'Bs I see about us? We'll book a big airy room with a large shower, perhaps a pool, and a nice veranda all within easy walking distance of an old and small but pleasant restaurant with a killer chef in residence."

Mary smiled with delight. Sounds wonderful. Sounds like you are reading from a tourist brochure." She pointed at the glossy pamphlet Tanner was holding.

"Ah, you know me too well, I fear," Tanner laughed.

"It sounds, as I said, divine. If you're bored with my browsing, why not run off to the place you have in mind and see if such a room is available?"

"My thought, exactly. I'll do that and meet you at the harbor yacht club for drinks in about an hour." Tanner bussed Mary's warm cheek and strode up the street toward the other end of town.

Twenty minutes later, having booked into a very nice room in a small hotel called the Ancient Mariner, Tanner was back on their boat, arranging with the harbor master to move the Beneteau to a slip reserved for visiting yachtsmen. He quickly packed a small soft-sided carry-on with a change of under things and their bathroom kits. Grabbing his new digital camera, a birthday gift from Mary, he stepped back ashore and paid the harbormaster. Then he sauntered back along the street, keeping an eye peeled for his wife.

An old black man looking the wrong way, stumbled over a small pile of dust in the street and collided with Tanner. "Oof!. Sorry, mon. I was looking the wrong way."

"That's all right. No damage and no harm." Tanner grinned at the man, raising him by one arm until he was steady on his feet again. "You haven't seen my wife hereabouts, have you?" Tanner went on to describe Mary.

The old man smiled, further wrinkling his face and slowly shook his head. "Well sir, I can't rightly say that I have, having just entered the street here, myself." He freed himself from Tanner's grip and went along, across the other's path. A little farther on, Tanner saw Mary exiting a small spice and tea shop. He waved to catch her attention. Then together, they walked lazily in the hot sun toward their temporary abode.

* * *

"Very, nice," said Mary. "What a fine room. Up here on the second floor, we'll catch the breezes, and those big palms are great shade over the swimming pool. I approve, I do." She grinned and bussed Tanner on the cheek.

"I thought you'd like it. Unless there are rowdies around, having the pool practically right outside our door will be convenient."

"The owner tells me there's a fine restaurant overlooking the bay just on the other side of the neck of land. It's called The Prince William. I thought we could have dinner there. This place has a tiny bar downstairs, but no dining room. Just snacks and a sandwich or something like that."

"How 'bout a sandwich and a Pussers Painkiller?" asked Mary. She surveyed the room again. It was large, with louvered windows on two sides. Opposite the big king-sized bed the door opened onto a narrow balcony. The walls were rough or textured plaster, the ceiling was heavy with, dark beams of some sort of tropical wood. Between the beams, the ceiling was white plaster, like the walls. Several prints in heavy wood frames decorated the walls. There were windows on both sides, assuring them of good cross ventilation from the trades constantly blowing across the island.

The balcony led past two other rooms to the small plant- surrounded swimming pool. In the other direction, one quickly came to a narrow staircase that led down one flight to the open flagstone patio surrounded on three sides by the hotel walls. There was a large heavy door set into the stuccoed walls that were nearly covered with thick ancient leafy vines. It led to the street outside and was secured by an elegant, if crudely fashioned, heavy iron hasp and padlock.

Tanner had looked at the hasp and the padlock hanging on the wall. It reminded him of scenes from some of the old pirate movies he'd seen as a boy. They went to the office and picked up literature about places and the history of Spanish Town. The heat and the humidity were oppressive in the late afternoon, introducing languor and sapping of energy. It was unlike the environment they were used to aboard the yacht where the wind and the restless sea injected a constant sense of motion and energy.

The tropical sun was falling more and more rapidly when Tanner roused from a light nap, sprawled in a rattan chair near the foot of their bed where Mary was curled into a loose ball of slumbering woman. He spied a radio on a nearby table. Switching it on he was surprised to hear the Dixie Chicks cover of a James Taylor song, instead of the almost incessant rhythms of salsa and Caribbean tunes.

Mary murmured and stirred. She stretched and found Tanner with her gaze. "Shower with love, hey?" she whispered. "Give you any ideas, boy?"

Tanner smiled and rose lithely to his feet. He stepped swiftly to the side of the bed where he leaned way over and planted a hearty kiss on Mary's cheek. "Oh, yes. Like a shower and a slow walk to the restaurant where I have planned ahead and made us a reservation for just a little over an hour and a half from now."

"Ninety minutes? Plenty of time." Grinning, Mary grabbed Tanner by the belt and pulled him down to her. She hooked one heel behind his calf and pressed him close. "Plenty of time."

9

The Prince William was a far cry from the Soggy Dollar on the island called Jost Van Dyke where they'd had to swim ashore with paper money in the pocket of Tanner's swim trunks. Mary looked around appreciatively. Her mother, Mary thought, would have approved. One of Seattle's leading society mavens, Louise Hitchcock Whitney had very exacting standards when it came to restaurants and their decor. She believed when one went to town for a meal, especially an important meal such as dinner, one dressed for the occasion. Dinner did not, ever, involve popping down to the local fast food restaurant. Louise Hitchcock Whitney was never able to persuade her husband, a man she loved desperately all her life, to leave the rough and tumble manners and mannerisms of the Seattle waterfront, but dinner was always at least semiformal.

Even after he and his family had risen from laboring as longshoremen and shrimpers to become lumber barons and international deepwater cargo shippers, he preferred the bars and saloons of the docks to the salons and drawing rooms of Seattle's high society. But he'd won the love of one headstrong daughter of a politically important state senator with vast lumber holdings in Washington and Canada. The union had produced two boys and a bright, mischievous girl whose love for the sea, her rapscallion uncles, and her father, had instilled a wide-ranging insatiable thirst for classical knowledge and worldly experience.

Mary Whitney smiled as she looked approvingly around. Multiple groups of white candles hung in graceful wrought iron arrays high up near the vaulted ceiling of polished timbers. The room sheltered by the roof was open on three sides. The multi-tiered room dining room allowed people seated nearest the solid white adobe wall to see the vast expanse of the sea over the heads of other diners. The tables were all square mahogany or teak with softly glowing smooth polished surfaces and gracefully sculpted legs. Snowy white tablecloths reflected the candle light, as did the huge mirror on one wall. The room was surrounded by a patio of slate with a row of swaying rustling palms just at the outer edges of the pool of light. Some of the patrons already seated were casually dressed but here and there scattered through the room, like jewels specially presented, were women in elegant evening dress, glowing silk blues and greens with the occasional white gown. The men with them were likewise clad in dark semi-formal dress as befit their sparkling companions.

The table for the Tanners was set to one side, at the edge of the stone patio. Mary chose to sit facing the interior of the restaurant so she could watch the interplay of the patrons, the waiters and waitresses moving swiftly and efficiently between the tables, offering interesting looking exotic dishes and drinks. Sitting, the couple ordered drinks and studied the menus.

After placing their dinner order, Mary looked over her shoulder to see a large cruise ship passing the island in the sea channel. Every deck was lit from stem to stern and she counted fourteen levels.

"Big ship," Tanner smiled. "Must be a thousand people aboard, not even including the crew and assorted attendants."

"It's like a moving city. Must have a terrific impact on the economy wherever they go."

"And no holding tanks," Tanner responded, "unless it's been retrofitted."

As Mary looked around at the dining crowd, her gaze fell on a handsome dark couple making their way slowly through the room. The man was tall, wore a light tan, conservatively cut suit, over a pleated, sparkling white dress shirt with a dark figured tie. The woman with him was as tall as her companion, but Mary couldn't tell if she was wearing heels because the full sweep of her white silk skirt nearly touched the floor.

The woman's dark brown, luxuriant hair, was wavy and full, swept up in an elaborate hairdo. They changed direction and headed for Mary and Tanner. She noticed that several people seated in the dining area were watching, both covertly and openly, as the couple made their way across the restaurant.

Mary reached and pressed her companion's wrist where it lay on the table before her. When he looked at her, she nodded in the other direction. Tanner swiveled his head to see the approaching couple.

"Silk?" murmured Tanner.

"I expect so."

Tand then he rose in an easy motion to greet Lieutenant Archambault.

Archambault smiled, white teeth gleaming as he took Tanner's extended hand. "Good evening, Mr. an' Mrs. Tanner. How pleasant to see you. May I present my wife, Clothilde?" He reached his other arm around the woman's waist and drew her close. She smiled and bathed the table with warm radiance.

Tanner gestured to the empty chairs in an invitation to the Archambaults to join them. "Thank you, no. We have already eaten. We'll leave you to your dinner which I expect will be excellent. We consider this one of our favorite restaurants."

Archambault glanced around swiftly and leaned closer. His smile broadened and he murmured, "I would greatly appreciate it if you would come to see me sometime tomorrow. I have some additional information that will be of interest. I think we've made some headway at finding some answers. Any time tomorrow. I'll be in the office the entire day."

Tanner inclined his head, smiling broadly. "Thank you. It was a pleasure seeing you again." He looked the other man in the face to signal he'd received the message.

Clothilde Archambault smiled also and nodded to Mary and turned at the edge of the patio and the couple strode out of sight. Tanner sat down and smiled at his companion who smiled back saying in a slightly louder than necessary voice, "What a handsome couple, don't you think?"

"I do think," chuckled Tanner. "Thanks for picking up on that little interchange. I wonder what's happened."

"Looks like they were doing a little improvisation. I noticed that the good lieutenant changed direction as they were leaving. It appeared he recognized us and decided to come deliver his message personally."

Mary leaned closer and said, "Let's try to forget it for now and enjoy our dinner." Tanner looked closely at her full red lips and agreed.

* * *

After an excellent dinner of roast lamb, fried plantain, braised potatoes and a lavish salad of locally grown fruits and greens, topped off with nicely chilled brandy ices, the couple strolled through the hot night back to their room. High overhead, above the humming of swarming unseen insects in the frangipani that grew thickly along the street, a gibbous moon appeared to ride across the star laden sky. It's light cast a warm glow on the passing clouds. The moon, seemingly close overhead, rolled its beams and shadows across the landscape. A few lights shown in windows of homes in the village. The couple, fingers entwined, paid little attention to their surroundings until they reached the big weathered gate in the wall surrounding their hotel.

"Will they open the portal do you suppose?" Mary smiled and leaned against the rough stone pillar.

"I told our hosts that we would be late and was assured that we would be most welcome at any hour." Tanner's questing hand found a rough rope loop and he gave it a yank. Inside he heard the clapper of a heavy bell. They waited and soon hurried steps sounded on the tiles. The latch was lifted and the door swung open to the smiling face of their host.

A single dim bulb on a pole near the stairs to the second floor struggled to illuminated the open patio. There were no lights anywhere else in the place and the shutters had been drawn over the small closet that served as a bar for the guests of the residence.

"Everybody else in bed?" Mary asked, slipping off her shoes.

"We have just two other couples in residence, elderly guests from England. They have stayed with us before and always take the same ground floor rooms."

Tanner thanked the man and followed Mary up the stairs to their room. At the door he produced the key and Mary whispered, "How 'bout a midnight swim?" She gestured at the calm pool behind them. He nodded and they went inside.

In a trice, Mary had divested herself of her clothes and wrapped a big beach towel around herself. Then she slipped out the door and headed down the short length of the dark balcony to the pool. Tanner followed her lead and walked carelessly, towel over his shoulder, after her.

When he stepped, naked, around the balcony wall, Mary gave a low whistle of appreciation. Tanner slid quietly into the cool water and swam to his waiting wife.

10

The next morning they took advantage of their host's kitchen and had a light breakfast in the small patio dining area. At a separate table across the room the four elderly Brits were engaged in a spirited if quiet conversation at their table. The two men had glanced up and nodded at Tanner, who preceded Mary into the room by five minutes. The women ignored him. He watched when Mary arrived. No one at the table paid the slightest attention.

Another cup of coffee in hand Mary leaned forward and said, "Well, slugger, shall we go back to the boat and run over to Road Town, see what the good lieutenant wants?"

"I suppose so. Seems a shame not to be able to spend the day here or just sailing, though."

"Why don't I pack our duffels and you can settle up."

Mary went back up to their room and Tanner sought out their host. Then they walked down to the marina to retrieve their boat.

"There is a message for you," said the harbor master. It was left here late last night. He handed the small envelope to Tanner who ripped it open. Mary watched as Tanner shrugged and said, "It's from the good lieutenant, a reminder that he wants to see us in his office today, preferably before noon."

"I suppose he left it before we encountered him at the restaurant. Either that, or he just wants to be very sure we'll sail over to Road

Town," Mary remarked, hoisting her duffel off the dock and onto *Passions Messenger*'s deck.

Saying goodbye to the busy marina in St. Thomas Bay, they motored into the passage and headed southeast toward Beef Island, then past Fat Hogs Bay and on into Road Harbor on the island of Tortola. This time they slipped inside the barrier to Little Wickham Cay where the harbormaster found temporary space at the transient's dock.

"Should we lock up?" said Mary, stepping aboard after tying off the stern line.

"I think so. There's a lot of foot traffic and the marina doesn't seem terribly secure," said Tanner.

"Okay. I'll change into shore togs and pack a handbag. I hope this meeting doesn't take too long."

Tanner nodded and checked the dinghy's painter, shortening it. The waterway was also busy and he didn't want an inattentive boater to hit the inflatable. He knew Mary would either hide or carry their passports and other identification along with money and other valuables. He finished taking another quick survey of topsides to be sure nothing appeared to be amiss or sloppily lashed. Just as he finished, Mary emerged and locked the sliding hatch. Neither the lock itself nor the hatch, for that matter, would withstand a determined attack, given time and opportunity, but at least there wouldn't be an open or easy invitation, should someone decide to try to learn if they were making progress in their search for the source of the waterlogged currency.

"Do you think we're still being watched?" Mary asked as they strolled toward the center of town.

Tanner smiled mirthlessly. "I expect so. In fact, if this is a laundering or funny money smuggling operation we've stumbled into, I won't be surprised to learn we've got a bevy of watchers, state and federal, maybe from more than one nation, hanging on our every act."

"Really? How exciting." It was clear from Mary's tone she didn't find the prospect of multiple agents trailing in her wake to be at all appealing. Side by side they went again into the Road Town Police Department building.

When Lieutenant Archambault ushered Tanner and Mary Whitney into his office, the atmosphere was definitely chillier than the previous evening at the restaurant. Without more than the barest preamble, the lieutenant laid out the most recent information.

"I have had several messages from Her Majesty's Home Office. Apparently it is the Home Office that has been tasked to handle this problem. We colonials don't rate a real examination."

Tanner raised his eyebrows briefly at this bitter sally.

"The late lamented Mr. Ian McGwean was indeed on a special mission. His brief was supposed to be fairly passive: to be on watch, as it were, for any activity that might be linked to the transport of counterfeit securities through the islands."

"I take it," Mary said, settling into the chair, "that his death has raised the stakes and agitated the watchers."

"We will shortly have an influx of agents from the Home Country to find these murderers and bring them to justice." Archambault shrugged elaborately. "Or so I've been advised. Now I have a few questions, relayed to me from the Home Office."

Tanner raised his hands, palms up, in the universal gesture of cooperation. "Anything we can do to help," he said.

Archambault smiled thinly and slid open the lap drawer of his desk, apparently consulting something within. "Have you ever met a man named Gordon Barnes?"

Tanner glanced at Mary. "I don't think so. At least not since we've been here in the islands."

"I agree," said Mary, "I'm sure I've never heard the name."

"So you are both sure. Perhaps you know him as Gordo or Bobo?"

Both Mary and Tanner shook their heads. "Sorry, nope. Never heard the name. Who is he?" asked Tanner.

"And what's his connection to this business of the soggy hundreds?" concluded Mary.

"I'm afraid I cannot answer either of those questions," said the lieutenant. "But I think that concludes our business."

"Really? We can go?" asked Tanner.

"Hardly. You are to be escorted to the airport here on Beef Island and shipped home. Forthwith."

Tanner smiled and nodded. "Hmm. That seems rather abrupt but our vacation is pretty well shot anyway, so I guess we won't protest."

Mary started to say something, but subsided after a quick glance at Tanner. "As you wish. We'll sail the boat around to Maya Cove and your men can ferry us to the airport for the next flight to Charlotte Amalie."

"I think not. My instructions are to have you driven directly to the airport where you can be protected until the next flight to the American side, which is in about four hours, at dusk."

"I'm beginning to feel like a protected witness. I'm surprised you let us sail over here from Spanish Town," Mary remarked, "instead of bringing us in under escort." She smiled faintly to reduce the sting of the words. "I guess that's about it." She rose and straightened her white slacks. "I can't say this has been the most pleasant vacation I've ever spent on the water, but it certainly has been interesting." She extended her hand to the lieutenant. They went to the door and exited to the front of the building.

Lieutenant Archambault shook hands with Tanner, saying, "A car will meet you at the wharf and help you with your belongings. We will contact the charter company and arrange to transfer the sloop to their marina. I am sorry it has come to this, but we want you both to be safe so you can return and enjoy our islands more fully at some future time."

Outside the headquarters building, Tanner turned to his wife and said, "We better get some cash before we go pack up our gear." They walked casually away from the building.

"All right, spill," Mary said. "What's going on here? Do you have a clue?"

"No but I thought it best not to raise the flag in there."

"I got that," replied Mary. "It feels to me that our good lieutenant has been given some orders from higher up."

"Maybe. Maybe not. There certainly is something odd going on."

"I'll say. Last night he said he had information to share and today he basically only asked about that Gonzo Barnes. Weird. It's like there's been a total change of plans by somebody, somewhere."

"Well, bank and then home," Mary continued. "But let's be extra vigilant from now on so we'll be better armed should the need for testimony or something else appear on our horizon. Some relaxed vacation this has turned out to be."

Tanner smiled. "At least no hurricanes."

"I'll hit the bank. I want to call Edmund in Seattle anyway. It won't take any time at all if you want to go directly back to the boat to pack," Mary said.

Tanner agreed. "Works for me. There's still enough daylight to let us get back to Maya Cove before the plane leaves. Maybe I can persuade the nice policeman, whoever's assigned to be our bodyguard, to let us sail back, in spite of Archambault's orders. Then we can pack up in the relative peace of Maya Cove before we get hustled to the airport." Mary leaned up and kissed Tanner decorously on the cheek as they moved down the dusty street. A few minutes later Mary Whitney waved goodbye and turned up the hill inland. Tanner continued toward the dock where their boat was moored. The street was not crowded, but there were people going about their normal activities.

Mary turned in at the first bank she saw with an ATM and withdrew some money. She took the five twenties the machine dealt her and then went to the counter. The cashier pointed her to a row of telephones in a narrow ell off the main lobby of the bank. When she turned around to go to the phones she almost collided with a nice looking woman who had been standing close behind. I wonder if she was watching me, Mary mused and then punched in her telephone card calling numbers. It took only a minute to alert Edmund Hochstein of their circumstances and to suggest some lines of inquiry he might initiate. Stepping through the door into the afternoon heat, Mary reflected again on the advantages of her position of wealth and privilege. Edmund Hochstein, long-time head factotum of Whitney Enterprises and of her foundation, would begin to learn many things about the smuggling business in this part of the world. The information would be valuable when she and Tanner sat down to evaluate their experiences back home in Seattle.

Five minutes later she stood on the wharf feeling the oppressive sun beating down on the broad-brimmed straw hat she wore, staring in consternation at an empty mooring. Tanner and *Passions Messenger* were nowhere to be seen. She checked nearby piers in case she'd stepped onto the wrong dock. No mistake. She stared out at the sparkling blue water, searching in what she realized immediately was a useless attempt to spot the sloop. There were dozens of boats on the water, including several sailboats using their engines. Some boats could hardly be seen at a distance, much less identified. Where had Tanner got to? It was inconceivable that he would take it into his head to sail alone around to Maya Cove, leaving her stranded on the beach, as it were. But where was he? Her instincts told her it was not idle circumstance. Something or someone had intervened to cause her husband, never an impulsive man, to move their boat. Her breath came more rapidly and alarm coiled through her. The possibility that her husband had been kidnapped rose in her mind.

Mary went trotted to the harbormaster to see the man who had directed them to the slip when they arrived from Spanish Town. But the tiny shack perched on the edge of the long wharf was locked. A crumpled note stuck into the crack in the door jamb indicated the man was gone until the next day. Growing increasingly worried, Mary stalked off the dock to the street and found a public telephone. She phoned the police to learn that Lieutenant Archambault had left the building but a detective would be dispatched to the marina.

"Ms. Mary Whitney?" She cradled the handset and turned her head. The woman who had been next to her at the bank was staring at her and holding out her hand with a card case.

"Yes," Mary said. "You were in the bank a few minutes ago. Are you following me?"

"My name is Hilda Martin, Ms. Whitney. Here's my ID. Yes, I have been following you. Ever since you returned here to Tortola this morning."

"You're a federal agent?" Mary Whitney examined the woman's credentials. "What does the U.S Secret Service want with me? I haven't time for this. Look, I'm sorry to be so abrupt but my husband appears to have gone missing and I don't think it was his decision to leave me on the dock."

"I was told he went aboard and immediately cast off in an ordinary way. Mr. Tanner appeared to be talking with someone standing in the companionway."

"My God, that's insane," Mary snapped. "That wasn't the plan. Talking with someone? This is just crazy! Wasn't there a policeman at the dock?"

The woman hesitated. "I never actually saw the other person until they were into the harbor, but Mr. Tanner appeared to be having a conversation as they left the slip No one nearby identified themselves as a policeman."

Mary realized that Tanner had to have been getting under way while she, Mary, was in the bank. This woman, Hilda Martin had been in the bank lobby at the same time. She couldn't have seen what she'd just told Mary, so there had to be at least one other person involved to tell her what happened. Mary gestured impatiently staring at Agent Martin. "Please! Tell me exactly what you know."

A short squat black man puffing heavily, trotted up to the women, extending a shiny gold badge. "Missus Whitney," he puffed. "Hello, Agent Martin, I thought I'd run into you pretty soon." He turned back to Mary. "I'm assigned to be your escort to the airport. When I saw your husband leaving on your boat I stopped to notify the Coast Guard and the other law enforcement folks. I knew he wasn't supposed to go off like that. I've put the word out so if that boat shows up anywhere in five hundred miles, we'll hear of it. Why did he leave? Surely you didn't plan this?"

"Of course we didn't! I went to the bank and Michael was going to the boat to pack our gear. Thank you, detective, for notify the other authorities, but I can't stop there. Apparently there was someone waiting for Michael aboard our charter. I have no idea who that could be or why this happened. My husband would not have gone willingly. He's in some kind of danger and I want Air-Sea Rescue notified immediately! This is kidnapping and hijacking! Piracy, right?"

"Not piracy, we're not in international waters at the moment. Look—"

Mary cut him off with a sharp gesture. She squinted against the burning sun, looking at the busy harbor. Michael was out there somewhere and she knew he needed her. Suddenly she was beginning not to trust this detective although she couldn't have said why. She whirled and stared at Agent Martin. Was she real or yet another lie?

11

"We need to get off the street," Hilda Martin said abruptly. "I have an office just down the way."

The short detective nodded. "I know where your office is located, Agent Martin. I must talk to my superior at headquarters and also to Lieutenant Archambault as soon as we can locate him. I'll find you after that." He took Mary's hand. "Try not to worry too much, Mrs. Whitney. We'll do everything possible to find your husband and your boat." With that he turned and hurried off, back the way he had come.

Mary watched him go. Was that detective to be trusted? Was Hilda Martin a real Secret Service agent? Then she realized she needed access to a telephone again. "All right. Do you trust him?" Mary asked, gazing after detective Emmett Smythe. She gnawed her lower lip. It was a habit she'd acquired years ago. Now it only manifested itself when she was worried or upset. And right now she was both.

"Yes, I do. I've worked with Detective Smythe on more than one occasion and known him since I first arrived. He's competent, smart and as far as I can tell, completely honest. He's married and has two very nice pre-teen children." She lengthened her stride. The two women strode rapidly along the dusty road.

Hilda Martin took Mary to an old but substantial stone and concrete one-story building next to one of the old hotels. Inside, in the stuffy afternoon heat of a shut-up room in the tropics, Mary found what appeared to be a down-at-the-heels small business office. There were two old wooden desks and chairs, a battered IBM electric typewriter on one and nothing on the other. Two side chairs of dark green plastic and an uncomfortable looking sofa under the front window completed the furnishings. There were no machines, no file cabinets.

"Look, Mrs. Tanner—Ms Whitney, I realize this is terribly upsetting." Hilda stared keenly at Mary for a moment. "And right now you aren't even sure if I'm legitimate. I assure you I am. In spite of the surroundings. This is a temporary station, until my superiors decide I should stay. But you'd better be sure." She watched Mary take in the shabby-appearing office. "You said you wanted to make a call?" Hilda sat down at the desk with the typewriter and pointed at the other desk. "There's a telephone in the left hand drawer. The bathroom is through there," pointing at the only other door.

Mary sank into the desk chair and pulled out the indicated drawer. The telephone instrument was shiny black, modern and had a thick cable running out the back and through the drawer. Three LEDs glowed orange on the panel. The sleek telephone console was at odds with the rest of the room.

"Use any open line," Hilda said, pulling out an identical console from her drawer. Mary saw her pick up the handset and a button glowed white. That left two unused and she pressed one while picking up the handset. The ordinary hum of the telephone line reassured her and she swiftly dialed a Seattle number from memory.

Two rings and a familiar voice said, "Yes? Edmund Hochstein here."

Mary released a soft breath and sagged slightly in the chair. She'd been afraid her old friend and mentor might be unavailable. His calm and reassuring voice even from thousands of miles away made it possible for her to believe that things would turn out all right and Michael Tanner would be retrieved unharmed. Efficiently she sketched the circumstances of her husband's apparent abduction, avoiding any specific mention of niggling suspicions that were taking root in her mind.

"Are you all right, my dear?" Hochstein asked when she finished explaining that Tanner appeared to have been kidnapped along with their chartered boat that very afternoon. After receiving her assurances that she was now well-protected by a member of the U.S. Secret Service, Hochstein agreed not to send his own security people to the islands.

"What about the local law?" he asked then.

Mary hesitated. "I guess they are okay, but it's a small force, geared mainly to the tourists, I think."

"I see. I will of course exercise some of our contacts to insure no effort is overlooked to secure Michael's prompt return and in approximately the same condition as when you last saw him. I will also check on the local situation."

"Thank you, I appreciate that. I'll call again tomorrow morning or sooner if there are developments."

Mary turned around to find Hilda looking at her oddly. "Do I interpret your remark about the local police correctly? You aren't entirely secure with us? Sorry, I couldn't help overhearing."

"I assumed you would be listening. Frankly, Agent Martin, I also assume the call was recorded." She grimaced. "At the moment I trust you. I tend to trust all law enforcement but I'm not so sure about some of the local police." She paused, stood suddenly and paced two steps to the wall and back again to the desk. "I'm not used to waiting around in situations like this. It's not how I was raised."

The other woman looked at Mary with no expression on her smooth face. She waited, sensing there was more to come.

Mary stalked to the window and stared out. "Do you know who I am? Have you done a background check?"

Agent Martin's eyebrows went up. "Ms Whitney, we haven't had time to do a thorough check. We started with your husband. We know he runs a well-regarded advertising agency in Seattle, that he's comfortably situated and has no police record, except for a few minor traffic encounters scattered over a dozen years, and he's married to you."

"Correct. My name is Whitney. And yes, I'm one of the Whitneys of the Seattle Whitneys. I'm sure your supervisors will fill in the details. I don't particularly like to trade on my family wealth and position but we have money and influence and power in Seattle and in D.C., and right now I'm desperately worried about my husband." She sighed with exasperation. Other than a slight widening of her eyes, Hilda observed Mary Whitney without overt reaction.

"The man I called, as you'll shortly discover, is head of Whitney Enterprises and he knows how to use the power we have." Listening to herself, Mary tried to slow down and remove the stridency from her voice. She detested people who threw their privilege around and in her growing concern for her husband she feared she was becoming one of them. She stopped talking. She gestured helplessly and sat down suddenly. Mary turned away from the other woman and curled forward, resting her forehead on the warm wood of the desk top. She could feel tears forming. "Oh, God," she whispered. "Please be safe, Michael."

The telephone rang. Two short bursts of sound.

Hilda Martin picked up the handset and mashed a button. "Yes? Martin." The woman listened for a few moments and then said, "Got it." Then she replaced the handset. "That was my supervisor in Washington," she said softly. She glanced at her watch. "It's only been five minutes since you talked with your guy in Seattle. Now D.C. calls me. Some kind of record for quick reaction. Confirms everything you just told me and more. Apparently he will coordinate things with your Mr. Hochstein so that we'll have all the cooperation from the Brits here in the islands that we could ask for. I'm impressed."

Mary raised her head and smiled wanly at the other woman. "That's fine, but you and I know they're thousands of miles away and we have to do whatever it is right here. Listen, Hilda, I don't like the way I acted a minute ago. That's not normal for me. Forgive me, please."

Hilda Martin reached out a hand and touched Mary on the shoulder. "Forget about it," she said softly. "I can't begin to imagine how worried you are. Right now I'd like you to go over everything from the time you found the money off Ginger Island to the moment I introduced myself. Bring me up to speed while we hope the Coast Guard is locating your boat." She sat down again and pulled a file from her lap drawer.

12

During the ensuing thirty minutes Mary related to Agent Martin her and Tanner's travels in the islands, from the moment the aircraft touched down on St. Thomas, from Tanner's happening on the three soggy hundreds, to their meeting with the now dead Ian McGwean at the Bitter End and their interrogations by the police in Road Town.

"And when you two met the lieutenant and his wife on Virgin Gorda, at the Prince William, neither of you sensed anything even a little off in the police handling of you up to that point?"

"No, not at all. Why do you bring up our chance meeting at the restaurant?"

"You are sure it was a chance meeting?" asked the agent.

"Absolutely," Mary emphasized. "When we sailed to Spanish Town, we hadn't decided to spend the night and we didn't choose the inn or the restaurant until after we docked. There's simply no way that meeting at the Prince William could have been anticipated." She stopped then and leveled a questioning gaze at Hilda Martin. The women were silent for just a second and then Mary went on. "I don't believe I mentioned the name of the restaurant when I gave you my overview of our time and activity while we've been in the BVIs. How do you know about that?" She leaned forward to maintain eye contact with Martin.

Martin hesitated and finally said, "You're very sharp. I'm breaking some rule, but I can tell you we've been watching you two ever since you first were contacted by Mr. McGwean at the Bitter End." She touched the file folder on her desk. "It started after he called our office."

"Is that so? And what did Mr. McGwean have to say about the two Americans who seemed to have found and then promptly lost three hundred dollar bills?"

Agent Hilda Martin smiled briefly. "He seemed to take you at your word. He did think the bills you found could be part of something he was working on. He suggested the owner of the bills you found might come looking for you."

"So you thought we could be bait? But the bills disappeared while we were ashore at the Bitter End. I assumed the smugglers or whatever they are got their money and just left."

"We knew that. We didn't know if there was anything else. It was all very iffy. Chances were nothing would come of it." She waved a graceful hand. "You'd wonder, McGwean would make some plausible excuse, then you'd finish your vacation and fly home. No entanglements. That's the nature of this business. Bits and pieces. Gossamer on the wind. Bad intelligence, good intelligence and lots of dead ends.

"But then McGwean is murdered and there was the matter of the radio finder somebody planted on your boat."

"I don't get any of this," said Mary. "And now Michael and our boat have disappeared."

"Tell me again," said Hilda. "You've never had any reason to wonder about the actions in this case by local authorities?"

"No. Absolutely not. At least not until we arrived here this morning. I don't understand why they would ask us to come in for another interview and then after we get here insist that we have to be escorted directly to the airport and flown to Charlotte Amalie. Even without surrendering our charter to the company in Maya Cove," said Mary. "That reminds me, I should call them to tell them about the hijacking. Damn!"

"I have a different idea," Hilda Martin said. "We need to get you situated in a room at the hotel across the street here. Not the one next door. Then I think you and I ought to run out to Maya Cove and talk with the people there."

"Do you think they're involved somehow?"

"I don't want to jump to any conclusions, so let's just say I like face to face contact." Agent Martin smiled humorlessly and ushered Mary to the door. Mary watched her press a sequence of buttons on her telephone console, stow the instrument in her desk drawer and the two women promptly exited the building.

As they left the building, Agent Martin said, "I know my office isn't much. Somebody felt we should keep a low and casual profile, so don't be fooled. This was supposed to be a temporary assignment. Now, we'll need to get you a few clothes. Let's go over here to this shop." Mary allowed Hilda to guide her to a small store two doors down where Mary purchased some necessaries and basic toiletries. The smiling native woman at the desk of the hotel escorted them to a large airy room on the second floor at the front of the building. Mary noticed that it overlooked the space being used by the secret service officer. She realized that it would be relatively easy for someone in the building across the street to keep loose tabs on her. She assumed that was the case.

They collected Hilda's Morris Minor and drove the winding road west along the coast to Maya Cove.

The man in the charter company office looked surprised. "Ah, Mrs. Tanner. I expected to see you arriving by sea in your boat. But not so soon. Is there a problem? His musical voice carried the peaceful rhythms of the island patois, but now they seemed out of place to Mary.

Mary took the lead. "I'm afraid I have some very bad news, Simon. *Passions Messenger* has been stolen. Hijacked."

"Excuse me? Piracy? But that simply does not happen here. Explain please."

"We came to port early this morning and tied up at Wickham Cay. We had an … an appointment today here in Road Town. After that I went to the bank and Michael went directly to the marina. When I left the bank to go aboard, the boat was missing. What's worse, people at the marina said they saw my husband leaving with the boat. One person said he appeared to be talking to someone who wasn't visible."

"How very odd. Is there some other possible explanation?"

"No. I'm convinced he was forced to sail away. It's been a couple of hours. I've notified the police and the Coast Guard. There's still no sign of either the boat or my husband."

"The Coast Guard! I see. Yes of course, we must do everything possible to find our boat and your husband right away. I shall call my employer immediately. We will also start a search. Oh, Mrs. Tanner, this is awful. Be assured we will do all possible. Is there anything now that you require?"

"Nothing right now, thank you, Simon. Here is where I'm staying, and the telephone number. Please call me the minute you learn anything. And of course, the police."

Mary and Hilda left the small office and went to Martin's car.

"What do you think?" said Mary.

"I think Simon isn't part of this." She fished a pair of high powered Nikon binoculars from a bag in the back seat of the tiny car and they walked to the wharf where Hilda stopped and examined the small cove and the several boats anchored there. "It's too bad you happened to choose one of the most popular sailboats down here. There must be dozens of identical sailboats in the BVI."

Outside the entrance to the cove, a helicopter emblazoned with the insignia of a private tour company scudded by at just over tree-top elevation. Martin watched it for a few moments and then nodded. Mary looked at her with a question on her face, but the agent said nothing. She lowered the glasses and the two women went back to the car.

Later, when they parted in the street outside Mary's hotel, Agent Martin gave her a private cell phone number and pressed her to call at any time if she learned anything new about Tanner's whereabouts, or was contacted by the kidnappers.

In her room, Mary looked out from the second-floor window over the town. The sun was getting lower and she knew it would be dark before long. Her concern for her husband grew as the light faded from the sky. The small office building across the way, the one being used by the Secret Service, was dark. Small low powered street lamps left dark shadows over most of the town. Where only a night ago the scene would have seemed warm and romantic, now Mary saw only menace. Beyond the shore, vast areas of dark restless water concealed…what? Now, finally, Mary let her guard down; alone she allowed the steely reserves she'd developed over the years give way. She let the tears flow, conjuring Tanner's image as she'd seen him last, smiling, turning away to return to the marina while she went to the bank.

There were people on the street then, weren't there? Not close. Mary sat in a chair beside the bed. She leaned her head back and closed her eyes. Concentrating, trying to reconstruct the hot street scene where she and Tanner had parted. In her mind, for the fleeting moments she'd surveyed the street, was there anybody looking? Watching them? Her memory scanned the street. Nothing. Wait. A man, an old man a few yards away seemed to be paying attention and his eyes had stayed with Tanner. Mary struggled to fix details of the man's appearance and his clothes in her memory. It might mean nothing, it probably did mean nothing, but maybe there was something. She snapped on the bedside table lamp and wrote down everything about that moment, the people there, that she could remember. Later, she recalled thinking she wouldn't be able to sleep, worrying about Tanner, and there were so many questions.

13

The ringing of the telephone in the hotel room woke Mary. Its insistent sound brought her up from some primal depth where the mind sometimes takes the body for protection from heavy emotional stress. It was morning, bright and sunny, and she realized that even while Michael was out there somewhere in danger, she had slept soundly in this comfortable bed.

She rolled over, scrubbed the sleep from her eyes and grabbed the receiver. "Yes?"

"Mary Whitney?"

"Who's this?"

"What's the first letter of the first name of your foundation's director?"

"What? Who is this?" She paused to take a breath. Now she thought she recognized the voice through miles of cable and satellite and wire connections. "Ed—, wait. Please. I just woke up." Mary took a deep breath, clearing her mind a little. "The letter is 'E, and isn't this a little melodramatic?"

"Possibly not, my dear. Are you alone?"

"Yes, unfortunately. Michael is still missing."

"Some disquieting information has come to us. It concerns the situation in which you currently find yourselves. You appear to have become entangled in some large multi-national activities. I will not go into specifics on this open line. Do you understand me?"

"What? I don't—" she frowned. "Wait. All right. I get it. Go ahead."

"Take every precaution you can. I'd order you home immediately if I thought you'd obey. But avail yourself of anything Ms. Martin offers. Are we clear? She may be young and inexperienced, but she is trustworthy."

"Mmm. Yes, thank you, sir." He severed the connection while she was still talking.

"Oh, Hell," she muttered. She lay back down and stared at the ceiling. Order me home immediately? He never talked that way to her. Never had. Obey? Another odd word. Mary knew that the old family friend and her head of the Whitney Foundation sometimes became overly concerned about her welfare and that he and Tanner conspired to weave a loose network of protection around her whenever possible, but this seemed a little over the top. Except... except that her husband was missing along with their chartered sloop. She ran over the rest of the conversation in her mind. Hochstein had never mentioned Tanner, but he obviously was not ready to give her whatever he'd learned because he feared being overheard. Somehow she and Michael had gotten tangled up with some pretty serious people who had the means of tapping her telephone. That possibility was ominous. The main piece of it was that Hilda Martin could be trusted.

Mary showered and dressed. She was about to leave her room in search of breakfast when the telephone rang again. "Yes?"

"Ms Whitney, this is Agent Martin. Hilda."

"Have you had breakfast, Ms. Martin? I haven't and I'm hungry. I think better if my stomach isn't distracting me. Can you meet me?"

"Yes, I'm downstairs in the lobby. I'll wait in the dining room."

Without saying goodbye, Mary dropped the instrument and stalked out of the room. Halfway down the staircase she stopped and clutched the railing. She took three deep breaths to slow her pulse. Being abrupt and snarling at people or trying to throw her weight around wasn't part of her normal makeup and she knew it wouldn't help get Michael back any sooner.

When she entered the small sunny dining room tucked into one corner of the main floor of the hotel, Agent Martin rose to greet her. Mary smiled at her and the two women sat across from each other. Mary cocked her head and sent the other a quizzical look.

"I've had a call, two calls, actually, from my superiors. You appear to carry a considerable amount of weight in Washington." Hilda's tone was respectful.

Mary leaned forward and stared into the other woman's blue eyes. "Yes, money is good for lots of things. I've had a call this morning also. You come with high recommendations. Here's the thing. I never apologize for the money my family acquired and passed along, but it doesn't make me any better than you or thousands of others. I want us to cooperate in getting my husband back safely, and as quickly as possible. Where my money, or his, can help, we'll use it, but your training and your agency's resources are what's really needed now. All my money can't match that."

Hilda bit her lip and said, "Look. I have to level with you. I'm fairly new on the job. I was shipped down here to the islands to liaise with the British, apparently because Washington wants to keep London happy. This is not a regular post for the Service and I don't have a lot of experience. I doubt my boss expected anything major to turn up here."

Mary reached across the table as a waiter approached. He carried a white pot in his hand. "Let's you and me be a team. I have money and you have training and access." She touched the other woman's fingers.

Hilda visibly relaxed and they both glanced about while the waiter poured coffee and took their breakfast order. There was a single woman at another table and an elderly couple nearby. "Your man in Seattle? Edmund Hochstein? What's he like?"

Mary smiled briefly. "He's eighty years old, he's been part of the family all my life. He can be abrupt sometimes but he's very bright. He runs Whitney Enterprises and oversees my foundation. Why do you ask?"

"He raised some dust in Washington. I like to get the important players clear in my mind. I've been authorized to give you some background on what we think may be going on."

"Think," echoed Mary. "So you aren't sure either. Based on my conversation this morning with Mr. Hochstein, we might be tangled up with a powerful criminal enterprise as somebody in the press called these gangs. I always call Mr. Hochstein 'mister,' always have. I think of him as a stern old, but very sharp, uncle." She stopped. Realized she was jumping around, her thoughts running in several directions. She had to calm down, think analytically. Do what she was good at. That was the best way to help Michael. Mary took a deep breath and sat back watching Hilda.

Hilda nodded and said, "There were rumors a few months ago that one of the big drug cartels in South America was moving into counterfeiting. Who knows why. We also heard that they had found a way to transfer some of the large amount of cash the drug trade generates through the American and British Virgin Islands Our informer claimed the smuggling was easily done with almost no chance of detection. That's why I was sent here as liaison to the British efforts to root out drug smugglers. Washington didn't give the information much credence, which is why I'm here alone with almost no facilities." She paused and fixed Mary with a steady look. "Never mind. I am here and we're going to do the very best we can to find your husband. Very recently we heard that a large amount of cash had gone missing, cash belonging to one of the cartels. That's one of the reasons we were interested when we heard about the hundreds you found."

Mary said, "I've read somewhere that the war on terror and other efforts at increased security have disrupted some of the routes used by drug smugglers." The women finished their meal and left the hotel for Martin's office across the street. Neither noticed an old man in ragged tan cargo pants and a loud silk shirt who sat and rocked slowly at the end of the veranda. He watched them go through half-closed eyes. When they disappeared into what he knew to be an office leased by a United

States law enforcement agency, he rose slowly as befitted his aged joints and shuffled inside the hotel lobby.

Hilda Martin sat at her desk and began to make a series of telephone calls to her contacts in the America Virgin Islands and to others scattered through the archipelago, seeking information and especially sightings of *Passions Messenger*.

Mary listened with half her attention. She was trying to imagine what she would do to conceal the identity of a stolen sailboat in this area where there were so many experienced eyes. When Hilda hung up her desk phone, Mary said, "I've been thinking about the boat. There's no way they'd have time or facilities to pull her ashore and repaint the hull. But if they were prepared, they could have renamed her by just painting over the transom. Nobody would notice except with a close inspection."

"I'm not a boater," Hilda said. "So I don't know much about these things, but other agents tell me there are only a few places here in the islands where a boat that large could be concealed and then only for a short time."

"I assume those places have been checked?"

Hilda nodded. "More than once."

Mary looked at the floor and said in a small voice. "If I was doing this, I'd sink the boat just as soon as I could. Somewhere in the channel at night. There are several places only a few hours away where she'd go undetected for years. There's another possibility." Her voice caught in her throat. "If they only wanted to get Michael away from Road Town, they could just set the boat adrift as soon as they transferred to another craft."

The telephone rang. Hilda answered and stood, forcing her chair back. "Where?" she barked. Then she dropped the phone and said to Mary, "There's been a sighting. A derelict sailboat, partially sunk."

"Where is it?" Mary stood, staring at Hilda, her worst fears rising to the fore.

"Out beyond The Indians. That's a jagged collection of rocks on the southern side of the main Francis Drake Channel, between Pelican and

Flanagan. It must be in Flanagan Passage."

"I've seen those rocks on the map."

Hilda held up one hand and dialed a number. It was clear she had called her superior and was asking for a helicopter or some other transport. After several minutes of discussion, Hilda said, "I—we don't have any way to get there now. The helicopter is still in Charlotte Amalie. I believe we shouldn't wait." She listened and her shoulders slumped. Then she cradled the phone.

"My boss thinks we should wait until the helicopter or the Coast Guard can pick us up. Could be hours. I'm sorry." She bit her knuckle. "Damn bureaucracy anyway."

"We'll get a boat," said Mary. "That's the best way. C'mon, Hilda. Your badge and my cash will do the trick."

The two women rushed out of the office. From the window of Mary's room, the old man in the ragged cargo pants watched them go toward the wharf. Then he went back to his methodical search of her sparse belongings.

14

At the municipal wharf, Mary's prediction came true. A charter company employee was quickly accommodating to the two pretty women with intense demeanors and an urgent request. The one assured him she could handle the thirty-six foot Grand Banks power yacht reserved for a wealthy Chicago businessman who was delayed by a late night party and too many Pusser's Painkillers. The hundred dollar tip was added incentive. The other waved very official-looking identification and demanded fast action.

The young man flipped the mooring lines off with practiced ease while Hilda and Mary scrambled aboard.

Mary ran her eyes over the control console at the steering station. Her fingers flew across the switches as she verified that the tanks were full and the twin engine ready indicators were glowing green. Lights flickered and came up when she pressed the starter buttons. Both engines came to life with no hesitation. Their throaty, reassuring rumble the women heard and felt beneath their feet, brought a quick curve to Mary's lips. She was at home here. This was a machine she could handle in a familiar environment.

She glanced at Hilda, waved at the boy on the dock and powered out of the slip, tapping the electric horn with three warning bleats as she did. She saw Hilda struggling to maintain her calm as the boat rocked in its own backwash and remembered then that the agent wasn't a boat enthusiast.

"Get a PFD," she called. "A life jacket. Look in those lockers." She pointed. Find one for yourself and bring me one."

Hilda nodded. When she turned and leaned to set her purse on a settee, her jacket flared open and Mary noticed for the first time that Hilda was carrying a small sidearm in a black holster at her waist.

Mary glanced around. Then she nudged the throttles up and they raced out of the marina into the harbor. She chose a route that brought her closer to an anchored cruise liner and avoided some of the smaller craft moving about the water. In minutes that seemed to take hours, they were outside the harbor, crashing through the big waves, slamming from crest to crest as Mary brought the power boat to its top speed. Fifteen minutes of teeth-jarring effort and she looked at Hilda who was clinging to a stanchion where she crouched on the portside settee. Hilda had a decidedly mournful green tinge to her face. Mary realized that they couldn't maintain this speed and arrive at the derelict in any kind of decent physical shape. She throttled back to half speed. Immediately the howling noise of the engines and the air rushing past the windscreen wound down. Their more comfortable ride in turn reduced the tension and the strain on the women in the cockpit. And now they could talk without yelling at each other.

Hilda stood and came to where Mary was standing braced on widespread feet at the wheel. "You're really good at that, you know. I'm impressed. But thanks for slowing down."

"It's mostly experience. I guess I have an instinct for boats, like some people are natural airplane pilots. I get a little airsick unless the plane has three or four jet engines. Do you have the coordinates, the location of the sighting?"

Hilda shook her head. Not exactly. The agent who called me just said it was a few miles south of those rocks. The Indians. He'd had a report from somewhere."

Mary nodded her understanding. "I hope this isn't a wild goose chase. Can you work a marine radio?"

"Not part of my training. Sorry."

"That's okay. Here. See this? Compass. It's electronic. It beeps and flashes if we get off course. I've dialed in the latitude and longitude of the rocks. This gizmo," she pointed to the gps screen, "uses satellites to give us our exact position and point us in the right direction. That thing is a radar scope. I turned it on to help me see other boats in our vicinity. Just in case." The two women looked into each other's eyes with unspoken understanding.

"Here," said Mary. "You stand here and steer. It's a good thing to know. And slip off those sandals. Bare feet is better, but I'll try to find some deck shoes for you."

Hilda nodded agreement and slipped into position. Mary showed her how to lightly grip the wheel. Once Hilda appeared to feel confident handling the launch, Mary explained the many controls on the steering console, her fingers flitting from place to place. "These are the throttles. They also control the transmission. See the notch? That's neutral. Pulling the handles toward you shifts to reverse, pushing forward, the boat goes ahead. If you change the transmission at high speed, it puts a big strain on the gear system and things can break. I always pause a beat or two when shifting from forward to reverse, or the other way, to allow the machinery to slow down. Less strain all around."

"Here, take control while I radio the marina. We need to find out exactly where the derelict boat is."

Hilda sighed and stared at the console. "Okay. Mary, give the radio operator my name and badge number and ask them to contact whoever called in with the original sighting so we can get the coordinates."

Mary raised the marine radio operator quickly but as soon as she identified herself, a message came back with the exact latitude and longitude of the derelict sighting. She tuned in the weather report and listened to some of the routine message traffic. It was a way to pass the time while they raced on toward whatever they might find ahead on the sea. These small routines didn't help. She found herself consumed by worry for Michael. Suddenly, she heard her name, rousing her from her brown study.

"What? I'm sorry. What did you say?"

"The Indians," said Hilda, pointing at the jagged rocks just ahead. "Can I have some relief?"

"Sure, sorry. Oh, there's a head—a toilet—down that stairway right there. But if you're feeling stomach upset, don't be long. Going below is a sure way to bring on seasickness until you get your sea legs."

Hilda soon returned, the green tinge around her eyes that had largely faded while she was at the controls of the speedy launch returned, but she soon recovered. She closed her eyes and held her face above the windscreen at the side of the cabin and let the fresh sea breeze flow over her.

Two hours later Mary throttled back. GPS told her they'd reached the reported location of the sighting. There was nothing but gently heaving, empty sea, all around.

"Now what?" asked Martin.

"The boat may have sunk, or drifted with currents or wind, depending on how much of the hulk is or was above water. Take the helm and stay on this course. I'm going up to the flying bridge with these binocs."

Mary ran up the ladder and braced herself against the canvas wrapped railing. Unlike the cabin, the flying bridge smelled faintly of old fish. Slowly, deliberately, breathing deeply to center herself, Mary scanned the horizon. Once. Twice. Then as they topped a big rolling wave, she saw a swaying mast upright in the water less than a mile downwind.

"Hilda, turn right and head northwest." She glanced at the repeater compass by her thigh. "Good. Hold this course. I think I see a mast."

Minutes later they were slowly circling a derelict sailboat, its deck about three feet below the surface. Its mast was bare, and the standing rigging was in a tangle, ripped sails trailed off the starboard side in the water.

15

Mary took the wheel, carefully maneuvering the launch as close as she dared go, avoiding wreckage in the water around the drifting boat. Lines streaming away from the hull could prove disastrous to the propellers. Hilda watched Mary as she assessed the sailboat. Sail cloth hung over the stern so the name was obscured.

Hilda could see that Mary recognized the boat. It was the sloop they had chartered. *Passions Messenger*.

"I'm sure that's our charter, Hilda. I need to go aboard."

"What? Not a chance. That thing could sink any minute. Uh uh. No way."

"Look, it's not going to sink this minute. I have to be sure, don't you see?" Mary had put the drive in neutral and went to stand at the rail beside Hilda, switching her gaze back and forth from the drifting hull to Hilda. "I have to know if... if Michael is down there, in the cabin." Her voice quavered and she took a deep, shuddering breath.

Hilda looked at her companion and shook her head. "Forget it. I can't run this boat alone. You know that. There's another thing: I was a champion swimmer in college. I'll go."

"I can't ask you to do that."

"There's no asking involved." Hilda quickly stripped off her PFD and her blouse and slacks and the borrowed shoes. "Give me that clasp knife." She pointed. Mary handed her the knife and watched as with shaking fingers Hilda stuck it into her bra. A pair of swim goggles had turned up in one of the cubbies. Hilda adjusted them around her head and then jumped feet first into the sea. Swimming strongly, she reached the stern and carefully lifted the torn cloth to reveal the name: *Passions Messenger*. Now there was no question it was the right boat.

Hilda eeled over the stern and paused, floating just above the cockpit floor. She took two deep breaths, glanced up at Mary and disappeared down the open hatch. Time passed, whether slowly or quickly, Mary couldn't have said. Her hands gripped the rail so tightly her knuckles turned white. Hilda had been underwater an impossibly long time. Suddenly there was a faint gurgle and an apparently empty water bottle popped out of the forward hatch.

Mary started and stared at the mast. Was the sloop sinking a little? It was hard to tell. With no warning the mast swung away and then back toward Mary. The hull lurched heavily and now there was no question it was getting lower in the water. Mary lunged for the electric horn and sent three ear-ringing blasts into the air. Again three quick blasts, the traditional warning to mariners everywhere. She ripped at her blouse, about to go over the side after Hilda when the other woman popped into view out of the forward hatch. She swam strongly straight up to the surface.

"The mast," yelled Mary. "Watch out! The boat's going down."

Hilda waved one arm and stroked hard for the side of the launch. Mary dropped a tethered life ring over the side. Panting heavily, Hilda grabbed it and hung on. "He's not in there," she gasped. "The boat is empty."

Shuddering with relief, Mary towed Hilda to the swim ladder she'd hung over the side just before Hilda reappeared, and helped her to the deck. "You're sure? You were able to look everywhere?"

The agent nodded, rubbing her arms with the towel Mary brought from below. "There were pockets of air in each of the cabins up at the ceiling. That's why I could stay under longer." She peered at Mary's worried face. "I went in every cabin, looked under bunks, pushed stuff

around. I even looked under the benches in the main cabin. There is nobody on that thing. I lost the knife. Oh, look."

Both women gazed again at the derelict as *Passions Messenger*
gave out one more gasp in release of trapped air and sank into the sea.
Mary watched the mast head get less and less distinct and then disappear. Glad as she was that Michael was not aboard, it was sad to see the
fine boat go down.

After a minute Hilda said, "I'm going to take off my bra and panties. Hope you don't mind. The sun will dry them quicker that way."

Mary nodded and then instinctively checked their horizon. "I guess
we better start back to Road Town." She went to the bridge.

Hilda wrapped a towel around her waist and followed. She laid a
gentle hand on Mary's arm. "At least we still have hope. Mary, that boat
was trashed. Even allowing for the water damage, I could tell somebody
did a thorough search of that thing and they weren't careful. What could
they have been looking for?"

Mary's head came up. "I really don't know. Without doing an in-
ventory there's no way to tell if anything was taken. We didn't keep a
log." She stopped, thinking hard.

"That could be it. Sailors usually do make a log, to record where
they went, the sea and weather states. But we didn't this time. Maybe
whoever wrecked the boat thought the log could help them, because
if we'd been keeping one, we'd have recorded where we were every
day and where we were anchored when Michael found those hundreds.
Dammit!" She pounded both fists on the control console in frustration.

Then she let go of it. Their sailboat was gone, but Michael had to be
still alive, a captive somewhere. She was sure of it. She would know if
Tanner had died. Agonizing over the why of it wouldn't help now. Getting back to Road Town to try to move the search was the best she could
do. She pushed the throttles forward.

"Mary, I'd appreciate it if you didn't mention my watery excursion
back there."

"No problem, I owe you. A lot. You didn't have to risk your life that way. I appreciate it more than I can say." Mary sent Hilda a tremulous smile. "Can we go to your office when we dock? I'd like to make some calls to the mainland."

"Absolutely. I need to report in as well," the agent warned. "Bureaucracy, you know. Records are required."

16

By the time they reached Wickham Cay, Hilda's underwear had dried in the sun and wind and she was properly dressed again. With Mary giving succinct directions, she hopped ashore and tied off the bow mooring line, returning the sport fisher to the anxious care of the charter company at the Village Cay Marina. The young man employed by the company went aboard immediately, muttering, "I hope you didn't mess things up too much."

"We didn't," Mary retorted tartly. "Thanks for letting us use the boat. We found the sinking sailboat. It's now on the bottom. We'll report to the authorities.

"You'll have to top up her tanks and if you send me a note at the hotel I'll pay for the fuel."

The women stepped off the boat and started for the center of town and Hilda's office.

"First thing," Hilda said," I'll report this adventure to my office, leaving out the swimming episode and make a few notes for my file. Then we see if there's been any other word."

While Hilda wrote her report, Mary called Seattle to inform Hochstein about loss of the boat and that there was little progress finding Michael. When she contacted Tanner's office, Christian only reluctantly agreed not to fly out immediately but said he'd wait with a phone for further word.

Mary went to the hotel, promising to rejoin Hilda in her office as soon as she had changed clothes and checked for messages. Unsaid was the hope that Tanner had been located, or perhaps had communicated in some way.

There were no messages at Mary's hotel. But something had changed. She sensed an alien vibration the moment she opened the door to her room. She stopped in the doorway and looked carefully around. Everything looked normal. Nothing appeared out of place, yet there was something. Something indefinable. After a moment she shrugged and closed the door. Outside her room in the hall, an old man shuffled spryly along the hall and down the stairs. He nodded to the desk clerk and went out onto the veranda. There he slumped into a well-worn rocker at the very end of the porch. He closed his eyes and resumed rocking slowly in the breeze.

Upstairs, Mary checked the time and called Seattle again. This time she called Tanner's family. There had been no communication of any sort, from Washington where the situation was being closely monitored, nor had anything else occurred that could be construed as a ransom note or a threat of any kind. She hung up the receiver and looked at it for long moment. The machine smelled different. Now she realized there was the faintest odor of tobacco in the air. She stood up from the bed abruptly. It could have been the maid. Since she'd left the bed had been made up and the towels in the bathroom replaced. But somehow she didn't think a maid had smoked in her room. Her gaze skittered around the room. There was no place to hide.

For a minute she considered moving to another room, but decided to talk to Hilda first. Mary left the hotel watching as carefully as she could to try to detect anyone watching her, but it was fruitless. Too many people were outside the hotel. Several young men stared boldly and frankly at the tall attractive woman who strode purposefully across the street.

Hilda sketched a quick wave when Mary walked in. "I've just been on the horn to Washington. They've been persuaded to let you have some more information about what may be going on here."

Mary nodded. It went without saying that Agent Martin had helped sway the decision makers in Washington to the view that Mary Whitney was trustworthy and could be a reliable asset in days to come if connections between Michael's kidnapping and the smugglers were developed.

"They faxed us some information and a photograph. It's not very sharp, unfortunately." She slid an 8x10 across the desk. Mary leaned over to peer at a fuzzy shot of a scruffy looking individual with what appeared to be a two-or three-day beard growth. His medium shaded hair appeared to be caught in an untidy pony tail that stuck out behind his head, under a sailing cap pulled low on his forehead. The harsh shadow from the bill of the cap obscured part of his face but the beakish nose was prominently in view. His lips were thin and formed a dark slash straight across his face. He was of stocky build but because the photograph had been taken from above, from a balcony or a second-floor window, Mary surmised, she couldn't accurately estimate his height.

The subject's clothing was casual, the sort one might see on the deck hand of a freighter or in the cockpit of any of the hundreds of water craft in the Virgin Islands. "Who is this?" Mary inquired.

"A very bad actor. His name is Gordon Barnes. Ex-British Special Forces, smuggler, drug runner, unproven killer, pirate. His heritage is obscure. Some say he's a Canadian, others that he emigrated from the U.S., maybe Iowa or Minnesota after things got too hot there. We don't know for sure. He's been jailed several times in various Caribbean ports for a whole raft of offenses, a few heavy, mostly minor. His list of known associates reads like a who's who of the criminal element in this part of the world. An international tribe of thugs."

Mary shook her head. "I don't think I've ever seen him," she said and slid the picture back.

She straightened and stared at Hilda. "I think my room was searched while we were gone."

"What? Searched by whom?" Hilda grimaced. "Forget I said that. Of course you don't know who did it. Do you want another room?"

"That was my first reaction. But then I thought, what's the point? I could hide, but maybe somebody will try to contact me. I shouldn't be unreachable."

Hilda nodded slowly. "Well, it wasn't us, and the Brits have no reason to do so since we're working closely with them here. Local law might, of course." Hilda paused a moment, then, "Mary, why do you think someone was in your room?"

"An impression, a feeling. I thought the telephone smelled like cigarette smoke."

"Okay, I understand." Hilda scribbled something on the pad in front of her and then changed direction. "What do you make of this?" She picked up a scrap of paper and handed it to Mary.

"It's damp."

"Yeah. I found it in the galley. In the sailboat," she said unnecessarily.

Mary looked at Hilda and turned the scrap over gently. The writing was faded and a little smeared. She stared down at the familiar script. Her breathing quickened. "Michael wrote this. It's a page from the notebook I always keep in the galley of any boat I sail on." A tear came to her eye and she blinked at the writing. "Letters and numbers but I don't recognize any of it."

She took a pen and copied the writing to another piece of paper. She sighed and tucked the paper into the pocket of her blouse. "I'll think about it. Maybe something else will come to me. Where did you find it again?

"It was wedged into the cupboard door over the sink. I just happened to see it when I swam inside the main cabin."

"Could it have floated there after the boat went under the water?"

Hilda shook her head. "Not likely. I had to open the door to free it."

"Uh huh. Okay. What else have you learned?"

Hilda picked up another piece of paper. "Washington advises they have no useful information yet on the serial numbers of the three bills you found. But they speculate the money is part of a large shipment either drug money going to South America or possibly a payoff of some kind going north. Why they think that, of course, they didn't bother to tell me. What's confusing is that drug money is mostly smaller bills, people on the streets of North America don't typically buy drugs with hundreds, they use ones and fives and tens."

"So, you don't think this is about drugs? Then what?" Mary's frustration was evident in her tone of voice.

"We just don't know for sure. There are some rumors of a huge shipment of cash from a bank heist. Maybe for a diamond buy, coming through the islands. Recent chatter." She waved her hands, as frustrated as Mary. "It's all so vague, speculative, you know what I'm saying? Typical though."

"I don't see how any of this helps me find Michael. At first I just assumed it could be for ransom, but there hasn't been a ransom call." Mary thumped the desk with her fist. "There's got to be something we can do now."

"I don't believe whoever has your husband took him and your boat for ransom. Think about it. That boat isn't the fastest thing on the water. If they'd wanted to kidnap him, why didn't they put him in a car? Or onto a cigarette boat? One of those long sleek over-powered jobs? Kidnapping for ransom usually involves planning. This has the feeling of an improvised or an opportunistic act. I think the smugglers were following you. Suddenly there was Michael all alone, boarding your boat with nobody around. Boom. They just grabbed him.

"There are lots of places on this island that are private and isolated that could be a temporary bolt-hole. We sometimes have boats stolen here, of course, but not when there are people aboard. If the idea was robbery, the perpetrators would have just done the deed and then left your husband tied up or something."

Mary didn't want to even think about what the "or something" might refer to. "So what's left is the damn money we found, right?"

Hilda nodded. "Yes. We think this is all because of the money you found. And we believe that's also why Mr. McGwean was killed."

17

"I'm going to talk to the police again," said Mary, an hour later. Fruitless speculation, based on fragmentary facts and speculations, had brought the women no closer to finding Tanner. They'd tried out every possible theory they could come up with as to why Tanner was abducted. What it came down to was information, information about the three hundreds and maybe about McGwean. There'd been one call from the agent's superior in Washington, but he hadn't any information to relay. Unspoken between Mary and Hilda was the concern that the longer Tanner was gone, the fewer the chances they'd find him alive. Or at all.

"Do you think that's wise," said Hilda, "getting cozy with the police? Remember we're concerned there may be a bad cop on that force."

"I know. But I can't just sit around here waiting for something that may never happen. Maybe I can find out something more from them. Whatever happened to that cop who came to the dock when we first discovered the hijack? Wasn't he supposed to get back to us after he reported in? I'd almost forgotten about him. We need to talk to that detective." Mary looked at Hilda and went on, "The police don't know yet what we found on *Passions Messenger* and I need to make a report on that. I'm surprised they haven't come looking for me."

"They probably haven't learned we're back from Flanagan's Passage," said Hilda. "It's a small force. They must be struggling to cover murder and now a kidnapping along with their normal duties."

"I'll go make a report. That'll give me a chance to talk to that detective again."

Hilda nodded. "Keep your eyes and ears open. Maybe you can find out if there's something hinky over there. At least, hinky about this funny money monkey business."

Mary stared at Hilda, who had the grace to blush and look away. 'Sorry," Hilda muttered. "I do realize how worried you are. It's just... I can't keep doing this job if I let it get to me too much."

"Cop humor. I've heard about it," Mary said. She turned and left the room, heading for the door to the street. At the last minute she deviated from her path and entered the bathroom at the back of the building. She trickled water into her hands and rinsed her face. Her skin felt hot to the touch. Through the thin wall she heard Hilda pick up the telephone and the chatter of the dial buttons.

"It's me. No, there was nothing in the boat. I don't know. No. She doesn't give me much. If she does, she hasn't given me a clue." There was a longer pause while Hilda apparently listened to the voice in her ear. Mary cracked the door so she could hear better. Who was Hilda talking to? Mary thought the agent had already reported to her home office. She listened some more, ear pressed to the crack.

"Nothing," Hilda said. "No. I told you. Frankly, if Mary is hooked up in this, the disappearance of her husband came as a total surprise. No. No one's that good an actor. Oh, give me a break!" Hilda slammed the phone into the cradle and muttered something that sounded like "jerk."

Mary quietly slid along the wall toward the outside door and eased it open. As she swung the screen door wider, one hinge squeaked. Mary grimaced and stepped through, eased the door shut and turned sharply to the left away from the street. She flattened herself against the hot wall, not wanting to be caught eavesdropping. She sensed Hilda at the entrance but the other woman merely stood in the door for a moment. Then the inside wooden door shut with a soft snick of the latch.

Mary exhaled, surprised to discover she'd been holding her breath. She walked quickly to the street and found her way down the block and then around the back of the hotel to the next block. She was unaware that the little drama had been observed by the old black man in the white painted rocking chair on the shady veranda of the hotel.

When Mary got to the police department building, she realized she couldn't ask for the policeman by name because he hadn't given it to her in their brief meeting in the street at Village Cay Marina. Fortunately, the department wasn't large and she described the pudgy man in sufficient detail that the receptionist recognized him. She placed a brief call and the detective, Emmett Smythe, appeared and ushered Mary into his tiny cluttered office.

He squinted at her and said, "I know this is very upsetting, and you have deep concerns. I admire your resolve and your demeanor, Mrs. Tanner. I assure you, we are doing every possible thing to locate your husband. May I be frank? It was not a good thing that you went off on that power boat to see the wreck. You must allow the police to do our job."

Mary stared into the man's seamed brown face. He radiated compassion and sympathy. "I understand and I'm sorry, but if we hadn't gone immediately we would never have located it. It sank in Flanagan's Passage just after we reached it. The charts say it's around thirty fathoms deep. That's almost two hundred feet. Retrieving anything from that depth, assuming we can even locate the hull, will be difficult at best."

"Yes, Madam, that is quite true." Smythe drummed his fingers on the edge of his desk. "Now we have had no real report on the derelict. Can you tell me, please, what you found? Was it your charter? *Passions Messenger*?"

"Yes it was, I'm sorry to say. When we arrived at the site, the hull was already underwater. Only the top five or six feet of the mast were above the surface." She paused to take a breath. Making this report was lowering her anxiety level, at least for the moment. "Sails were loose in the water and one was draped over the stern. It covered the name of the boat." She watched the detective laboriously print the information on the form he'd dragged from his desk drawer. The air conditioning didn't seem to be keeping things cool. Mary felt sweat trickling down her sides and she wiped her moist fingers on a tiny napkin she'd carried in one hand.

"So you cannot say the boat was yours? Is that right?"

"No, Detective. We were able to get close enough to move the sail cloth to one side to see the name. It was definitely our charter boat, *Passions Messenger*." Mary remembered not to tell anyone that Hilda had gone into the water to move the sail. She wouldn't tell him about Hilda swimming into the flooded cabins, either. But she still wasn't sure how she felt about Hilda. That overheard telephone conversation raised a question about Hilda's place in this mess. And how far could she trust this detective? Her instincts said he was honest, but her instincts were sometimes wrong.

"We were on site of the wreck for about twenty or thirty minutes. Then she rolled over and sank. There was no sign of damage to the hull, but topsides was a mess. Tangled rigging, the wheel appeared bent but I couldn't swear to that." Mary's voice trailed off and she sighed. Why had she said the sailboat rolled over? It hadn't, but she didn't correct her statement.

"And it goes without saying there was no sign of a bod—your husband?"

"That's correct, Detective Smythe. Have you had any word? Anything at all that might help us find Michael?" Mary stared across the desk.

The detective looked sympathetic, but not overly concerned. Mary supposed it was the same dis-engagement Hilda and other police officials practiced to avoid burning out with emotional upheaval. She rose. "I'll be going to my hotel room now. You can reach me there when there's any news."

She left the building, realizing that she had no idea whether the detective had anything other than strictly professional interest in Tanner's disappearance and the loss of the charter boat. He'd even seemed so reticent as to be almost uninterested except for that one moment when it felt as if he was reaching out to her.. But now he was a closed book to her. Discouraged, she wandered back to the hotel and went to her room. For a few minutes she thought about detective Smythe and about agent Hilda Martin. For the time being, at least, it seemed was obvious to her that of the two, Hilda Martin, was someone she would have to trust. At least for now. Exhausted, she lay down fully clothed on the bed and drifted off into restless sleep. The thick dark tropical night had fallen over the islands when she awoke hours later.

18

She was disoriented. Where was she? With a clutch of her heart she remembered. A hotel on the British Virgin Islands. In Road Town. Michael was missing, their boat with all their belongings, their stuff, was gone, sunk deep in the sea. She'd watched it go down. And all she had was that piece of paper that Hilda had found, probably by chance, in the galley. She sat up in the thick darkness, slipped her feet over the edge of the bed onto the cool wood of the floor. Breathed deeply, trying to center herself. Her head was full of randomness, images, impressions, memories. Tears came. Maya Cove, checking out the boat, missing a winch crank, their first exhilarating sail across Sir Francis Drake Channel. Making love in their bed in the forward cabin after they'd anchored. Tanner finding the damn hundreds while they swam naked the next morning. Then the great day of sailing to the Bitter End and meeting Ian McGwean; Spanish City, Lieutenant Archambault and Michael's disappearance.

Mary's memory swirled back to the scene at the Bitter End resort on the outer edge of Virgin Gorda. She remembered sitting in the shade on the broad patio, looking out at Gorda Sound and their sloop resting easily in the anchorage. Her bitter divorce from a brutish East Coast investment broker had left her with a healthy distrust of the male animal until she'd encountered a damaged but forthright man, Michael Tanner, struggling to recover from his own loss.

She was waiting for Tanner to return from his inquiry inside the resort. A long rakish yacht had anchored behind *Passions Messenger* and two men had come ashore in a motorized dinghy. She remembered thinking it had taken them a long time to make the transit from boat to the dock. Part of the time they were out of sight, she now remembered, behind the Beneteau.

Mary jumped to her feet and stalked to the window, heedless of her rumpled clothing. She envisioned two men coming up the sand toward her. They were grimy. The one in front wore a stubble beard and a soiled yachting cap with elaborate braid on the visor. He was shorter than the other man, who looked nervous, she now recalled.

If the boat that had anchored behind them, she considered, carried the men who had stolen the hundreds back from *Passions Messenger*, she needed to find out if they were known to the authorities. And if so, how? Fully awake now, Mary concentrated on the images in her head, trying to remember every detail. There was something about the man who led, the man in the dirty cap. What was the dinghy that brought the two men to the dock? Motorized, not rowed. It was a faded red, maybe almost a dusty sort of red. Two men. One tall and thin, dark hair, she thought. The shorter man who seemed to be in charge was heavier, maybe a little shorter than Michael. How did she know that?

Mary couldn't decide how she knew. Maybe she was wrong. It was difficult to be certain. The images wavered. She went over them again, seeing the two strangers as they landed at the dock and then as they came toward her. When she was through with the images in her head, she had looked beyond the two men and seen them against familiar images, boats in the harbor. The images faded and, exhausted, Mary went to her bed and fell back to the pillow.

In the morning she went to breakfast in the hotel dining room, but with no appetite she ate little. After picking for a time at the pancakes she didn't want, she left the table and walked onto the veranda. Gazing toward the harbor, she saw the old back man she recognized from having encountered him in the hotel a few times. He was shuffling across the open lawn by the marina office. A squat white man in dungarees, a tee shirt and a dirty yachting cap stepped out from the other side of a building. The two men stood close together. It was apparent they knew each other. Mary glanced away, scanning the street, her random thoughts tracking nowhere in particular. Where was Michael? Where was Hilda? What were the police doing to find him? Was it a maximum effort? Her nerves started screaming again in her frustration.

She thought of the scribbled note Hilda had found. What was its meaning? Then she looked back again at the two men still standing together at the corner of the marina building. There was something.... The squat man turned away and Mary saw him as she'd seen an overweight man in a yachting cap stalking toward her on a sun-washed beach, toward the resort office at the Bitter End on Virgin Gorda. Suddenly she was sure of it. It was the same man, the one who'd come ashore at the Bitter End. She remembered bits of a conversation. Michael had said he suspected that man of following them from Ginger Island to Gorda Sound, and probably of slipping aboard *Passions Messenger* to steal the hundreds. The target of her scrutiny turned in the shade of a building, and suddenly she wasn't quite so sure.

Her heart speeded up, she could feel it pulsing in her throat. Her inclination was to run down the steps, cross the road and confront him. She resisted, knowing she couldn't restrain him and it would endanger Michael if the man knew she recognized him. If he was one of the kidnappers. What to do? She wished desperately that Hilda was with her. The two men separated and the old black man turned and walked slowly to the south away from the marina. There was a street there, lined with shops, and he disappeared behind the buildings.

Mary started slowly down the steps in the general direction of the marina. The man in the yachting cap strolled through the gate to the docks of the marina. He seemed in no particular hurry so Mary had no trouble keeping him in sight from sixty yards away. She lost sight of him for several nervous moments as she went around a low building and then stepped up beside the fence that surrounded the marina. The man was no longer visible on the dock. But then she saw him just clambering aboard the afterdeck of a large motor launch that rested at the transient wharf. He leaned over and leisurely unhooked the stern mooring line, tossing it to the dock. A cloud of smoke puffed from the underwater exhaust of the yacht.

A few minutes later the man she was watching disappeared into the after cabin of the reddish-hulled boat and the craft eased away from the wharf.

Mary felt a presence at her side and realized she had been joined by Hilda Martin. "What's so interesting out there?" she asked.

"The reddish-bronze-hulled yacht. Let's go find out who she is."

The two women walked swiftly around to the entrance to the marina and to the harbor master's shack. The old man smiled appreciatively when he saw who approached.

"Nice looking boat," Mary commented, pointing. "Locally owned?" She saw Hilda staring at the lettering on the stern and then casually turn and look in a different direction. Mary stepped to one side so she was partially shielded from anyone on the boat who might be looking back at the marina they had just left.

"Yep. Some retired fella, name of Jensen, I think. He lives back up on the mountain there. Nice fella. Don't see him around much anymore. Can't say the same for his crew though. That Gonzo Barnes is a surly fella. Never smiles, never even a howdy. Only talks to issue orders or demands." He hawked and spit over the edge of the platform into the bay.

"Did you say Barnes?" asked Hilda.

"Yep. Don' think that's his real name though. He's been around a few years. Rough cob." He winked at Mary. "You'd do well to avoid the likes o' him." He winked at Mary again and started polishing the brass fittings at the side of the shack, all the while keeping his eyes on the two women.

Hilda stared across the widening band of water at the yacht. *Maid Marian* was picking up speed and her white-water wave widened as she pulled into the bigger basin. She was headed out away from the island.

"That guy looks sort of like somebody I saw once. At the Bitter End. I'm almost positive he came ashore with another taller man, I think it was."

Hilda stared at Mary a moment and then tugged her arm saying, "C'mon we've gotta get to the office."

Mary said goodbye to the harbor master and the two women walked swiftly back onto shore. "What's the deal?" Mary followed Hilda into her office.

Hilda stopped abruptly and turned to stare at Mary. "You still don't entirely trust me, do you," she demanded.

Surprised, Mary was silent. She looked away from the other woman's intense gaze. "I'm just not sure. I'm sorry. I'm so worried about Michael I'm not thinking straight."

Hilda grabbed Mary by her arms and said fiercely, "You have to trust me. I am on your side, all the way. Look, I think you overheard part of my conversation on the phone yesterday and that worried you. I was talking to a division director in Washington. You can have your contacts check it out." Hilda released Mary and bent over her desk, scribbling on a note card. "Here's his name. Call."

Mary took the card and said softly. Hilda, I'm sorry. I apologize. Can you forgive me my addled suspicions?" As she spoke, something told Mary she was going in the right direction. The card slipped from her fingers and drifted to the desk top.

"Okay."

"So, what's the deal?" Mary asked again.

"The deal is that Gonzo Barnes is a known felon here in the islands. He's a dangerous man. We're sure he's responsible for drug smuggling and probably laundering money from gambling and drug deals in the states. Both we and the Brits would love to nail him. If he was near you at the Bitter End and now here, it's got to be more than just coincidental or casually interesting."

Mary stared at Hilda. "Ian McGwean alluded to a big case he said he was working on when we saw him at the Bitter End. Could this

Barnes be part of it?"

"Sure could," Hilda said. She was paging rapidly through a tele-phone book. Her finger stabbed a name on a page. Mary looked over her shoulder at the line she indicated. Homer P. Jensen. The address meant nothing to her.

"Jensen," she murmured. "H.P. Jensen. Why do I know that name?" She stared unseeing at the wall of the office for a moment but nothing suggested itself.

Well, this gentleman, H. P. Jensen, has a house in a seriously up-scale part of the island. I wonder how much he knows about his yacht crew."

"I wonder what he knows about where my husband is being held."

19

"Mary, I can accompany you to Mr. Jensen's home, but we don't even know if he's on the island."

"I understand, Hilda, and I know you'd like to get some background on the owner of the yacht Barnes seems to captain now before talking to the owner. Ordinarily I'd agree, but every hour, every minute that goes by decreases chances we'll ever find Michael and this seems like a possible lead."

"Just let me make a couple of calls, then we'll see what's what." Without waiting for a reply, Hilda punched in a number on her telephone. Mary turned away and picked up the island phone book Hilda had set aside. She found the Jensen entry and scribbled the address and the number on a scrap of paper which she slid into her pocket.

Then she had a thought. Somewhere on the island she knew was an office that had records of all the boats resident in the British Virgin Islands. It was something island authorities and especially the Coast Guard would of necessity require from time to time. Calling the Coast Guard office number she reached a young-sounding female.

"I'd like to know if you can give me the registration or owner of record of a motor vessel here in the islands."

"Of course, ma'am, if you can give me the name of the vessel."

"Yes, it's the MV *Maid Marian*, port of registry Road Town, BVI."

"Just a moment, please." Mary heard a hum and faint rustle of paper. "Yes, here it is. That vessel is registered as owned by HPJ Corporation, a United States Corporation registered in Delaware."

"Thank you." She read out the local address that Hilda had found for Homer Jensen. The voice on the phone confirmed that the two addresses were identical. She severed the connection and turned to look at Hilda. Agent Martin was making notes at a furious rate, scribbling away, nodding and muttering into the phone as she did so. While Mary watched, Hilda blew out a long breath and hung up the phone.

"Well, hell. I have good news and bad news, I guess you could say." Hilda shuffled her notes. "This guy Jensen. Neither he nor his corporation have any kind of profile with our jurisdictions."

"Meaning nothing around counterfeit or smuggling money, right? No threats against the President or the Queen."

A quick smile flickered over Agent Martin's face. "My office in D.C. is contacting DEA and who knows, maybe the CIA? But they don't think there's anything there about drugs either.

"I think we ought to go talk to Mr. Jensen. Maybe the company doesn't know who their captain really is and what he's doing with that yacht."

"Give me another hour then we'll go visit Mr. Jensen. Maybe my folks in D.C. will have something else for us."

The hour passed and a call to her home office in the states resulted in no additional information. Hilda closed up and the women went to Hilda's vehicle. As they opened the car doors, Mary looked over the hot top of the car and caught Hilda's eye. "Do you always carry a weapon?"

Hilda hesitated and said, "Not always, but sometimes, like now."

The women drove off up the mountain into the setting sun and the dusty heat. The road curled around on a high shoulder of Mount Sage, with grand tree-speckled vistas of Cane Garden Bay and a distant Jost Van Dyke sparkling in the blue sea. They arrived at an impressive Italianate villa nestled among tall tropical pines and lush mimosa bushes. Interestingly, there was no wall or gate.

Martin parked the Minor at the edge of the wide driveway, and they walked up the slight incline to the veranda. Martin's hard heels clacked on the stone steps. The big wooden door loomed before them. In the center of the door, below the small window was a large plaque with elaborate raised brass letters in a heavy gold-painted circle. HPJ.

Mary glanced at the door and then stopped in mid-stride, doing a double take. HPJ! She suddenly remembered. "I know about this company. They're a West Coast TV production house. I think they did some work a few years ago for some family friends. Or maybe Tanner and Associates worked with them. Michael's firm does a lot of work for smaller independent film companies."

"Small world, but I'm not sure if it helps us."

"I'll think about that." Mary examined the windows she could see on either side. They were all dark, shades drawn against the tropical sun. Hilda raised the tarnished knocker made in the form of a monkey head and dropped it. The door vibrated and magnified the sound when the monkey's chin hit the strike plate. There was no reaction from the interior. Hilda glanced at Mary and raised the knocker again. This time she used the muscles in her forearm to good effect and banged the monkey twice on the striker plate. The reverberations boomed through the house with a cavernous sound. Again there was no result.

"I'm going to look around," said Mary and turned to walk off the veranda.

"Wait," said Hilda. "We can't do that. It's trespass."

"Maybe you can't, but I can. I'm just going to look around. I'm not going to damage anything. You can wait here." She went off the veranda and started around the house. Moments passed and when she stepped onto the grassy verge beside the driveway, she heard Martin's footsteps on the concrete behind her.

Mary resisted an urge to bend over and skulk around the house. She tried to look casual as she strolled to the back of the place where a stone walkway led from a rear door under an open breezeway to a three-stall garage. She saw impressive-looking padlocks hanging from each hasp on the doors. Clearly, someone didn't wish to chance anyone entering the garage without leave of the owner of the locks.

Hilda hissed at her and when Mary turned, she saw Hilda pointing toward the expanse of lawn on the other side of the breezeway.

"What is it?" she murmured.

Hilda flinched at the sound of Mary's voiced and said. "Actually, nothing, but there's a pool."

She was right. A sturdy above-ground pool squatted in one corner of the yard, backed up by the windowless garage wall. "Why is it above ground? The pool," Mary said.

"The mountain is mostly volcanic rock. Too expensive to dig," Hilda remarked.

"I'm going up here," Mary murmured. She turned toward the step leading to a back door. It was set into the stuccoed wall with no windows. She couldn't see any other entrance from the back of the house.

Wondering about the alarm system she assumed was installed, Mary tentatively tried the door knob, actually a sturdy brass lever. It turned easily and noiselessly in her hand, but the door didn't budge. She pushed against the door with no result. Mary walked off the breezeway and along the back of the house. Peering through the deep shadows along the other side, she realized that thick foliage crowding a high fence on one side, and the house itself, would make passing down that side toward the front nearly impossible.

She turned to find Hilda coming toward her, arms forward, palms up, indicating she'd discovered nothing unusual. "The pool is filled and clean. But there's nothing else to see. What say we get out of here?"

"Okay. I guess no one's home right now."

"Right," said Hilda. "We can come back later."

The women walked briskly back to the front of the home and entered their vehicle. Even in their heightened state of alertness, they failed to see an old black man across the road standing in the deep shadows of a large banyan tree.

20

Mary slammed the flat of her hand against the Morris Minor's dashboard hard enough to sting. The smack startled Hilda, maneuvering the little car down the mountain. "I'm so tired of just doing nothing. Dammit! We have to find Michael now."

Hilda winced. "I can't imagine how you must be feeling. I'd be useless in your place. But it isn't as if we're doing nothing. There are a lot of people in Washington trying to help."

"I'm going to offer a reward," Mary said abruptly. "I've thought about this and thought about it and I've got to stir things up."

"Wait a minute," exclaimed Hilda. "You better let me check with D.C. before—"

"Screw that!" barked Mary. "There isn't any more time. Where's the local radio station? Or TV. I'm going to make a personal appeal." She dug into her purse, searching for her seldom-used cell phone.

"Damn it. It's dead. Battery, I suppose." She closed it with a snap and dropped the phone back in her purse. She twisted toward the Secret Service agent who glanced worriedly back. "Look. I realize you're in a bind with your superiors. I'm not. You don't have to come. In fact, I insist you let me out and I'll find a cab. You go back to your office and warn your people. I'll go to the station."

Hilda didn't slow down. She wove skillfully through the light traffic toward the hotel. "Maybe you should talk to Lieutenant Archambault first."

Mary shook her head. "I don't think so. He'll tell me to wait, just like you did. I don't see any sense in waiting. I have a picture of Michael in my room. I'll ask the TV people to show it. Maybe somebody will recognize him."

Hilda blew out her breath in a long gusty sigh. She wrenched the tiny auto into its accustomed parking place and said, "Okay, okay. But let me come with you. Maybe I can help." She was talking to an empty seat. As soon as she'd stopped the car, Mary leaped out, slammed the door and trotted to the hotel. Hilda left the car and hurried into the office to check her messages. Then she ran back out and waited, watching the front entrance to the hotel. After a minute Mary appeared, coming swiftly off the veranda. The Secret Service agent started to raise her hand when she noticed movement behind Mary on the veranda. As she stepped down to the road a man rose from a chair and slowly came toward the steps. Hilda recognized him.

It was a man she knew as a suspicious character around the islands. He seemed to be paying an inordinate amount of attention to Mary Whitney. Hilda watched for a moment and then beckoned to Mary across the street. When Mary drew closer, Hilda said, "I think you're being watched. I just noticed a man who I already know is not exactly on the side of the angels; seemed like he was paying you a lot of attention."

"Can we have him arrested?"

"Let's wait a bit. We can always pick him up. The police here on Tortola also know him. If he is watching you we'll learn for sure after while and he might lead us to whoever's currently paying him."

"He's a mercenary?"

"Something like that. C'mon, I'll drive you to the station." She opened the car door.

"You don't have to do this, you know. And it can be risky, calling attention to your husband."

"I know, but I've thought about it some more. Publicity could be a good thing."

Mary got in the car on the passenger side. "I called Lieutenant

Archambault. He agrees with me—with us. He's even talking to the people at the TV station so they're waiting for us. The radio station will take a recording of the interview."

Hilda nodded. "Okay, I guess we'll run with it."

"I think it would be different if there'd been a ransom note or any kind of communication," Mary said quietly. She grabbed the window frame as the little car jounced through a sharp dip in the road.

"The station is just over this rise," Hilda said. She glanced in the rearview mirror at the car behind them, the one she was pretty sure had been following them since they left the hotel.

* * *

The television station, the only one in the islands, was in a modest concrete block building on a side street above the main part of Road Town. Mary, who was no stranger to television back home in Seattle, might have smiled at the relatively limited setup in other circumstances. However, as soon as the producer of the local news program met her, she sensed the tall slender black woman was a consummate professional. Fifteen minutes later Mary emerged from the studio and looked around for Hilda. She found the agent standing at the entrance to the station building gazing pensively at the street outside.

"They were very professional. Sympathetic," said Mary, wiping a tear from her cheek. I did a short interview, maybe two minutes or so. They said they'd broadcast it several times over the next couple of days."

Hilda Martin nodded. "It could help. If it turns out that money is what the kidnappers are after."

"I think I covered it if there's anything else."

Hilda looked at her, a question in her face.

"I implied I might know something, or I might have something to trade."

"You what?"

Mary winced. "I know, I know. We talked about what I should say on the way to the station. It's just at the last minute I had to try a little harder."

Hilda frowned, and blew out her breath. "I suppose you realize you've probably turned yourself into a target? If the kidnappers think you have information about their missing cash, they'll come looking for you."

"Yes, but I just felt I had to do something to push ahead."

"I get it. But did you think that if you have what they want, they won't need your husband any more? What's more, the man who apparently has been watching you is either getting careless, or he's getting different instructions now."

"What does that mean?"

"I have the feeling he's been watching you for some time, probably ever since you came back to Road Town and Mr. Tanner was taken. Because of his history, I suspect he's the one who searched your room the other day when you were gone."

Mary blew out her breath. "I think it's time to talk to that detective, Emmett Smythe, again. He told me he's been assigned to this case. I don't really expect to learn anything, if he's anything like the police I've dealt with in Seattle. I just want to get another read on him. Do you know him?"

Martin nodded her head. "As I mentioned earlier, he's a relatively recently promoted detective. He's been on the force for several years, but never come to our attention. I've met him once or twice in the past."

"Will you come with me? I'd like your assessment after I talk to him."

Hilda nodded and piloted her automobile to a parking spot near the Police Station. Inside the station the receptionist Mary and Tanner had seen before nodded and said, "I'm sorry to learn of your troubles, Mrs. Tanner. I certainly hope we'll have your husband back to you unharmed. Good afternoon, Ms. Martin. How may we help you?"

"We'd like to talk with Detective Smythe, if he's available."

"Certainly. Why don't you go into the conference room right behind me here? I'm sure he can see you in a few minutes."

The two women had barely had time to seat themselves in the small sparely furnished room, when the door opened and Detective Smythe appeared. "Good afternoon, ladies. Can I get you something? Tea perhaps?"

"Thank you, detective," said Hilda. That would be lovely."

Impatiently Mary drummed her fingers on the shiny table top and glanced around the windowless room. The bare painted walls had no pictures and no concealed observation mirror. It was a small, stuffy, anonymous space, depressing in its ordinariness. Or maybe, that was just because of her circumstances, Mary mused. "Oh, God," she thought. "Michael, I hope you are still safe."

A black woman she'd never seen before entered on silent feet carrying a tray with small cups and saucers, spoons and a steaming tea pot. She looked sympathetically at Mary and favored Hilda Martin with a small smile. After she deposited the tea makings she left without saying anything.

Detective Smythe replaced the tall woman in the doorway. He was carrying a thick file of papers. He sat down and clasped his hands together on the table top.

"How may I help you, Mrs. Tanner?"

Mary didn't bother to correct the man. "I wanted to know about your progress finding my husband."

"Yes, I see. Do you recognize this man?" Smythe slid an 8x10 glossy photograph across the table. Mary studied it. Although it was a little grainy, having been taken, apparently, from a distance, it was sharp enough.

"Yes! That's the man who may have been in the companionway of our boat when it was hijacked from Wickham Cay with my husband aboard. I'm sure of it. Who is he?"

"His name is Gordon Barnes, sometimes called Gonzo. He works currently as the captain of a large luxury yacht berthed here in Road Town. The yacht is owned by HPJ Enterprises. They're a United States film production company."

"Is that H. P. Jensen?" asked Mary.

Detective Smythe nodded with a questioning glance at Hilda Martin. She looked placidly back, giving nothing away. "Yes it is. He has a large home on the island. It is located up on Sage Mountain."

"Can we speak to him? Maybe he's involved."

"Regrettably, Mrs. Tanner, he is in the States tending to business. We understand he is not expected back for at least a week. I doubt very much he has any knowledge or connection to this affair. He has a long history here on the island; he supports many civic activities."

"Tell me about this Gonzo Barnes, please." Mary twisted her fingers together in her lap. She forced herself to maintain an outward calm, in spite of the turmoil inside her.

"He is an unsavory character with a long record of accusations, but only a couple of arrests and no convictions. He is a competent and experienced captain, hence Mr. Jensen's willingness to employ the man. At the same time Mr. Barnes is a known associate of several, shall we say, unsavory individuals here and elsewhere in the Caribbean."

"I assume there will be no attempt to recover our charter boat," said Mary. Her mind skipped over everything she knew about their trouble. It was pretty clear there was nothing more to be learned from the Road Town Police Department.

"It is very sad. I'm afraid the water is too deep where the boat sank. It would require an experienced deep sea diver. You told me you observed no evidence of violence nor the presence of a body. It is unlikely anything of value would be found, assuming we could locate the hulk and raise it. Nevertheless, let me assure you we are using all our contacts and resources to find and restore your husband to your side." Smythe gazed expressionless at the women.

Mary rose. "I'm sure you are. Thank you for seeing me today." Anxious to leave, Mary began to form a plan and she needed some supplies.

21

"Okay," said Mary as soon as they reached Hilda Martin's car. "Tell me what you think about that detective."

"As I told you, we haven't anything on Detective Smythe except his name on a file and a few vital stats. He's honest, a hard worker with a family. He went to school in the UK and came back here as soon as he could for a job as an ordinary patrolman." She paused and licked her lips. Then she inserted a key in the ignition. "I also think he's been assigned to a sensitive case with a lot of serious implications for the BVI so his superiors are watching him closely."

"Why is this so sensitive?" Mary interrupted.

"Mary, you have to realize the context here. This island counts tourism very high in its financial profile. The authorities have to be quite nervous over the kidnapping of the husband of a wealthy and powerful heiress. You were known before you arrived here. I told you that. And your husband isn't exactly anonymous. There are probably people who regularly vacation in the BVI that he's done work for. Add to that the possible involvement of a long-time well-known wealthy, nearly permanent, resident of Road Town, the Jensen guy. This thing has high messy potential right now so the police and civil authorities are anxious to keep a lid on it. I don't think detective Smythe has told you everything he knows."

"Yeah, okay, I get it. Look. I need to find a store. Hardware and some clothes. Can you find me one?"

"Sure but whatever for?"

Mary waved a negligent hand. "Oh, never mind. I've taken up enough of your time. Just point me in the right direction." Hilda shook her head. "Boy, I hope for your sake if you ever get arrested for something serious you do a better job of lying. This sudden shift to casual Cathy isn't playing well." She paused and said, "the chandlery at the marina will have pretty much anything you need. For what, I can't imagine, of course."

Hilda started the car and drove into the marina parking lot at Wickham Cay and got out, ignoring Mary's quiet protest. The two went inside the large store where they were confronted with almost every possible tool and part a savvy ship's crew could want for boat repairs and maintenance. There was also a wide selection of clothing, from light summer wear to serious off-shore foul-weather protection. "These people also own the sail loft on the other side of the harbor, in case you want to buy a shroud."

"That's good," said Mary absently.

On one wall a multitiered rack of spools held ropes and lines of every description and size from light waxed line for whipping rope ends to stout halyard and shroud lines. On another lower rack were several different sizes of anchor chain. In the narrow aisles Mary .plucked off a large black cotton tee-shirt with long sleeves and a pair of dark blue pedal pushers. She then found a pair of black cross-trainers in her size. While she was trying them on Hilda glanced around the store. "What an incredible variety, but I would have no reason to shop here. Do you really need all this stuff to sail a boat?" She poked her finger into a tray of shackles and rattled the packages.

"Different sizes, but yes, boats can be complicated. "Mary stood up.

Hilda leaned closer. "I bet they'll have a slim jim and a set of lock picks somewhere here as well."

Mary appeared to ignore the semiserious remark and turned away. She went to the tool section where she selected a small hammer and reached for a narrow wood chisel.

"That's good," Hilda said. "I'd go for one at least an inch and a half wide, though."

With a quick glance at her companion, Mary chose a two-incher and started for the checkout lane. A box-cutter with a wicked-looking retractable blade caught her eye and she added it to her collection.

Hilda murmured, "What about some theater makeup? You'll need to darken that white skin."

Mary shook her heard. "Mud. I'll carry a small bottle of water and smear mud on my face and hands."

Mary was not into small humor at the moment. She started toward the checkout counter and then detoured to pick up a pair of latex kitchen gloves. She raised her eyebrows at Hilda and added a second pair.

Hilda looked around the store. She'd been more alert since Mary's broadcast, watching for anyone who might show up repeatedly or someone who seemed to be paying them too much attention.

"Coming?" called Mary from the door to the chandlery.

"You aren't, you know," she said back in the car. "I really appreciate your attention, but I can't let you go with me."

Hilda snorted and started the Morris Minor. "Listen, Mary, you can't do this without me. I'm willing to bet breaking and entering wasn't part of your upbringing. Well, it wasn't part of mine either, but I've learned a few things along the way. Odd stuff like how to find alarms and disable them. Recognition of evidence at the scene is another. I saw you add that second pair of latex gloves."

"What if we get caught?"

"You're more likely to be if you go in alone. If we get caught there's a chance I can talk us out of being chucked into jail. Our best bet, though, is not to get caught. There's another reason. I'm more likely to recognize anything significant if there's anything there."

Mary sighed in frustration. She understood the logic of the other woman's arguments and she recognized that Agent Martin was a lot like her in several respects. In spite of the danger Hilda was determined to accompany Mary on her B&E of the Jensen home up on Sage Mountain.

The tropic night fell dark and thick and sudden. By ten that evening things were quiet on Sage Mountain streets. Even the insomniac dog walkers had retreated to air-conditioned comfort. Hilda parked the car down the hill about a block away from the house and they waited and watched for several minutes. No vehicles passed. No one walked near and no dogs barked in the night.

Mary opened the car door and slipped on the tee shirt and pants. She wrapped her own shoes in the clothes she'd shed and stuck them in the back on the floor. Martin was already dressed in dark clothes and she changed shoes for a pair of low-heeled black flats she carried in the car as a matter of course.

The women walked quietly and casually up the road to the driveway, and with no one around, turned in and went directly to the house. "There's a dim light in two windows on the second floor," said Hilda.

"What do we do?"

"Knock. Have some kind of cover story ready. If the overhead light goes on, try to keep your face in shadow." She reached the door and pounded hard. There was no response. Martin nodded and said, "Good. Just a night light I bet. C'mon."

They skulked carefully along the side of the house until they reached the patio at the back. Stepping carefully over the tiled surface they approached tall glass patio doors.

"These are sliding doors," whispered Mary.

"That's lucky. Maybe we won't have to break anything. Look for any sort of barrier or barricade on the inside meant to keep the doors closed."

There was nothing.

"Okay." Hilda blew out a nervous breath. "Put on the gloves and give me the chisel." She squatted by two of the glass patio doors.

Mary looked at the door latch more closely. "These doors are wood and they're set in tracks so they roll open. The front roller should be right about here." She touched the wood frame lightly with her forefinger. "Pry the door up and the roller should come free so we can disconnect the latch."

Hilda muttered and gently forced the chisel under the edge of the door. She lifted it slightly. Mary wrapped her fingers around the door handle and pulled up at the same time. With a click that sounded louder than expected, the spring-loaded roller snapped out of the trough and the door tilted forward. The bar of the latch slid out of its nest and they pivoted the door far enough to slip through into a room cluttered with scattered casual furniture on a bare wood floor. Hilda raised a cautioning hand and the two burglars stood still for long minutes listening for any human or animal sounds in the house.

Moving cautiously, they walked to the central hall. "We'll start on the third floor," Agent Martin murmured.

She led the way, cautioning Mary yet again to remember to stay low in the second floor hallway to avoid throwing moving shadows on the windows from the weak night lights.

The third floor was a single large empty room given over to storage of boxes and crates scattered about. The women resisted an urge to poke around, knowing they couldn't take the time. They had to search all the rooms and get out as quickly as possible before the owner or one of his staff showed up.

Coming down the stairs to the second floor hall, Mary stopped and pointed at the floor. "Look," she hissed. In the dim light there were clear tracks in the light coating of dust of two people with small feet. "Our tracks."

"Or children," Hilda responded. Nothing we can do about it. We're not going to clean the house."

In short order they searched the second floor. Every bedroom, dressing room, closet and bathroom was cursorily examined for evidence of recent occupation. There was none except in the master bedroom suite and another nearby suite. Time passed and Mary felt her hopes falling.

The main floor including the large well-appointed kitchen provided evidence that the house wouldn't be empty long. Dry goods and canned food were stocked in abundance. "Look at the refrigerator and freezer," commented Hilda. Both units were locked but humming.

She ran a finger across the island counter. "No dust here. C'mon we can do a quick look at the basement. We gotta get out of here. If there was a silent alarm I missed seeing, the cops will show up any minute."

Mary found the basement door and eased it open. The steps led down from a small rough wood platform into stygian darkness. She flicked on her small flashlight and played it into the dark silent void. A musty odor rose from the space. It carried a faint trace of moldering food. "Smell that? Recent food. Hello? Is anybody there?"

Nothing.

They ran down the rough steps, flashing their lights from side to side. Hilda's hand brushed across a switch on the wall and she stopped.

"No windows, I don't see any windows." Hilda flipped the switch and two dim bulbs hanging from cords attached to the ceiling beams flickered on. The light brought only disappointment. As with the rest of the place, they were the only humans in evidence. Mary sagged and leaned against the work bench that was positioned at one outside wall. "Damn. Nothing."

"Take a look at that chair beside you. Look at the floor, at the foot-prints."

Mary looked where Hilda indicated. There were dragging marks and footprints, large ones, in the dust on the floor. There was residue from duct tape and the imprint beside the chair legs showed stress move-ments. "No one sits in a chair like that with their feet tight against the legs unless they are tied. Or taped. Hilda's fingers touched the silvery scrap of duct tape still clinging to one chair leg. Mary wasn't listening.

"Look at this," she said. Her heart thumped. "He was here! Michael was here. He's doodled my initials on the dust of this bench, just like he used to do in meetings when we first got married. Hilda, he was here!"

"He's not now and we've got to get out. Mess up that dust and come on. We'll take a quick look at the garage." Mary smeared the scribbling on the bench and they ran up the stairs. At the back of the house they replaced the door in its track and shut it as best they could manage. The door slid back and forth okay but they couldn't reset the latch.

Agent Martin produced a pair of lock picks and quickly managed to open a side door in the garage wall. A late model dark blue or black Cadillac Escalade sat in one bay. The other was empty revealing only a thin layer of undisturbed dust. The film on the windshield and hood of the Cadillac assured the pair that the car had been unused for some time.

They walked carefully to the road and back to the car where they stowed their tools and extra clothes and left the neighborhood. They didn't talk much on their slow and circuitous drive back to the waterfront and Mary's lonely hotel room.

22

The next morning after breakfast Mary went across the street to Hilda's office. "Any news?" After the emotional high of last night's burgle, and finding evidence that Michael or someone had been recently in the basement of the Jensen home, Mary had admitted to herself that they were making scant progress, but Hilda had news.

"The *Maid Marian*, the Jensen motor vessel, was sighted docked at a harbor on St. Martins. They left there late last night on a heading that will bring them back here. That's a common occurrence. We assume they pick up a package and deliver it here for transshipment to the U.S. or sometimes the Bahamas."

"If you know that, why don't you stop and search them?"

Maritime laws forbid it without extenuating circumstances or a warrant. What if we boarded them and didn't find anything? All that would do is alert them to how much we know. Both the UK and U.S. authorities are pretty sure Barnes and his vessel are just part of a much larger smuggling network. We'd like to nail them with a big shipment or something really major which might leverage one of Barnes's crew into talking about their adventures and about the people they work with."

"Wouldn't finding a kidnap victim be big enough?"

Hilda smiled. "Sure, but far as we know, nobody's seen Tanner aboard that boat since they left Wickham Cay."

"So we wait some more."

"'Fraid so."

Mary groaned and then sat down to look at photos the Secret Service had collected over the years, pictures of proven and suspected felons resident in the islands or suspects visiting. It seemed fruitless, but it served to pass the time. She thought she might be going crazy with worry and inaction. At two in the afternoon, the British Coast Guard reported identifying the Motor Vessel *Maid Marian* inbound for the BVI. Her course was apparently calculated to bring her close to Tortola at the eastern end of the island in three to four hours.

Mary glanced at a chart of the Caribbean hanging on one wall of the office. "They're not on a good course for Road Town harbor," she said. "They'll make landfall much nearer Guano Island. Assuming the sighting was accurate, they're making an arc to stay to the outside of the islands."

"Is that important?"

Mary stared at the chart and the spot her finger marked. "I don't know. You say Barnes is an experienced captain. Why would he take that course today? To get here he'll have to turn in the Anegada Passage and then bump along the coast of the island near dark. Makes no sense, if he's coming to Road Town."

Hilda went back to her files.

Mary started to pace. After a few minutes she said, "Hilda, do you have a cruiser's guide to the Caribbean?"

"I think there's one around here somewhere. Check the desk drawers. Mary eventually unearthed a well-thumbed dog-eared copy. It was several years out of date, but it would serve her purpose. She found the section on Tortola and then pages about Tortola and its northern and eastern shores. She read several passages and checked the wall chart again.

"Maybe it's not so dumb. What does that boat draw, do we know?"

Hilda looked at Mary, distracted from her work and now wondering where this was going. "It's pretty big, 60 feet hull length I guess. Is that how you say it? I bet it draws eight maybe ten feet. I know it has bow thrusters to help maneuver in tight spots."

"I've figured out what he's doing, although it may be a wild leap of faith," Mary said. "Look. He's staying well out to sea, outside most of the islands. Keeps from being trapped against a shoal or a shore. More maneuvering room if he's spotted. Who saw him? Was it a Coast Guard plane?"

"No." Agent Martin shook her head. "We share some confiscated civilian planes with the Brits. We don't keep 'em very long. One of our pilots would have done a straight-on over flight. He was instructed not to go down for a closer look or to circle."

"So he could be wrong about the ship."

Hilda shook her head. "Not this pilot. And he remembered to use the special radio frequency. Of course, Barnes is pretty wily. He probably finds our frequencies and breaks our codes pretty fast, just as we do his, but this is a new radio beam so it's unlikely."

Mary smiled a wintry smile of satisfaction. The facts were lining up. "Okay. Here's what I think. Somehow they got Michael to the house because they knew it would be empty for a while. But then Barnes had to go to Martinique or St. Martins, somewhere down there. He may have figured Michael would be safer with him, so they took him aboard Maid Marion. It's a lot harder to escape a fast power boat, especially at sea." She swallowed hard.

"It's also easier to dump bodies or incriminating cargo in deep water. But they're now heading back here and staying east of the islands in open water, probably until the last minute to make port. There aren't any sheltered anchorages along the northeast edge of Tortola so it's pretty isolated until you get inland a way. It's especially bumpy out there right now so the chances of them encountering other boat traffic is even more unlikely."

Hilda interrupted. "You think they plan to offload contraband and maybe Michael this evening somewhere along that coast?"

"Exactly. And I plan to be there when they do."

Hilda looked at the map and shook her head. "You're right. That is one wild guess. That coast is a long piece. We're going to need some help, some backup. The timing is gonna be real tight." She reached for the telephone.

"Wait, Hilda. I know you trust that detective, but he might let something slip and he has to go through official channels. Can't we do this on our own?"

"Nope. Too much real estate to cover by ourselves. We'll leave the local police out of this. I have a couple of contacts on the British side. They'd love to be part of solving a big crime like this, since none of us has done very well nabbing smugglers. There's also this: they're MI5 and they knew Ian McGwean."

Mary nodded, remembering the smiling face of the agent they had known so briefly. "All right. Arrange to meet us there. We'll need more than one vehicle anyway."

Hilda was already dialing. She explained what they needed and why. It was a brief conversation and she hung up.

"All set. Both my friends are eager to help and they come with equipment. We'll meet them at their motor pool. We can't take the Morrie where we're going. No roads to speak of. Let's go."

The women grabbed two duffels with the gear they'd used the previous night and went to Hilda's car. Impatient as they were, they nevertheless managed to walk casually, appearing serious but in no hurry to get where they were going. Both women kept an eye out as they drove to the opposite end of the island to the official British compound near Soper's Hole. Hilda was so intent on keeping an eye on the rear-view mirror, she almost sideswiped one of the ubiquitous island taxis which blasted its horn at them in a rare expression of outrage.

Thirty minutes later Mary met Hilda's friends and explained the details of what they were looking for and gave them another description of Tanner and of the boat. MI5 had graciously provided four special walkie-talkies, four four-wheeled landrovers, two of which were even painted in camouflage. The other two were plain, but so dirty their paint scheme wouldn't matter. They spent several minutes pouring over large-scale charts, choosing spots from which to watch for *Maid Marian*.

Hilda and Mary chose to find places of concealment midway along on the target coast, between the two young MI5 agents who set up at either end of the stretch of coast where they hoped the yacht would come ashore. Mary wanted to be in the center so she'd have the least distance to travel if hers was the wrong spot.

The agents wanted her, as the lone civilian, to be as protected as they could manage.

"What about weapons?" Mary asked. The agents looked at each other. This was an unsanctioned, unofficial mission and they already had their necks out a long way.

"We can't do that, "said Hilda firmly. "You are a civilian and if there's any shooting and somebody gets hurt, especially you, we're all in hot soup up to our eyeballs. Plus any arrests we made would probably get thrown out."

"No warrants, you see. No time-consuming hemming and hawing by the higher ups," said the younger Brit, a smiling slender man of no more than thirty. "Speaking of which, we'd better get a move on."

Mary nodded, she hadn't really expected them to provide her a weapon along with the radios, field glasses and vehicles. Hilda stepped closer. "Are you familiar with weaponry?"

"Sure. My uncles saw to that. I've used a number of rifles and pistols, including the Springfield thirty cal., a Webley or two, Glocks and that good old weighty Colt .45. Even fired a Python once." Her lips curled. "But I understand."

She turned away and started toward one of the Landrovers where the two men were already firing up their own vehicles. The camouflaged vehicle looked tired and old so she veered toward the newer-looking one at the head of the line. Dust blew a little whirlwind across the compound.

"Take that one, Mary," said Hilda from behind her. "Be sure you stuff your duffel well under the driver's seat. These open machines have a tendency to blow up a good breeze and things get lost along the road."

Mary shrugged and changed course, carefully stowing the radio and binocs in holsters provided. When she went to place her duffel under her seat she saw there a flattish hardboard box. She recognized it as a case for a hand gun of some sort. When she pushed it aside it, it was too heavy to be empty. She jammed her duffel around the box, crumpling the clothes inside, concealing the box.

The drivers moved out in the afternoon sun in a loose caravan. They didn't want to attract attention from anybody so they each took slightly different streets through the island, although there wasn't a large number of choices.

Mary and one of the Brits had chosen the same route past Mount Bellevue and the entrance to Maya Cove where she and Michael had picked up their yacht in those happier days that now seemed so distant in the past. He waved her to stop at a small store and he ran in and returned with several bottles of mineral water. He handed her three. "Thirsty work, this, so you'll want these." He hesitated and then said, "This is a huge gamble, you know."

"I know. Thanks for all your help."

The agent grinned wolfishly and trotted back to his Landrover. They got underway. No one paid them more than passing attention. Traffic thinned out to nothing after they passed the entrance to Maya Cove.

Mary knew this was the road to the small airport on Beef Island. She realized that Barnes could anchor near the airport or even at Grand Camanoe, in which case this was a waste of time. But she thought that everything she knew about her enemy—and it had become very personal since Michael had been kidnapped—indicated that he would make landfall soon after dark in one of the lonely indentations along this coast.

She and the agent in close attendance behind her would enter the area from the east while Hilda and the other agent would arrive by traveling up the coast on the northern side of Tortola. She glanced at the sky. It was clear. She hoped it stayed that way. Regardless of the phase of the moon, the night sky gave off light that would help them.

They drove past Bascule Bridge and the road to the airport. Almost immediately the pavement became rougher and as they passed Long Bay and Little Camanoe Island on their right, the road disintegrated even more. The other Landrover dropped back to stay out of her dust cloud and at some point, Mary wasn't sure when, the agent turned off into the desolate sand dunes of the coast. He was going to find a spot where he could see Monkey Point on Guana Island. She continued to an area near Cooten Bay and Rogue's Point. Privately, Mary believed this was the most likely beachhead. She was sure that if the yacht they were waiting for was *Maid Marian* and if Tanner was a prisoner aboard, and if they were bringing him back to Tortola, this was where it would happen. She didn't know any of this for fact, but Mary had always trusted her instincts.

She parked almost a mile east of her intended spot in a warm sand hollow, changed into her dark tee and slacks she'd worn the other night at Homer Jensen's. She substituted lace-up trainers for her usual deck shoes, figuring she'd acquire less sand that way, especially if she had to do any running.

Then she started a careful examination of the map of her sector. If she was right, there had to be a vehicle waiting somewhere near and she didn't want to stumble over them unexpectedly. From under the front seat she took the hardboard box and found in it a Glock nine millimeter handgun with two loaded clips and a lightweight holster. She stuffed the clips in a pocket of her pants and checked the weapon as she'd been taught. She'd load it later if necessary.

The radio crackled when she turned it on to the correct frequency.

"Pit two, pit three calling." The sign was repeated. They'd agreed on a simple one-syllable alphabet, using clipped phrases to keep chatter to a minimum and more easily understood.

"Pit one, three and four, check in please." Mary was station two and while the agents were uncomfortable with it she knew, she was nominally in command and she asserted her authority immediately.

They expected that the British agent positioned the farthest east would be the first to see the target vessel. He reported after several minutes that he had pretty clear vision beyond Guana, but the mists were rising. Mary hoped fog wouldn't become a problem. She reported that she'd done a careful reconnoiter to the beach but had found no parked cars or loitering picnickers. None of the watchers reported any anchored boats or vehicles parked on the beach. It wasn't surprising. The coamers built and rolled in smashing in great frothing foam lines along the beach. Any boat that didn't anchor well out risked grounding in a trough or having an extremely rough ride. The onshore wind, now freshening, bode ill for any unwary mariner. Wind and currents had put more than one boat hard on a windward shore with frightening suddenness.

Time passed achingly slowly. Far off shore lights of passing steamers and cruise ships punctuated the dreary hours. Stakeouts, Mary mused, must be the most bone-boring job for any policeman or woman. She lay near the top of a warm dune that was sparsely sprinkled with sea grass. Occasionally the radio hissed or coughed softly. Once in a while her scattered companions checked in or verified a passing ship.

Then, just when Mary was figuring that she'd been wrong, the man at the far eastern perimeter coughed into his radio and said quietly. "I have a vehicle approaching on the beach road. Traveling west at a slower than normal rate."

A few minutes later Hilda verified a black Ford Explorer had gone by her and turned off to the water's edge just east of Rough Point, a particularly exposed promontory at the foot of Mount Healthy. What Mary knew was that the depth of the water right to the land was ten to fifteen feet around that point. Nobody would risk anchoring at that place, but off-loading some cargo and even a person or two could be accomplished if they were quick and careful. Tricky business, but the whole enterprise was tricky.

The radio spoke again. This time it was the agent at the other end of the area. "This could be it." The excitement was obvious in his voice as he reported a motor vessel that fit the silhouette of *Maid Marian*, traveling at a sedate speed with the minimum regulation lights showing.

"Whoa," said the agent. "She's passing Rogue Point and their lights went off. Their radar must show zero bogies in the area."

"This must be it," said Mary. Fear landed on the back of Mary's neck. What if they were discovered? What if her presence with their little reception party made Barnes panic and he killed Tanner? What if.... Her breathing stuttered in her throat. Her tongue seemed suddenly swollen and dry. She dropped to her knees. Fingers clutched the warm sand and she peered seaward. So much could go wrong.

"Collapse the net slowly," cut in Hilda, taking command. "No lights or challenge until we verify what we're dealing with. Pit two—that was Mary's sign—stay put."

Mary bit her lip and wormed her way to the top of the dune. She stayed flat to the ground, but knew that if anybody was watching with night glasses they still might pick her out. A pale weak moon made its appearance in the east. The beams could bounce off the glass of her binoculars and be seen as light flashes by an observer on the beach or aboard the oncoming launch. She tried to be careful, but it was dicey and she knew it. She couldn't help it. She had to watch what was happening.

Below her, about three quarters of a mile away, she was able to make out a dark blob on the beach that hadn't been there before. That must be the vehicle. The headlights flashed once, as if offering confirmation. Her long-range inspection showed no figures standing beside the Ford.

"I'm gonna block the road to the east," whispered the radio.

"Go," responded Hilda.

"I don't see any people by the SUV," whispered Mary.

"Stay away," hissed Hilda. "We're coming in on the beach side of the road from the west. About a quarter mile out."

Suddenly the hair on Mary's neck lifted and she swung the glasses toward the sea. Mist thrown up by the waves crashing on the rocks and beach reduced her ability to make out objects, but there was a large motor vessel now hanging off-shore a couple of hundred yards just outside the surf. Partway to the beach east of Rough Point was a long low shape that could only be a smaller launch of some kind.

She turned the glasses back toward the vehicle on the beach and saw two people get out and run toward the shore line. The launch paused, rolling heavily in the sea. The dark shapes came together and a figure that looked vaguely human was dropped in the shallow sea and the boat turned away. Faintly, over the crashing sounds of the surf, Mary heard the throaty sound of a marine engine. The craft headed at high speed, crashing through the seas, directly back toward the larger vessel.

Mary watched as the figures at the beach edge grabbed the blob lying in the surf and begin to drag it toward the vehicle. Could that dark lump be a body? Could that be Michael? Chucking caution to the wind, she rose to her feet and began to run down the dune's slope toward the scene, sliding in the loose sand. At the same time, flashlights flicked on west of the scene and two agents rushed toward the big vehicle and the figures struggling to haul whatever it was up the sand toward the vehicle.

Shouts over the pulsing surf that sounded vaguely like official commands came to Mary's ears as she hurtled across the sand toward what she felt must be Michael in the clutches of these criminals.

The vehicle's engine roared to life. Flashes from one window indicated somebody was shooting at somebody else, but she couldn't tell which way the bullets were flying. In a great spewing gout of dirt and noise the big station wagon spun around in the sand and fishtailed onto the sandy beach road. It roared down on Hilda and the other agent who flung themselves aside to avoid being run over by the oncoming automobile.

Mary continued to run toward the scene. Toward the prone figure lying so still in the sand. "Michael!" she screamed. Sprawling to a crouch beside the figure she played her flashlight on the dripping tangled hair, the pale calm face with silver duct tape across his mouth. He rolled his head slightly to the side and opened one eye. Mary's tears dripped down her nose and onto Tanner's face. Hilda and one agent slid to a sandy stop beside them. Mary carefully peeled the tape away from Michael's lips, causing him to wince.

"Nice to see you again, babe," he whispered. "Wondered if I ever would." Then he passed out.

23

"Mr. Tanner, you are looking much better than when I first saw you yesterday in this room."

"Thank you, lieutenant. I'm feeling much better and ready to get out of this hospital room."

Lieutenant Archambault nodded thoughtfully. "Yes, of course. The doctor will be in to release you directly. I assume you have nothing to add to your statement of yesterday? That you happened to encounter some unknown assailants in the dark of the night who were apparently bringing your husband ashore?" This was directed at Mary who sat beside the bed holding Tanner's hand. The policeman scowled when she shook her head. "Please do not leave the island without speaking to us again." He gave Mary a sketchy bow and stalked out.

"I think he's unhappy with us," she said.

Tanner grinned at his freshly coiffed wife in her long raw silk skirt and subtly patterned off the shoulder blouse. She looked great even with three broken fingernails as a result of the B&E and the scramble at the beach. "Can't say I blame him."

The kidnappers waiting on the beach had made good their escape in the black van, heading east and disappearing into the slopes of Mount Bellevue. The two MI5 agents gallantly agreed to join Hilda and Mary in defending their actions with the local law, but Hilda declined their offers. She and Mary agreed on a simple straightforward story that cast the British assistance as mere happenstance.

They had been exploring the north coast of Tortola, they explained, and were discussing Michael's kidnapping when they happened on a dark vehicle just leaving the coast at Rough Point. A long low power boat had also been glimpsed departing seaward. It seemed obvious to the women that they had interrupted some kind of dark-of-the-night smuggling transfer. Curious, they went to the beach. At the edge of the sea they had been astounded to discover the bound and unconscious body of Michael Tanner. They'd immediately called the police and emergency medical people.

That there was no way to verify the timing of the sequence of events the women related and there seemed to be no suspicious gaps in their tales. That made it impossible for the authorities to question the story they told. The story was tissue-thin, but the authorities were not inclined to be too hard on a tourist woman who had somehow got her kidnapped husband back alive and in reasonably good shape.

Both women had willingly returned to the same beach a few hours later to talk with police and watch the fruitless examination of the crime scene. Mary had already been assured that her husband, though weak and dehydrated, was in no immediate danger health-wise. He had numerous days-old surface contusions and bruises, none of which was dangerous.

It was painfully apparent that neither Lieutenant Archambault nor his men entirely believed the story Mary and Hilda had told them in multiple interviews. Agent Hilda Martin's status as a member of the elite U.S. Secret Service didn't hurt. The question of multiple Landrover tracks on the road and a pair of military issue binoculars discovered along the road were left unanswered.

Midmorning the doctor brought in a clipboard holding several forms for Tanner to sign. Then he was released to the willing and anxious arms of his wife.

"So, what's next?" said Tanner.

They meandered slowly down the sun-washed street from the clinic toward the hotel where Mary had already moved their accommodations to a larger, more pleasant room. Only a close look betrayed Tanner's stiffness and the yellowing bruises on his arms and legs. True, his eyes appeared a bit sunken and prominent bags framed them, but that could have been the result of a night or two of hard drinking. They stopped for tea and a late brunch of fresh pastries at the Tortured Turtle, a small open-air shop on one of the side streets. Although they adopted a studiedly casual attitude, their conversation was anything but.

"We've done a lot of research and collected all sorts of information while you were away," Mary said, sipping from a tiny cup. "My, this is good tea. I've hardly paid attention to food the past few days."

Tanner nodded. He stretched a hand to touch her fingers. "I noticed you seem to have lost that sleek smooth and satisfied air you had when we were in Spanish Town.

"Just wait 'til I get you upstairs to our room, I'll show you sleek and satisfied. Unless you're just too worn out from your ordeal."

"A very tempting offer, my dear," Tanner murmured, leaning closer. "Tempting indeed. Given the state of my health and our crowded plate perhaps a rain check? Just for a few hours, you understand."

Mary tilted her head in mock frustration and sighed, "that's the trouble with you, it's always business." She sent Tanner a quick air kiss.

"Seriously, I wish I could be more helpful about identifying my kidnappers. I think it's fortunate they were careful. If I'd seen or heard more they would have just dumped me in the ocean. I'm still not sure why they didn't anyway."

Mary shivered at the thought.

"I don't even know where we went except it took a long time and the trip was pretty rough." Tanner stretched, ate the last crumbs of his flaky Danish and said quietly, "are we being watched, do you think?'

"I'm pretty sure of it. Especially since I made that radio and TV appearance. I wonder if those creeps even saw it."

"Oh, they heard it at least. I know that because they changed their plans. I'd learned enough to assume we were heading toward South America, or at least one of lower Windward Islands when Barnes ordered the boat back to Tortola."

"How odd. Why were they taking you to South America?"

"I think to get me off their hands. The South American end of this trail ordered it."

"You seem to have overheard quite a bit. Maybe you know more than you realize," Mary said.

"Yes, well, snatches of bad Spanish and English. I never let on that I knew any Spanish, but it didn't help much. My language skills are rusty and besides, when you study a foreign language at school they always seem to leave out a lot of jargon, not to mention the more creative obscenities.

"I've been lying in that hospital bed for almost two days, you know, mostly thinking about what I heard and saw. I'm pretty sure the money we found is from a very large shipment of cash that was headed for the drug makers in South America, probably Colombia. Somehow it got lost and nobody knows where it went."

"Did Barnes and his crew hijack it?"

"Could be," Tanner said, squinting into the bright street, "but I don't think so. He'd have been killed if somebody in one of the cartels thought he'd stolen it. If he did make off with the cash, he's a pretty good actor."

"I think he's been assigned to find it."

"I promised Hilda that sometime today after you got your release we'd go and sit down with her to fill in some information," Mary sighed.

"You are referring to Agent Martin? Let's do that now. I take it you two have become close?"

Mary nodded. "Yes, she's a brick. I don't know how I would have managed if she'd been somebody else. Stuck her neck out more than once for us, too." Mary hadn't yet related how the two women had burgled the home of the wealthy media businessman, H. P. Jensen.

The couple first toured a few of the shops in Road Town to replenish Tanner's wardrobe that had been lost and Mary acquired a few more things as well. Except for the clothes they were wearing, almost their entire vacation wardrobe had been lost when *Passions Messenger* was scuttled at sea.

When they entered Agent Martin's suite of two tiny offices across from the hotel, Tanner was grabbed up in a spontaneous embrace by a delighted Hilda Martin. "I'm so glad you are all right, Mr. Tanner. It's been a pretty harrowing time for your wife." She colored and stepped back into her usual role.

He grinned at her. "I can't begin to thank you enough for your help and your support. Mary's been telling me something about it. I gather this kind of thing is unusual for your tenure here."

Hilda smiled. "You could say that again. If it wasn't for the murder of Mr. McGwean and the other violence, this might have even been sort of fun." She stopped and blushed. "Sorry, I seem to be getting carried away here. I know you've been interviewed by the locals but I do need you to go through it for me personally. So far my superiors haven't decided to send someone with more experience down to take over the case. I'm hoping to keep that from happening. One way is by filing timely updates. I've alerted them that you were rescued and they're pressing me for whatever information you may be able to supply."

Tanner nodded. "I'm happy to help, although I'm afraid I won't be able to add much. The goons who had me were pretty careful to keep me isolated. I suspect they might have killed me if they thought I'd learned anything useful. The cabin I was in had a shuttered port-hole and it was pretty well stripped of any amenities. The door was always locked and while I had a portable toilet, they never let me out for any reason. Two men, always the same except once, brought me food and water. The food was adequate, barely. So far as I can tell, there may have been one or two other men aboard. I heard voices one night to indicate that, but that's all.

"Right after I was grabbed at Wickham Cay I was at gunpoint. There were two men on board. As soon as we got away from the slip they shut the hatch and locked me in below deck. I could see from the instrument repeaters at the nav station where we were, so I scribbled a note with latitude and longitude on it just as they met with a big power boat. The questions they kept asking in different ways the entire time I was in their hands always were about the money. Where had I found it? How many containers? What had I done with it?"

Hilda frowned. "So we were right all along. Barnes and his people think you found a shipment of their money and hid it somewhere."

"Yep," agreed Tanner. "They whacked me around a little, nothing serious, but it was obvious they were getting more and more frustrated when I kept insisting the only money I'd found was the three hundreds that somebody had subsequently stolen when we were anchored at the Bitter End."

"We found the note you left," said Mary, "stuck to the inside edge of a galley cabinet."

"That's amazing. I take it the boat was already sinking when you found it?"

Mary looked at Hilda. "Yes, well actually, it was almost down. The deck was well under water. It was Hilda who found the note."

Tanner swiveled and looked at the young agent. "How was that?"

"A question of expertise. Mary is an experienced boat handler. I'm a good swimmer, so I went in the water to uncover the name of the boat. I needed to be sure of the identification. After that, even though we could see we had only a few minutes, I swam into the cabin and saw the edge of the note. Pure happenstance."

"Over my strong objection, I might add," said Mary. "Scared me to death when she disappeared inside. But she was right. I could handle the power boat we borrowed. Hilda couldn't and she's a much better swimmer."

Tanner looked back and forth between the women for a moment. "I sense there's more, right?"

Mary smiled and looked at Hilda. "See? I told you he was too sharp not to tell him the whole thing."

Hilda looked back and stood up from her desk. Then she sat down again and blew out a sharp breath. "Okay. But you have to promise me not to tell anyone else. My career is in the toilet if some of this gets out. I was okay with it when we were trying to save your ass, but now that we seem to have gotten away with it, I'd rather revert to my buttoned down role as an agent shuffling paper to try to keep track of counterfeit trafficking in this part of the Caribbean. For a while, anyway."

There was solemn silence for a minute, then Mary started to giggle. "I'm sorry, Hilda, I really am, and we will keep quiet, but you have to agree it's been quite a ride."

Tanner watched and said, "Okay, I'm not going to tell anyone anything, but I've sensed from right after I woke up in the hospital that you two have been up to quite a bit. I'm with Lieutenant Archambault here. I don't buy the scenario that you two just happened to come on the transfer of me from sea to the island one dark night."

So they told him the rest, including their nocturnal perambulation of the home of H. P. Jensen, film producer and impresario.

"Aha," exclaimed Tanner when they had finished. "After the initial hijacking, they did take me ashore at one point. Because of the timing, I guess it must have been here on Tortola. I had a truck ride up hills and then was dragged into the basement of some place that had an empty feel to it. I think there was confusion about what to do with me. The whole kidnapping may have been a spur of the moment act."

"That's one thing that worries the authorities, including the sticks in Washington." Hilda dug into her desk looking for something. She gave up. "They wonder if you're part of some gang or conspiracy because they didn't dump you overboard after they figured out you didn't know anything useful."

"I wondered that too," Tanner said. "I think the one guy I saw only once wasn't sure. He spoke very bad English and I tried to persuade him I didn't understand most of what he was saying. Or asking. He might have been from Eastern Europe. He stank. Old garlic mostly."

"That's not Barnes," said Hilda after Tanner described the big white man in more detail.

"So what do we know?" They'd completed sharing their separate adventures and now Mary wanted to move ahead, either go home or figure out a way to solve the mystery.

"Not much more," said Hilda.

"There is one thing more," said Tanner looking at the weekly island newspaper.

"What's that?"

"Homer Jensen will be returning to Road Town tomorrow. He's throwing a party to celebrate the successful conclusion of his latest film project. That's a party we should attend."

"Short notice. I wonder how we wangle invitations."

"I know people who know people," said Tanner grimly.

24

"But why?" asked Hilda. "I really don't see why I should attend this soiree you two seem so excited about."

Tanner smiled and pointed two fingers at his eyes. "Observers, my dear. In fact it might be a good idea for you to have an escort. Perhaps one of those gentlemen who helped you two out the other night at the coast?"

"I have nothing suitable to wear. My formal things are still in Washington. Pack casual, they advised me. It's hot in the Caribbean, they said. You won't be there long enough to settle in, they said."

"How long ago was that," asked Tanner grinning at Hilda.

"Almost three years."

"Listen," Mary, interjected. "I haven't anything to wear either, since our boat sank. We'll just go shopping. "You're sure you can arrange an invitation to Jensen's party?"

"I told you, I know people." Tanner blew her a kiss.

Mary nodded and waved away Hilda's continued demurrer. The two women left the table that had been set for them on the wide veranda.

Tanner leaned back with a drink in his hand and crossed his legs, looking very much the recovering and relaxed vacationer. It was partly an act. He watched carefully but unobtrusively and made note of anybody who seemed more than ordinarily interested in his two companions. His observations were more difficult in that the two women cut striking images as they sailed off the veranda and down the street. They were watched by several pairs of appreciative eyes.

An hour later Mary returned saying, "We didn't find anything suitable. Hilda's taking the rest of the afternoon off and we're going on the ferry to Charlotte Amalie, where, I am assured, we will find dresses to suit the occasion."

"All right. I'll be here and make some phone calls. You two stay alert and take no unnecessary chances."

"Hilda will be heeled," smiled Mary. "We'll just try to play relieved, flighty vacationers for the next few hours." Hilda arrived and the women went off to the ferry dock.

Tanner called Lieutenant Archambault and arranged to meet him later at police headquarters. Then he called a client in Los Angeles. "Jack, it's Michael Tanner."

Tanner explained where he was and what he wanted. The other man promised to arrange it. An hour later a clerk at the hotel approached Tanner where he sat reading still on the veranda of the hotel.

"Mr. Tanner, I have here a message. The boy said he would wait for an answer."

Tanner tipped the man and beckoned the boy forward.

"You are Mr. Michael Tanner?" he said softly.

"Yes, that's correct."

"Oh good. Mr. Jensen was not very specific. He just said to find you and give you this." The young man handed over a thick envelope. Tanner quickly confirmed that it was an invitation for Tanner and his guests to a celebratory gathering at the H. P. Jensen Productions Caribbean site the following evening. Tanner nodded and tipped the young man. So, he mused, they'll write the thing off as a business expense.

Hilda and Mary returned from their trip to St. Thomas with several packages. "I think you'll be happy with our purchases," commented Mary. "Fortunately, we found what we needed with little trouble. Did you get a dinner jacket?"

Tanner shook his head. "Not necessary. I've received our invitations which are unspecific enough as to numbers so we could bring an army. The women will wear summer cocktail dresses and the men will wear whites. No ties or coats, thank God."

"I'll be back and we can all go in the Morris," said Hilda. "Tommy will be here at seven and we better have a light supper before we go. Tropical punches are often heavy on the rum, or so I've heard. I just don't know where I'm gonna conceal my gun in this dress." She smiled and left with her packages.

Tanner and Mary went to their room to prepare. "If you aren't wearing a coat, you won't be able to conceal a weapon, either," Mary said later.

"I hardly think that's necessary. Besides not having a pistol handy, carrying one would be illegal."

Tanner smiled widely and appreciatively as his wife appeared in a light blue dress with darker blue abstractions. The dress had a filmy skirt of thin linen, sporting an uneven hem. The deep décolletage of the bodice showed off Mary's figure and her golden skin to excellent advantage. "My, my, you're gonna knock 'em dead."

"Thank you, kind sir. I just thought we might need some distraction." Her tiny bow and smile belied the tension she was feeling. "Wait until you see Hilda. That girl is going to be the star of the party. Incidentally, I'm assuming you're all right that this party is our treat. Hilda and I almost came to blows when I insisted on paying for her dress." Mary smiled to show she was kidding.

Tanner, who never questioned his wife's money management, merely nodded. They went to the hotel dining room to meet their companions. Tommy Corwin, Hilda's escort for the evening was a slender man of average height with reddish-blond hair. He had a sparkling smile and ready conversation. He offered to wait on the hotel veranda for his "date."

"I should have picked her up. It's not like my position here with the office is a secret, you know."

"We understand, Tommy." Mary said. "Hilda wanted it this way. Oh, and tell her to park her car. We've made other transportation arrangements."

A few minutes later Hilda and Tommy appeared in the dining room. They made an eye-catching couple. Hilda in particular was dressed in a stunning deep red long dress that fell in two panels from the waist. When she walked the skirt separated to reveal a flash of tanned skin. The bodice was held by thin straps that left her smooth shoulders enticingly bare. The dress set off her excellent figure to perfect advantage.

After a light supper and a little wine, Hilda leaned in and said, "Can we go? The anticipation is starting to get to me."

Tommy nodded agreement, drumming his fingers on the white table cloth.

"Yes, we can. The party should be going well by now. But remember," Tanner fixed each of his three companions with a flat stare. "This is not a time for any kind of searching. We're going to Jensen's party to observe and perhaps learn a few things. Poking about behind closed doors or asking a lot of embarrassing questions would be a mistake. Let's just try to have a good time and see what develops. Even noting who turns up may be helpful."

Three heads nodded solemnly and they departed in an open Island taxi Tanner had reserved. There was no room to park nearby in any case, as they discovered. A long white limo was just leaving the driveway when they arrived and they waited a few minutes. Hilda started to get out but Mary restrained her.

"Just wait. We'll be delivered right to the door, as we should be in these elegant clothes with these so-handsome escorts." She drew her hand down Tanner's sleeve and lightly pinched his wrist, revealing her still unsettled emotions.

They descended from the vehicle to appreciative glances and eager assistance from the young island men standing by who had apparently been hired for the occasion. Soft music flowed from somewhere inside the well-lit home. Oil torches dimly lit the perimeter of the lawn. Most of the conversational noise and laughter seemed to emanate from the patio at the rear of the place. Walking through the dining room, Mary noted with approval the rearranged table and chairs to make the flow of traffic easier. At one side of the white-walled room a long sideboard was laden with large tubs of ice and a variety of bottles of wine and other spirits. Mixes were arranged at one end. Two smiling bartenders efficiently handled drink orders for the people scattered about.

Mary took Tanner's arm and they went through the casual room that looked out onto the patio. The furniture here had been moved as well and she noticed several original oils on the walls. Everything was polished to a high sparkle from the candles and soft electric indirect lighting. She saw signs of an improved locking mechanism on the door she and Hilda had forced open on their previous visit.

Tanner caught her glance at the door and murmured, "My wife the cat burglar inspecting the results?"

Mary smiled serenely and drew Tanner onto the patio. Hilda and her escort had been left to go their separate way. On the back lawn at a temporary bar set up near the pool, Tanner and Mary found a short florid man the center of a shifting crowd of admirers. In mid-sentence he caught sight of Tanner and Mary Whitney approaching.

"Mike! Michael Tanner. Look here, everybody!"

A lot of people looked and both Tanner and Mary unobtrusively observed the crowd watching for unusual reactions.

"Folks, this here is Michael Tanner. He's one of the best public relations people in the country. Out of Seattle. I'm delighted to see you again. And this lovely creature must be Mary Whitney. Am I right? Yes? I always said you have excellent taste, Michael!" He took Mary's hand and drew her closer where he could kiss her fingers. Jensen was noticeably shorter than Mary and she'd elected to wear high heels this evening so she almost towered over him. His eyes rested placidly on her cleavage.

Mary smiled down at their host. "You are too kind. Tell me, Mr. Jensen, what are we celebrating this evening?"

"Ah, my dear as I'm sure your husband has explained, I've been a minor player in the motion picture business for quite a few years, low budget industrials, specialties, short subjects, commercials, and so forth. But last week we completed a full-length entertainment motion picture that I feel confident is destined to become an acclaimed blockbuster."

Tanner smiled, recognizing Jensen's hyperbole.

"Really. I applaud your success," Mary said.

She had heard such dreams articulated several times in the past as would-be producers beat paths to the investment doors to her family's fortune. Those doors had remained resolutely closed. The Whitney Foundation had no interest in funding Hollywood dreams, yet here she was, in the midst of a swirling group of the beautiful people. Not the triple A list, perhaps, but there were several individuals present she recognized, a character actor or two, a gentleman she was sure was a well-known director, and a young man who had stood very close for several minutes while he explained that he had a wonderful job for her in Hollywood.

What, Mary wondered, would that be? The young man who said his name was Abner something-or-other, she never got his last name, began to explain at length that the job was in development.

"You would be responsible for taking the germ of an idea and developing it into a concept."

"A concept."

"Right," he smiled waving his drink casually and dangerously near her bosom. "Of course, you'd then shepherd the concept into treatment and ultimately pass it on to the production department." He smiled again as if that completed a most satisfactory and detailed explanation.

Mary was about to ask another question since she didn't want to be rude and slap this puppy down. A presence came to her shoulder and she glanced at Tanner, who said, "Sorry, sir, I need to speak with my wife."

The other man blinked and said, "Your wife? Oh, of course. Sorry, old man." Abner slugged some more of his rum punch and wandered off.

"Thank you, my friend," murmured Mary.

"You looked like you needed rescuing and since you did it for me, turn about is only fair. Anything interesting develop?"

"I'm afraid not. Hilda's young man almost got into some kind of dustup with one of the locals a little while ago out by the pool. It wasn't related to our reasons for being here, something about a separatist movement here in the islands. I do feel just a little odd being here in these rooms, you understand?"

"Sure," said Tanner. "I have noticed that a couple of the larger fellows standing around here seem to be staring closely at us. But I admit it might be a spurious feeling."

Hilda glided up, her face shiny and glowing. "Wow, she said, so this is how the other people live. I could get used to this."

She was attended by three young men whose pale skins betrayed their recent arrival in the tropics. "Where's Tommy?" said Mary.

"He found a kindred spirit, somebody who I think works for the production company and is into shooting. Skeet or birding. I'm not sure which. Maybe both. They're off in a corner of the patio comparing weapons." Hilda giggled and blushed, covering her mouth with one hand.

"I see the trio has packed up and left along with several guests. Maybe we should go along too," said Tanner. "I'll call the car and collect Tommy. He flipped open his recently acquired cell phone and touched a key.

Mary and Hilda sauntered slowly through the room looking for their host. When they found him he rose from a bench on the veranda and took Mary's hand. "Ah, Mrs. Whitney and the equally lovely Hilda Martin. Thank you, ladies, for bringing a touch of class to our evening."

"Thank you for the invitation. I hope your film is very successful."

"Thank you," Jensen smiled expansively. "I wonder if you and Mr. Tanner would join me for lunch on Friday? I could send the car."

"Thank you, that would be delightful. If my husband isn't busy, I'm sure he'll be happy to be included."

Tanner appeared with Tommy and the two couples turned to the taxi just arriving at the front steps.

"Nobody even mentioned the kidnapping," said Tommy. "Some of them must know about it."

"Odd, isn't it?" said Tanner. "We'll go over this little outing once we get back to the hotel."

25

Disembarking at the hotel the couples took a table at the end of the veranda where they could talk privately. The street was dark and warm, illuminated by an occasional yellow glow of a street light. Most of the lights in the hotel were extinguished. Hilda kicked off her shoes and Mary promptly followed suit.

"An interesting evening," said Tommy.

"Anything specific?" asked Tanner.

"I saw two people I'm sure are on a watch list at the office. There was another man I think I've seen before in, shall I say, questionable circumstances, but I can't be sure."

"Well, that's good for you, I suppose. The best I can do is tell you I heard someone in the kitchen who sounded awfully familiar. He could have been one of the crew on *Maid Marian*. But when I went into the kitchen, there were several people there who I'm sure I've never seen before."

"Nothing at all?" said Mary.

"Not a clue. In fact of all the people at that party, the five guys in the kitchen seemed the most friendly of all." Tanner shook his head.

"I had a couple of openings when I could have asked some leading questions, but I restrained myself," Hilda said. She pulled one foot into her lap and began to rub her ankle.

"Here," Tommy said. "Give me your other foot."

"Ahh." Hilda smiled, half-closing her eyes as Tommy's fingers began their ministrations. "I think I'm happy I don't have to attend these stand-up-all-night-and-smile sorts of gatherings. Although this is nice compensation." She smiled at Tommy and extended her other foot to him.

"How much do we know about Jensen productions and this film wrap they were celebrating?" Mary asked.

Tanner first glanced at Mary, then away. When he looked back again she carried a calm, almost innocent look. Tanner glanced at Tommy and Hilda and a smile broke across his face. "Here, you two," he said and chuckled. "You hear that tone? You see that look? You don't know this woman the way I do and I can tell you, when she looks like that and asks a question in that tone, you'd better have at least the nub of an answer right in your fingers."

Hilda nodded. I get it, at least part of it"

"We have to find out about the financials of this company," Mary said waving off Tanner's comments. "Let's just speculate about this for a moment. Suppose Jensen's company took a real gamble on this feature. And suppose it went over budget. Suppose further, the company got into serious financial difficulty and ran into trouble paying all its bills."

"Sure," Tanner continued. "If Jensen mortgaged the company's assets to this project and they ran into trouble, he'd be facing ruin and loss of face, a real problem in Hollywood."

"Now Mr. Jensen starts looking for new money," Mary continued her thread. "He's employed his captain for some years and I can't believe he hasn't heard the stories about Barnes. At least some of them. So just maybe he talked to Barnes about how he needed a big cash infusion and the banks wouldn't lend any more money."

"Mary, how'd you come up with this?" Hilda was eying Mary with amazement.

"I've been hustled by all sorts of people for all sorts of projects, some very sophisticated and some not. It was pretty clear that once Jensen had been asked to invite us, he—or more likely one of his minions—did some research. Jensen knew who I was and probably exactly how much I'm currently worth."

"Could you have reasonably invested in Jensen's company?" Tommy asked.

There was a pause as Mary considered the question. This was a little more personal than she liked. She smiled at Tommy. "The short answer is yes, I could have afforded a large investment were I so inclined, which I am not. The foundation doesn't invest in film projects.

"The hustle was subtle; after all, they've completed the film and, I gather, most of the editing. Release is scheduled for the Christmas season." She smiled in recollection. "A nice youngster offered me a job. Something about project development, I believe it was. But Homer Jensen and his financial people had me in their sights from the moment we walked in." She yawned and stretched. "If we're done here, I'm for bed. She caught a quizzical look from Hilda. "Experience. I've developed sort of a sixth sense about these things. Michael wangled the invitations, but I sensed Mr. Jensen was waiting for me to appear." And he's invited us to lunch." Mary yawned again and said, "We can rehash tomorrow and see if anything else comes to mind."

* * *

Breakfast the next morning was late. The tension of revisiting the Jensen home and the long night had taken more energy than any of them expected. Mary spent the morning sitting on the shady veranda of the hotel making lists. Her priority was to reach out to the experts of her foundation to learn as much as possible about the financial state of Jensen Productions.

"I'm going to call some people I know on the Coast," said Tanner. "I should be able to scare up at least some gossip about the company. Then I'm going to drop in and have another chat with Lieutenant Archambault and maybe your detective. What's his name? Oh yes, Smythe. I talked with the good lieutenant yesterday. He seems to want to stay close. Doesn't act quite normal."

"All right, but no dark lonely alleys. I just got you back."

Tanner bent and kissed Mary's warm cheek. On the street he stayed near the center of the dusty road and kept track of people around him. He avoided big crowds of people, whether they looked like residents or tourists. At the same time, he chose his route to avoid deserted streets.

The lieutenant was not available but Tanner found Detective Smythe eager to sit down with him. They had coffee and the detective pulled a sheet of paper from the file in the center of his desk. He glanced at it and then at Tanner. "This is a report on the observed movements of Maid Marion that covers the period from the morning of the day you disappeared to yesterday evening.

"The yacht was anchored in the marina in Spanish Town at about the time you went aboard your boat here in Road Town."

"That's Virgin Gorda, right?" said Tanner.

"Correct. After that there are no reports until the next day when she was seen just leaving St. Martins. I don't have any information about the boat's performance, but we know she would have had to travel most if not all night to get to St. Martins. I am assuming you were in one of the lower-deck cabins by then."

"Yes. As I explained to Lieutenant Archambault at the hospital, I went aboard our charter after telling the harbor master we were leaving shortly. Then I went below to change. The next thing I remember is waking up several hours later in an unfamiliar locked cabin. I have no idea how I managed to sail out of the marina, apparently alone. When I awoke, we were definitely under way."

"Yes, the doctor says you were subdued and drugged. Some derivative of rohipnol, apparently. Is there anything else you can remember, particularly in regard to that first awakening?"

The detective's gaze and his expression were placidly neutral but Tanner had the sudden impression the question was an important one. He looked back at Detective Smythe for what seemed a long time. "The porthole was covered so I had no real sense of time of day and my watch was gone, but after some hours, I have the impression that we stopped. Not in a harbor. There was activity above me, on deck, I assume."

Tanner's gaze shifted to the bare wall. He tried to concentrate.

"Don't push your memory too hard," said Detective Smythe. "My training at Scotland Yard leads me to believe your memory may have stored bits and pieces of impressions which I can add to what we know to build a more complete picture." He smiled. "That's what we do. We collect fragments from many sources and when we assemble them we often have…" he paused, "…nothing of real value."

Tanner laughed and the detective grinned, having accomplished his task.

"When we were stopped I think there was another boat. I heard and felt a bump against the hull, that was probably on the opposite side of the hull from me."

"You were questioned by a member of the crew, correct?

"Yes. I was instructed to blindfold myself when two men came in. When they brought me meals, I was instructed to turn away. Only once did I see the man who came into my cabin. That was because he opened the door without warning."

"But I am sure you formed some impressions of your captors?"

Tanner nodded. Yes, of course. The man who interrogated me was large and he smoked. Cigars, I think."

"How do you know he was a big man?"

"He put a hand on my shoulder once. His hand felt large and he seemed to fill the cabin when he was there."

"Did the captain of the vessel, the man we believe to be this Gonzo Barnes, ever talk to you?"

"I don't believe so. The English of the man who questioned me showed a reasonable level of education."

The detective's eyebrows rose fractionally.

"I mean to say my impression was that he'd had at least a solid high school education. His use of vernacular Spanish was similar to what I remember from my college Spanish classes. The rest of the conversations I overheard were street Spanish or a patois of some kind. I could follow most of it fairly well. I never let on I understood them and some of the conversations were just outside my cell, so they had no reason to think I even heard them."

Tanner stretched and stood up, watching the detective continue to scribble notes as he had throughout the interview. The walls seemed a little closer and the air started to clog his lungs. "It was most difficult when I heard references to what they would do with my body."

Detective Smythe stood also. "Let's get out of here and take a walk. Clear the atmosphere?"

Tanner nodded and the two men left the building.

26

It turned out Detective Smythe had exact ideas about what, precisely, taking a walk meant. They went out a side door from the city building where the police department and jail were located. Smythe directed them up a small hill to the east and they soon found themselves strolling briskly along a shaded street of small, mostly white, bungalows built against the side of the hill.

"Are we headed somewhere specific?" Tanner was pretty sure of the answer, but he asked because whether his companion answered truthfully would tell him a lot. There were a few island residents on the street ahead of them so he felt no anxiety.

Detective Smythe smiled and pulled a large brilliant white handkerchief from a back pocket. He nodded. "In spite of my attempt to mask my motive, you are correct. It is benign, but I think you will be interested and we may both learn something worthwhile. The next house there is that of my sainted mother who is aiding us this afternoon in our investigation."

Tanner was silent, but his mind buzzed with questions.

"It occurred to me while I read the reports of your first interviews at the clinic, that if you could identify the ethnic character of some of the voices you heard, we might make more rapid progress."

"I get it. But why are we doing this here instead of at the station?"

"A very good question. Let me just say that the people we will have

tea with this fine afternoon would not have been comfortable at the police station. Perhaps we may leave it at that?"

"Of course. Lead on, Detective. I am more than a little interested." He remembered Mary's admonition to stay out of dark corners, but
somehow, Tanner thought the trail was definitely becoming intriguing
and thick with possibilities.

The two men turned in at a white bungalow at the very end of the
street that was a little larger than others they had passed. Tanner glanced
to the side. Through the trees he saw glimpses of the blue waters of
the Caribbean and the snowy white flash of a sailboat. It's a shame, he
thought, that I have to be here dealing with these crimes instead of relaxing on the deck out there with Mary.

The big woman who greeted them as they stepped onto the porch
clearly was pleased to have them arrive. Tanner quickly learned that she
was enormously proud of her detective son. In the shadowy interior of
the home Tanner was introduced to five men whose names he made no
effort to remember. He suspected at least two of them were using names
adopted for this afternoon alone. Except for Madeline Smythe, the detective's mother, everyone simply used first names. Tanner thought that,
if pressed, they would all own up to being members of the Smith or
Jones families.

Madeline Smythe offered tea which everyone accepted and she disappeared into another room. The front room where the seven men sat in
silence after the cursory introductions was lit only by the sun so it was
dim enough that Tanner knew he'd have trouble recognizing any of the
men on the street.

Finally the smallest man, short with arthritic fingers, nodded and
said, "Well, we aren't going to help this man unless we talk, right?" He
addressed Tanner directly. "My nephew here thinks if you can listen to
some different island dialects he might develop some, what-you-call-
'em, leads?"

"That's right," Tanner smiled. He knew now what was going on,
although the odd circumstances still were a mystery. "I heard fragments

of speech, conversation and some orders while I was being held captive. Maybe it will help to know the languages or dialects?" He glanced at Emmett Smythe.

"You are not English," remarked another man in a strong accent. "Canadian or American, I should imagine."

"American," said another. Definitely American, probably from the West Coast. Seattle possibly?"

Tanner acknowledged the man's accuracy. Madeline reappeared with a tray, a steaming pot of tea and several small cups. Tanner recognized the tea as Earl Grey breakfast tea. It was hot and strong and surprisingly refreshing. At times during the next several minutes he closed his eyes to more closely replicate the circumstances of his capture. The conversation ranged from local school board elections to plans by a developer to build a big complex of condos or town homes near the British Customs House along Sopers Hole.

"Dey prob'ly goin' to do it, one way or t'other,' said one, shaking his dredlocks. "Dey jus' better be sure de boat people can get in there when they winds come."

Tanner pricked up his ears. Conflict over building development happen everywhere, it seemed, even here is this tropical paradise. He decided to move things along. He asked a question in Spanish. It stopped conversation for a moment. Then, "Formal, old-style classic Castilian," said a tall spare man with small wire-rimmed glasses perched on his nose. He was the only one in the room wearing a tie.

Tanner grinned. "Right. It's my high school Spanish. I heard Spanish while I was locked away. But not like that."

The man stared in concentration, then he spat a torrent of words for a few seconds. When he stopped, he stared at Tanner. Then he nodded. "Yes, it's not so uncommon in the islands."

"Boy," whispered Tanner. "That's exactly what some of it sounded like."

"You heard someone who grew up in the Windwards, maybe St. Maartan; it's a mixture of Indian, Dutch and gutter Spanish."

After an hour or so and more tea, they tried a few tricks. One of them, a heavy man who seemed to perspire constantly, said in a high tenor, "It helps our trade because of all the tourists to be able to recognize off-island accents and jargon." He stopped and then repeated himself only lowering his voice two full octaves.

Tanner started and then nodded. "I heard a voice like that, and just about that range."

The small group went on, sometimes poking fun at each other and eventually at Tanner and Detective Smythe.

Finally Emmett looked at his watch and said. "It's growing late and I'm sure Mr. Tanner grows tired of our little exercise. Tanner admitted it was wearying to listen intently for such a long time. They shook hands all around and Madeline took them to the door. Emmett leaned over and kissed his mother on the cheek. She returned the favor and placed one strong hand on Tanner's arm. "He's a good boy, and smart too. He'll get to the bottom of this, you'll see."

The two men left and started the trek back to the station.

"Well, now," said Tanner. "That was very interesting. I never would have thought of it. Do they teach such things at Scotland Yard?"

Smythe laughed aloud. "No sir, but life teaches such things."

"Did it help, do you think?'

"Most definitely. I now have the names of at least three people, crew members I believe, who were part of the crew that abducted you."

"Seriously?"

Smythe smiled. "Yes. When I put these language recognition factors together with other information we already have, or have developed since you found those hundred dollar bills, I know three men who fit the profiles and who currently or recently crewed for Gonzo Barnes. It isn't proof. Wouldn't hold up in court. Wouldn't even get to court. You understand?"

Tanner nodded.

"But what we do have is some solid leads that may take us inside Barnes organization. That is huge. At least it can be. We've been trying for more than a year to develop some leverage with those people."

"Let me guess. Other leads you people developed either went no place or somehow just dried up."

Smythe nodded. "That's true."

Tanner looked at Smythe hard. "Why am I not surprised? You have a problem inside your department and I think you know it."

27

Mary sat at a desk in Hilda's office where she had been burning up budgets with several lengthy long distance calls to Seattle and to some of her contacts in California. Edmund Hochstein had made several suggestions as to how to ferret out needed financial information. He also encouraged Mary to call some of her friends who might be tuned in to current gossip in Hollywood.

"I will of course employ our contacts to collect similar information, Mary, but it would be good for you to use your own personal channels. Queries coming from you will be treated differently from questions I would ask."

"Of course, Mr. Hochstein. My mother's long-time friend Isabella Carter has contacts all over the Hollywood area. I'll call her right away.

"If we can get information from multiple sources that will help you verify its accuracy. I guess I can assume that will also make it more difficult for anyone listening in to determine why we're asking. Am I correct?" Mary winked at Hilda as she spoke.

"Yes, my dear. I also think it would be wise to treat these queries as straightforward questions. Don't ask your contacts to be more than normally discreet."

"Of course, that way any leaks will seem unimportant."

"Quite so." Mary heard him sigh gently and then he murmured. "And please try to keep yourselves out of harm's way. I'm not sure how much more my heart can take."

Mary smiled into the phone and offered a small reassurance as she hung up.

"You sound like a different person when you talked to whoever that was," remarked Hilda. Her fingers rattled over her computer keyboard. She was creating a database for the information they were collecting.

"Edmund Hochstein is a very old family friend and the executor of my mother's estate, plus he heads up my foundation. Michael says the same thing. He treats Edmund differently, too. There's just something about him. I suppose it's his age and demeanor. But I really do think of him like a favorite uncle, even though technically he works for me."

"Your lunch with Homer Jensen tomorrow ought to be really interesting. I only met the guy briefly at the party, but he seems nice. My gut says he's not involved. On the other hand, my gut has been wrong before."

"I wonder how Michael is making out with the police."

"He's doing quite well, thank you very much," said a familiar voice from the door. Tanner strolled in smiling wearily. He collapsed into a nearby folding chair after kissing Mary lightly on the cheek. "I'm still not entirely recovered from being imprisoned."

"How did your session with the police go? Did Lieutenant Archambault have any news?" Mary swiveled around in her chair.

"I have had a most interesting afternoon. Police methods on this island, at least in this case, are a bit unusual."

"How so?" asked Hilda, pausing in her typing.

Tanner proceeded to explain how he had met Detective Emmett Smythe's mother and friends in a private residence.

"Interesting approach," Hilda said. "Any results worth mentioning?"

"The detective told me he'd been able to identify two or three men who were part of the crew that abducted me and sank *Passions Messenger*."

"Wow," said Mary.

"But it's not evidence that can be used in court, I'll bet," said Hilda.

"Correct, but he feels what he now knows will help him leverage the gang somehow."

"Tommy told me they're really anxious to find Mr. McGwean's killer. That's one reason we've been able to call on them for help. McGwean was sort of on his last legs, but MI5 hates to lose an agent, especially to violence. I get the impression from Tommy he was something of a loose cannon in his last few years because of his drinking problem. But that doesn't really matter. He was murdered." Hilda shook her head.

"Do we have any information as to exactly what he was doing?" asked Tanner.

Hilda pursed her lips as if she was considering several possible answers. "After everything that's happened, I suppose I can stretch the rules some more. We share some information with the Brits, of course and presumably, they share with us. We don't normally share anything with civilians. Mr. McGwean insisted for some time there's a massive counterfeiting operation based in South America that is smuggling bogus bills into the U.S. through the Caribbean. There are other routes of course, but there is some evidence Road Town is a prime route."

"Gonzo Barnes?"

"Yes. I'm sure he's part of it, but we have absolutely no proof. We also think some local officials are probably on the take."

"I'm going to the hotel for a little while," Mary said abruptly and stood up. She looked at Tanner for a long moment and touched his hand. Without another word she went out.

Tanner watched Mary go and then said, "I have no proof either, but I got the distinct impression that at one point the people who were holding me were planning to dump me in the ocean. Then something or someone changed their minds." Tanner paused, looking into the unknown distance, and said in such a low voice Hilda almost missed it, "We were docked somewhere. I had overheard remarks about dumping unwanted cargo, which I assumed meant me. Lunch was late that day."

Tanner glanced at Hilda and bent his mouth in a poor excuse for a smile with little warmth. "Funny what I remember. They had my watch and they didn't beat me much. Just pushed me around. I have a pretty good internal clock. So I knew roughly what time of day it was, although I wasn't sure if it was day or night for the first couple of days. The meals always came at the same time. Within minutes. So I noticed it the last day that lunch was late. I remember there was a scramble, men running overhead. Loud talk, not quite shouting. There was an upsurge in the level of tension. Things got urgent somehow and then we got underway. It just seemed hurried to me, as if their plans had suddenly changed." Tanner shrugged.

Agent Martin had been making notes. "MI5 thinks the whole operation is run out of South America. We neither agree nor disagree. It sounds like the captain, Gonzo Barnes, I presume, got orders to return you here to Tortola. I wonder why.

"We know the ship was anchored in harbor at St. Martin about a day after you went missing. It takes the better part of a day to get back here, even wasting fuel at high speed. One of our spotter planes saw the boat heading this direction earlier the same day we got you on the beach. So your recollections pretty much square with what we know. I was pretty impressed the way Mary figured out where they were landing you so we could be a welcoming party."

"Me too," Tanner said.

For another hour Hilda and Tanner went over everything they knew so far.

Steps sounded and the door swung open. Mary paused on the threshold for a moment. Then she pulled the office door wide and came in. Without a word she grabbed Tanner and soundly kissed him. "Sorry, I just had to get out for a little while. But I made a few calls as Edmund suggested."

Hilda looked at her carefully.

"So what have you two been talking about?" Mary said.

"We're comparing notes," Hilda said. "Putting what your observant friend here remembers together with what we know about *Maid Marian*'s movements during the same time period is helping us figure out what may have been going on. At least I think so."

"I get it," Mary said. "I just talked with some people in San Francisco and in Los Angeles. There seems to be a fair amount of excitement about Jensen Production's move into feature films. It that's what it is."

"And why is that?" asked Hilda scribbling more notes. Tanner watched Hilda put some things into the computer in front of her and at other times write notes on a pad beside her keyboard. He wondered about that. Then he wondered if he was seeing double meanings everywhere.

As if she was reading his mind, Agent Martin said, "There's some stuff I want to develop a little more, so I do hand-written notes. I'll add this to the placeholders in the document later. Probably tonight or early tomorrow."

"There's more," Mary went on. "Word on the street, the street in LA that is, is that Jensen is stretched a little thin, may be over-extended, blah blah blah…" her voice thinned and trailed off.

Tanner looked at her and saw her hands beginning to shake. Mary sat down suddenly, as if her leg muscles had lost their ability to hold her up.

"Ah, rats." Tears appeared in her eyes. "It's happening again. This is why I left a while ago. I thought I was over it." She stared up at Tanner, mouth working, fingers trembling. "I'm, I'm sorry. I don't know what's wrong with me."

"I do," said Hilda. She rose from her chair and came around the desk to offer Mary a wad of tissues. "You have been incredibly strong since Michael was taken and now you're having a delayed reaction. Coming down from a long adrenalin high."

Tanner placed his arm around Mary's shaking shoulders and said, "I think we need more rest."

"Absolutely," said Hilda. "We had a little training on signs to watch for after a big emotional upheaval. You guys go back to the hotel. Spend some time with each other. I'll stay here and monitor the phones. If anything significant happens I'll come find you."

"Some vacation," Mary muttered and let Tanner raise her from the chair. Arms entwined, they went slowly out into the afternoon sun.

In the middle of the street, Mary paused and looked at Tanner. "What I want now is to have a bath, then a nap. Then I want a little to eat and then I want to go to bed with you, my dear, and make love for a long time."

Tanner smiled at his wife and brushed her cheek with his lips. "Sounds like a very good plan."

28

At twelve-thirty on another bright day, the black Caddy that Hilda and Mary had spied in the Jensen garage on Mount Sage, drew up to the front of the hotel. Mary Whitney, shining in a bright yellow sun dress and strappy low-heeled gold shoes, tripped down the steps to the vehicle, her husband beside her. He looked satiated and well-fed in a loud short-sleeved shirt and light-weight ducks. A long evening of intimacy had reduced Mary's delayed bouts of anxiety and allayed most of their joint fears. Now they were ready for the next chapter. Both Mary and Tanner anticipated an interesting luncheon

An elaborate spread of locally processed cold cuts, a massive fresh salad and a cold boiled rice dish had been prepared by Homer Jensen's cook and served up with icy crisp white wine. Mary and Tanner were Homer Jensen's only guests. After a few glasses of wine and partway through the excellent repast, Jensen wiped his mouth ostentatiously and put down his fork. He'd been cool and businesslike up to then.

"You have an excellent chef," Tanner said. "And if this is any indication, a pretty outstanding wine cellar." He saluted their host with a smile and a tip of his wine glass.

"Thank you, Michael. May I call you Michael? I've always believed in living well, if not beyond my means. Fortunately, my means have always been rather plentiful." He spread his hands. "I make no apologies for living as well as I am able. We," he included Tanner with a wave of his hand as he turned to address Mary directly, "are business-men and we strive to be successful while employing increasing numbers of individuals who help whatever enterprise we pursue. Isn't that the way it should be? I was frankly startled when I received word the other day of your presence here on Tortola. I think it's most fortuitous, if un-expected. Your husband, as I needn't remind you, has a successful and powerful advertising and public relations agency in Seattle."

That's right, Mary thought, *you needn't, so why are you?*

"You are heir to a large fortune due to similar efforts by your fore-bearers. Oh, yes, I've done my research." He smiled widely. "Of course, the expansion of your wealth and the many successful activities in which you and your foundation engage are becoming well known, if not truly legendary, if I may say."

Mary smiled and nodded, concealing her impatience. Tanner smiled inwardly. He knew this kind of flattery was just as likely to get Mary to reject whatever offer was coming as would a bad business plan or weak financials.

"Thank you, Homer." If he was going to switch to first names, so was she. "I appreciate the kind words. Are you going somewhere spe-cific with this gambit?" Her smile didn't reach her eyes.

Oops, thought Tanner.

Homer Jensen faltered only a little. "Quite right, my dear. There's no need to beat around the bush. All right. I've asked the two of you here to discuss the possibility of a joint venture. As you know, we've just wrapped up the shooting for a major feature film, the first feature for HJ Productions. I intend to use this film as the vehicle to launch a new era of studio production. More, I intend HJP to become a studio to rival an MGM or a Paramount of the twenty-first century.

"I am now actively seeking investors in what I plan to be a com-prehensive and wide-reaching promotion and advertising campaign. My plan is to raise funds with a private placement among sophisticated in-vestors. The advertising plan will be timed to give the film the greatest exposure at precisely the best time for maximum influence on the Oscar voting. There is time, while the work is being edited. Not a great deal, but enough time." Jensen smiled, showing his teeth, and spread his arms wide, nearly upsetting a crystal carafe of wine beside his plate.

"I intend to release the film simultaneously world-wide. I'm hoping I can enlist the creative genius of Tanner and Associates to plan and execute the film's release and I would also like to enlist the financial resources of the Whitney Foundation in this venture. There will be appropriate compensation, of course, in the form of shares in the studio. Naturally there will be other attractive compensations as well."

"It sounds intriguing," Tanner said after a moment of silence. "I assume you have developed some sort of business plan and ancillary materials to go with your presentation."

"Of course, although I had not anticipated encountering you as potential investors here on Tortola. I am having some preliminary projections and other information delivered to your hotel."

Jensen sat back with what Mary decided was a self-congratulatory look on his face. Tanner and Mary thanked Homer for his interest in them and without making a commitment of any kind. Mary had made it clear from the outset she didn't wish to dwell on Tanner's kidnapping and subsequent rescue, so talk turned to other topics.

Eventually they parted company and Tanner and Mary were driven back to their hotel. Even though Mary had received some attractive offers to move up the mountain to one of the more up-scale and exclusive resort hotels, they had decided to stay where they were in the center of town. There were a number of advantages, not the least of which was the proximity of the hotel to Agent Hilda Martin's office and to local law enforcement. The busy town also afforded them a measure of protection that would have been lacking in a quiet resort hotel and spa.

"So, what do you think about Mr. Jensen's proposal?" asked Tanner. They were climbing the stairs to their room.

"Umm. I think that first I want to read the material he's supplying." Mary reached for the latch to their room when Tanner's hand shot out and stopped her.

"What?"

"Hang on. I want to look at the door jamb." Tanner ran his eyes carefully over the crack between door and frame. The hair he'd placed there when they left was still in place. He plucked it out and showed it to Mary who nodded and then opened the door.

"I'll read it too," Tanner said, "but frankly, my dear, the idea sucks. Not necessarily what he wants to do. On that I'm not ready to comment. But we have a policy at T&A, since almost the very beginning. We do what the lawyers call pro bono work, but we don't accept stock or shares in enterprises as payment for our work, even for good causes. If we did we'd own pieces of hundreds of cockamamie schemes, and we'd be broke. He did sort of extend an offer of employment, but mostly that was to add to your possible interest. Jensen must know we don't have a lot of expertise in the kind of promotion I think he's going to need."

"Would you be willing to go over his plan and offer a pointer of two if it doesn't take too much of your time?

"Yes. Sure, of course. Does that mean you are interested in HJP as a possible investment opportunity?"

"Yes and no. I think Homer may be over-extended and getting a little desperate, but I know that up to now they've been a good profitable company so they have possibilities. Not for Whitney Enterprises, but for somebody. You know, they should have been working on a marketing plan long before they finished the film."

"That thought had occurred to me," Tanner said. He may have wanted to see the film finished first, because of his financial circumstances."

"If he's desperate, might he have done something foolish? Like go to questionable sources of money?"

Tanner nodded.

"Now, husband, I intend to swim a few laps and then nap by the pool. I have my eye on a comfy shaded chaise only steps away. Be a good boy and arrange tall cold drinks in about two hours, yes?" By now Mary had stripped out of her clothes and donned a modest bathing suit. She grabbed a towel and went to the door.

"Arrrr," Tanner growled. "I love it when you give orders like that. Makes me hot."

* * *

Two hours and thirty minutes later, a shadow fell across Mary's recumbent form. She squinted upward. It was not her husband who stood there. She couldn't make out his features in the shadow.

"Excuse me, Mrs. Whitney. I am sorry to disturb you. I have some news that concerns you. Your luncheon host, Homer Jensen, has just been found dead and I must ask you some questions."

Mary sat up with a jerk. "What? Homer? How?"

Tanner appeared next to her chaise and sank down beside her. Lieutenant Archambault watched the couple without expression. Apparently he had just informed Tanner of the news as well.

"Hell's Bells," Tanner muttered.

"That's tragic," said Mary. "He was so optimistic, so full of plans. He had very high hopes for his film, you know. Did he have a heart attack or something?"

"He was murdered." The flat statement fell like a stone in a placid pond. For a moment nobody moved. Then the lieutenant dragged over a nearby wicker chair and sat facing Mary and Tanner. "One of the staff, a housekeeper, found him in his bedroom. Someone stabbed him in the throat with a steak knife. What time did you leave Mr. Jensen?"

"It must have been around three," Mary said. "We got there about one and had lunch. Then we talked for a while."

"That's right," Tanner agreed. "I wasn't checking my watch, or anything like that, but the time frame seems about right. The driver dropped us off and I assume he went back up the mountain to Jensen's."

"What did you talk about?"

"Jensen was interested in having us join him in a business venture to promote and distribute his new film. We haven't made any decisions one way or the other."

"Who else was there?" Archambault took a small notebook from his pocket and started making notes.

"No one other than staff. A woman served the lunch and the wine. We mentioned the meal and then wine, but I never actually saw the cook."

"Do you know the name of the woman who served you?"

Mary frowned and thought for a moment. "I don't think so."

"Did Mr. Jensen give you any indication of trouble with his businesses?"

"No." Mary shook her head.

"Were any other subjects discussed?" The lieutenant scratched rapidly in his notebook.

Tanner shook his head. "If you mean my recent kidnapping, no. Apart from general talk about the weather and some mutual acquaintances."

Lieutenant Archambault's head came up and he shot a questioning glance at Tanner.

"By that I mean this was primarily a business invitation. I'm sure you know we were at his recent party. But today Mr. Jensen was definitely in a business frame of mind."

"Would you care to enlighten me?"

"Hollywood people are always on duty," said Mary. "You know I represent an investment possibility for a film studio, and my husband has vast marketing and promotional experience. Mr. Jensen seized an opportunity when he learned we were here on Tortola. That's all." She laid her hand on Tanner's bare thigh.

"So you have no information that might help our investigation." Archambault didn't sound exactly disappointed.

"I'm afraid not, lieutenant," said Tanner.

"Is there anything else you can tell me about this luncheon or about people at the celebration you attended the previous night?"

Mary and Tanner looked at each other and then shook their heads. There was nothing either could contribute.

"Lieutenant, do you think this is connected to my husband's abduction? Or to the death of Mr. McGwean?"

The lieutenant stared at the palm frond hanging over Mary's chaise. "There is no evidence to suggest it, at least not yet. I will have my notes transcribed into a statement for each of you to sign. If you think of anything else, please let my office know immediately. After you review and sign the statements, you will be free to leave the island. I am sorry that our local problems have invaded your lives so thoroughly. Good afternoon."

The lieutenant stood and left them.

"Well," Tanner said.

"Well, indeed," said Mary. "That's a real tragedy. Homer was so up at lunch. I thought the lieutenant asked some odd questions."

"You mean about things he should already know. I suspect he just wanted to double or triple check his other sources."

Mary sighed. "Things seem to be going completely out of control. What do you think we should do?"

"Talk to Hilda and then go home as soon as we can arrange a flight."

"That'll take some time. I just realized that we don't have any proper identification. Picture IDs for the security people at the airlines, and our passports, are gone. Not even an overdrawn credit card."

"Let's talk to Hilda about that, too. I imagine the Secret Service can be of some help in that regard," said Tanner.

"Did you notice he called me Mrs. Whitney?"

"Yes." Mary looked at her husband. "Odd."

29

"Do you think we're in any danger?"

"Do you think you're at risk?" countered Hilda. The air conditioner in her temporary office muttered. Still early, the tropical sun was already making itself felt.

Tanner looked at her. "With Jensen's murder, I'm beginning to wonder. What a mess. How soon can we leave, assuming the police don't decide to change their minds and hold us for some reason?"

"Already in the works. I've asked Washington to expedite things so you'll have valid identification to get you through security and on a plane. The airline has a record of your original reservations and the changes you've already made, so that helped."

"You know, if we put it out that we're about to leave, it might flush out the killers—Barnes and his cronies, presumably," offered Mary.

"Set ourselves up as targets, you mean," said Tanner. "I don't think I like that idea at all."

"It might just bring this to a conclusion, that's all. By now they must realize we know nothing about the missing money." She paused and stared at Hilda. "Fact is, we still aren't even positive money is what this is all about are we? I'm just really tired of constantly looking over my shoulder and wondering about the intentions of every stranger who gets too close."

Tanner changed the subject. "What do we know about Barnes's whereabouts?"

"*Maid Marian* docked at the HPJ dock in Soper's Hole later the same night you were released," said Hilda. "We don't know exactly when, just that it was after midnight and before dawn. The crew apparently dispersed immediately. They didn't even clean up or leave anybody aboard."

Tanner looked at her with a quizzical expression.

"We, ahh, looked at her after we discovered the boat had docked."

Her telephone rang. "Agent Martin here."

She listened for several seconds and then thanked the caller. "Important development. The Coast Guard has found something off Ginger Island. They think it relates to our case and McGwean's murder. They've called for a salvage boat that's about to leave for the site. If we hurry we can go aboard. I suppose you'd like to be there?"

"Just try and keep us away," said Mary, grabbing her purse and standing. The trio fled the office and minutes later were driving to the industrial docks on the west side of the harbor.

A big ugly well-used tug showing a lot of rust and stained superstructure was already maneuvering beside a long open barge nestled against the aging but solid-looking wharf. From the wharf the barge sides towered above their heads. The rusty hull was festooned with an assortment of enormous worn truck and construction vehicle tires to cushion the wharf and the barge hull from damage. A member of the crew stood braced at a narrow ladder between the high gunwale of the barge and the wharf. The captain of the salvage tug waved at them and pointed toward the ladder at the forward end of the big barge.

Agent Martin flashed her badge at the crew member, who beckoned them aboard. The three climbed the ladder and stepped gingerly onto the barge, then made their way across the steel bottom through clutter and debris to the stern. The barge was nothing more than a huge steel bin with high rigid sides, several massive mooring bollards along the sides and ends, and what looked like random piles of dirty ropes, cables and unidentifiable detritus scattered about.

Toward one end a huge counter-balanced crane hunched on the

deck, its long latticed boom resting with one end slanted onto the deck. Waves smacking against the side of the barge sent hollow booming tremors through the thing. Small diesel engines attached to massive drums of gleaming greased cable were situated at each end.

"Glad I'm not wearing whites," Mary mumbled as she slowly climbed a chipped green painted steel ladder to the bridge of the tug.

In the wheelhouse, the man at the controls nodded and explained. "There's some weather moving in. Coast Guard wants us to get whatever it is they've found up out of the water so it isn't lost again."

"Do we have any idea what it is?"

" Nosir. Just large crates that appear to be wood and sheet steel was the only word. You lot can wait in the ward room down that passage. It'll take us a couple of hours to reach the site." He turned his full attention back to the delicate job of getting his boat and barge straightened out and moving toward the mouth of the harbor.

* * *

Two hours later the rig was on station, held tenuously to the bottom by a pair of thousand-foot cables. During the trip, Tanner had explored the salvage barge, a 200 by-70-foot floating structure.

"The crane will try to hook whatever is down there with a grapnel of some sort." Tanner pointed at the crane, now extended over the side of the barge. " I think they have a lot more muscle here than they need but it was apparently the only vessel immediately available."

The captain looked worried. He frowned at his radar screen and then at the sky to the east. The sea seemed in a restless mood; waves weren't particularly large, but there was no regular pattern. Bigger waves boomed against the sides of the barge while smaller ones sent spumes of spray high in the air to drape over the sides and rapidly drench the men working the crane and the winches. Crew members who had mostly been out of sight during the trip now tended the anchor cable engines, while another man delicately adjusted the controls of the big crane's boom as crew connected the huge grapnel to a cable. The noise and stink of several diesel engines became increasingly penetrating.

A British Coast Guard patrol boat stood on the windward side, offering some small shelter from the trade wind that blew almost ceaselessly across the Sir Francis Drake Channel. Sophisticated side-scan sonar aboard the Coast Guard ship had found an anomaly on the bottom of the Francis Drake Passage, according to the tug's bos'un.

"What exactly did they find?" asked Mary. She stood braced on an upper deck of the salvage tug watching preparations for lowering an elaborate-looking grappling apparatus into the water.

"Three cubes," said Tanner, who had talked at length to the crane operator. "Whatever they are, they're definitely man made. Nature just doesn't create objects that are so regular."

"I don't get it," said Mary. "Why would somebody dump cases of contraband way the Hell out here?"

"Those crates, if that's what they are, are pretty deep," said Hilda, who had examined the sonar and video scans. "It occurs to me that may be where this all started. If the crates were dumped in the wrong place, here where it's pretty deep, the smugglers might have had trouble retrieving them."

"Sure," Mary said. "Look around you at this rig. A big ocean-going tug, a salvage barge. Those aren't vessels you just have hanging around and they are sort of noticeable. So maybe the criminals couldn't retrieve the stuff as quickly as they wanted because of the depth of the water. They thought we were down here to steal their merchandise and grabbed Tanner to keep us away while they located rigs like this to hire."

"I suppose my finding those hundreds triggered the whole thing," Tanner said.

"The currents are right. If one of those cubes contains cash and broke open when it hit the bottom, it could be the source of those three hundreds you found," said Mary.

"It's actually kind of a clever idea," Hilda said. "If they're like crates we've found before, they have big metal loops that stick out on all sides. They're designed to be quickly drowned. I've seen reports that the crates are weighted and stored near an underwater hatch built into in the hull of a freighter. If the freighter gets into trouble, like they're about to be boarded, the crew can jettison the cargo without bringing crates up on deck. The idea is that a radio homing beacon attached to at least one of the crates lets the smugglers find them and retrieve them at some later time."

"Clever is right," said Tanner.

"In this case, apparently the goods were dumped in deeper water than intended and either the beacon didn't work or it tore loose or something else happened. Maybe the currents moved the crates away from the dump site. We still aren't sure what delayed the retrieval," Hilda explained further.

"How'd they find this stash?" asked Mary.

Hilda just smiled. "Lots of detective work, tips, bits and pieces. The Royal Coast Guard has been searching for this stuff for months. Even with the tips, this find is mostly luck. I gather the Brits began to concentrate their search in this part of the channel more urgently after you happened on those bills and after McGwean's murder. The location of the bills you found apparently helped a great deal to focus the search. It's always been assumed this water is too deep for retrieval except with specialized equipment like you see here."

The tugboat captain came to the deck where the trio stood watching. "We've deployed an underwater camera to help locate the crates again. We've got some pictures but it's deep enough to be uncertain. The grapnel is almost to the seabed. With luck we'll see the first crate in an hour or so. Assuming nothing goes wrong." He scowled. "Which it often does in these situations. But at least we've got a secure beacon close by on the bottom. We'll be able to find the place again."

"Captain. Are you doing a GPS plot also?" asked Mary.

The captain stared at Mary, apparently surprised to hear such a knowledgeable question from a woman. "Yes, ma'am. Between GPS and the beacon we sent down we should have a good fix 'case we have to leave before gettin' all of it up. Fact is, I think we'll be lucky to have more than one of the three crates aboard before that storm hits." He pointed back over their stern to a long cloud formation looming on the horizon.

"Interesting, isn't it," said Tanner. "Except for hurricanes, the weather here is pretty good almost all the time. But here we are, racing an oncoming storm."

"There's no foolin' wi' the sea and the weather," drawled the captain. A shout from the door of the main cabin brought the captain's head up. A donkey engine with a huge spool of cable attached changed its tone and with a puff of angry-looking black smoke from its stack, began to reel in the cable.

As the captain turned to retrace his steps to the bridge, Tanner asked, "How deep is it here?"

The captain smiled grimly. "Over there on the island side, she's about twen'y fathom. But just on the other side, she's more like a hun-nert." He went off to more closely oversee the retrieval.

"Wow," Mary commented.

"Translation," Hilda requested.

"A fathom is six feet. So the bottom where the crates are is only a hundred and twenty feet. Still deep enough to be a problem for retrieval without experience and expert help. We're right at the edge of a trench that drops way off."

"Six hundred feet down," said Hilda softly. "Yikes. So if the crates had gone down only a couple of degrees south, they'd probably have been lost forever."

"I expect that sea currents may have had something to do with their location as well," mused Tanner. "I wouldn't be surprised if the next big storm through here sends them over the edge into deep water." The sun disappeared for a few minutes behind a fluffy white cloud, bringing momentary respite from the heat of the afternoon.

"That's a harbinger of things to come." Mary pointed toward the southeast where the low-lying cloud formation they'd glanced at before was noticeably closer. The wind suddenly freshened and an afternoon shower drenched them with warm rain. It only lasted a few minutes and didn't cool things except briefly. The retrieval operation continued.

Finally there rose shouts from the other end of the ungainly craft and a whistle from the Coast Guard ship. A crate streaming salt water was hoisted above the edge of the barge and swung inboard where the crane operator dropped it neatly to the bottom of the barge. The grapnel hook had caught one of the four heavy wire rope loops that were fastened to each corner of the crate. The crate itself measured approximately six feet on a side. It appeared to be constructed of a steel frame overlaid with heavy wooden planks. One corner was severely damaged. A large crack ran from the crumpled corner down one side. and a plank had torn loose at one end. Pieces of thick plastic shrink-wrap protruded from the jagged crack. Sea water continued to stream from the holes all around the perimeter of the crate and run down into the scuppers of the barge. Tanner fished a pair of binoculars out of one pocket and peered at the crate.

A lieutenant of the Royal Coast Guard from their escort craft was already aboard the tug. His clean white uniform and polished holster strapped to his waist contrasted to the more casually dressed crew and passengers on the tug.

"Sir," he said sharply to Tanner." He looked at the binocs making it clear he didn't approve of Tanner's attempt to examine the crate more closely. Two crew on the barge floor grabbed a big stained canvas tarpaulin and draped it over the still wet crate to conceal it. The lieutenant made it clear no one was to approach the crate. While Tanner, Mary and Martin watched, crew snaked ropes around and over the crate and lashed it to the deck.

The lieutenant took Tanner by the arm and drew him away from the women. They spoke for a few minutes and the man clambered down and went to take a position near the mysterious crate where it stood still leaking sea water across the stained deck.

The Captain of the salvage barge had evidently been conferring by radio with the Coast Guard vessel because no sooner had they retrieved the single crate then the crew turned to maneuvering the barge and winching the anchors back aboard. The crane operator also retrieved the slender vulnerable boom in preparation for returning to the harbor.

When Tanner and the two women returned to the bridge of the tow boat, they were informed that it was considered too dangerous to wait out the coming storm in this location. The little fleet would run to Road Town and return to the site after the storm passed and the sea returned to its normal state.

Mary looked a question at Tanner. "The lieutenant offered his thanks for our help. He said that when I pinpointed where those damn disappearing hundreds showed up, I helped the authorities find the goods."

"And set yourself up for kidnapping," Mary said.

30

When the salvage barge and tug returned to port with her escort, a man identified as the section chief of MI5 in the Caribbean was waiting at the dock. He approached Hilda as she stepped ashore and they conferred briefly. While Tanner and Mary watched from the bridge of the tugboat, where they'd been firmly requested to stay, the crate was off-loaded to a small pickup truck to be driven to a presumably secure location somewhere inside the confines of the port. Exactly where, no one would say. Tanner and Mary were not invited along nor were they told what was to happen next to the contents of the crate.

Tanner and Mary joined Hilda on the dock. She she'd try to get whatever information was released but she didn't seem hopeful.

"You'd think, considering everything that's happened, they'd at least tell us what they found," groused Mary.

Tanner shook his head. "I think they aren't entirely sure of us. Some officials may still believe we are more involved in all this than we are. I'm sure Hilda will tell us anything she can, but I get a feeling they aren't going to be very forthcoming for a while."

"Surely they don't think we're part of the group doing the smuggling, do they?"

"Who knows? I say we go back to the hotel and just relax. Have a true vacation day. We can't leave until day after tomorrow."

"Vacation? What's that?" But Mary smiled and squeezed Tanner's hand.

Since their official companions had all gone off, Mary and Tanner strolled through town back to their hotel, expecting the rest of the afternoon to be a relaxing time beside the hotel pool.

It was not to be.

When they arrived at the hotel, Detective Emmett Smythe was waiting for them. The grim expression on his face foretold serious business.

"While you were retrieving the mysterious crate, there have been some developments," he said without preliminaries.

They sat close together on the veranda and Mary thought, not for the first time, that police routines were often quite different in the casual atmosphere of the British Virgin Islands.

"I can now reveal to you that our investigation has reached inside my own police department. A customs official and Lieutenant Archambault appear to be heavily implicated in this money smuggling business." Smythe sighed loudly. "You must have noticed that there were occasions when I avoided answering some of your questions. I have been almost a year in this investigation of local corruption.

"We are convinced you are innocent bystanders, inadvertently caught up in a large smuggling conspiracy. There is still a good deal to learn. Lieutenant Archambault and his wife have disappeared and the customs official is in custody."

"What about the murder investigations? Are they part of this?" asked Mary.

Smythe nodded, a sorrowful expression on his face. "We are now virtually certain that is the case. It appears that Mr. McGwean either developed some leads, as we say, or stumbled upon the smuggling operation. We aren't sure which. What we do know is that he was not on an assignment here in the Islands working on the smuggling operation. We do not yet know for sure who killed him. Most unfortunately, Mr. McGwean appears not to have maintained regular contact with his superiors. Nor did he keep meticulous personal records."

"What about Homer Jensen?"

Smythe grimaced. "I blame myself to a degree for not making my case against the smugglers and corrupt officers sooner. I think that Mr. Jensen found himself short of funds, and because he knew or suspected that his yacht's captain was involved in illegal activities, talked Mr. Barnes into stealing from Barnes other employers. According to our sources Barnes was persuaded that he could make a tidy profit if he diverted some of the funds for temporary use by Jensen. It was apparently all about his new feature film."

"Sure," said Mary. "I'll bet they took some money from the illegal side of things, but then Jensen couldn't replace it before somebody found out."

"I wonder about that," said Tanner. "In all my dealings with Jensen's corporation, I never picked up a hint of corruption or even of any financial troubles. Did Gonzo Barnes kill Homer Jensen?" he asked.

Detective Smythe raised his hands. "We don't know, but the little evidence we have so far suggests that is the case. It's possible his gang found out about the money that went to Jensen and told Barnes to replace it and get rid of Jensen or he'd be the one to pay for the loss. But you should remember that some of this is just speculation and street talk, with almost nothing in the way of concrete evidence to support it. There is much to learn and verify before we can turn the case over to the Crown Prosecutors."

"Do you know where Barnes is?"

Smythe shook his head at Tanner. "Not at the moment. We're looking for him. The yacht *Maid Marian* is locked up at Jensen's slip in Sopers Hole. We presume he and his crew have access to another boat, or they are hiding on the island."

"I wonder if I could go aboard? If I can see the boat again I might be able to identify the cabin I was in," said Tanner.

Smythe was silent for a moment. Then he nodded. "That would be another bit of useful confirmation. We have an officer keeping watch for the time being. I'll let him know you are coming. He'll meet you at the dock. There's still time to do that this afternoon if you could."

"That's good," said Tanner. "We'll do it."

Smythe whipped out a cell phone and with two brief calls set it up.

Tanner had the hotel call a taxi and he and Mary parted company with the detective. Tanner promised to call Smythe and leave a message or talk to him in person after he and Mary had inspected *Maid Marian*.

Half an hour later Mary and Tanner had found the cop who was waiting at the Jensen slip with the keys. He said there was no reason for him to go aboard with them, after admonishing them not to take anything or damage the boat. He went back to his station, a chair on the dock beside the yacht's gangway.

Mary and Tanner stepped aboard. Tanner stopped and Mary walked around him to the other side of the cockpit. She turned and looked at her husband, silently assessing his reaction to being back aboard a place previously so fraught with danger and tension.

"Huh," he said and stepped to the glass door of the salon. He fiddled with the keys until he found one that fit. The door slid noiselessly open and they stepped into the dim interior. The porthole curtains were all pulled to cover the glass. Mary went to the port side and pulled back on the curtains to let in more light.

On their left was a polished bar. On the other side against the bulkhead was a padded two-seater sofa and three captain's chairs. All the furniture was heavy and made with widespread bases to maintain their stability in a seaway. Two doors led from the other end of the spacious salon to the ship's interior. Both pocket doors were open. One showed a set of stairs that led up, presumably to the captain's cabin and the bridge. The other led below decks to private cabins and crew quarters.

"I assume the engine room is down there," said Mary. She didn't like the look on Tanner's face.

"That would be a safe assumption," he responded. "It's a basic fact of marine vessel design that the machinery should be fairly low in the boat. It helps the stability of the thing." His lips twitched and he winked at Mary. "I'm all right, I think." He took a deep breath.

"Okay. Do you want to look over the rest of this truck before we go below?"

"Nope. Let's get it over, 'cause if this isn't the boat I think it is, we needn't waste our time."

They moved to the stairs leading down and went below. Mary found a light switch at the head of the stairs and flicked it on. Small recessed lamps provided minimum illumination. The narrow corridor, paneled in light tropical mahogany, ran down the centerline of the yacht. There were three doors on each side, two side by side at the center of the boat at approximately midships, the third toward the bow. At the end of the corridor was a steel door with heavy duty dog latches at all four corners. The dog levers were sizeable and the cams that would secure the door were also large.

Mary pointed at the door. "You dog down that door and it'd take explosives to get it open. Seems unnecessary to need that level of water-tight integrity."

Tanner grunted and walked to the end of the corridor where he hesitated, looking down at the floor. He tried the door that was the last one on the starboard side. It was locked. Tanner rattled the knob and Mary started toward him. He looked at the keys in his hand and selected one. Sliding the key into the slot Tanner twisted the brass knob and the door swung open. With Mary waiting at the threshold, he stepped into the dark interior. A light went on. Mary waited.

There was almost no sound. *Maid Marian* rocked gently against its mooring. Mary put her head around the door to see Tanner sitting on the single bunk. He was smiling and he beckoned Mary closer.

"This is it. This is the cabin where they kept me those days." His voice was low.

"How can you tell?"

"Look here, see the tape residue? They had the porthole taped over part of the time and when I lifted a bit and looked out, it left a little of the adhesive they didn't notice when they cleaned up. But here's the clincher. I want you to witness this, just in case it ever becomes necessary. Put your fingers up here. He indicated a small crack between the wooden paneling and the inside frame at the head of the bunk. It was just large enough that Mary could wedge her little finger into the hole to her second knuckle. Then by twisting her finger she touched something loose. Feel it?"

"Something loose. A piece of paper maybe?" Mary wiggled her finger some more. "I could fish it out if I had a hairpin or tweezers. What is it?"

Tanner reached in his pocket and produced a new Swiss Army knife that replaced the one that went down with *Passions Messenger*. He handed Mary the tweezers.

After a couple of tries, she tweezed a tiny piece of paper out of the hole. When she unfolded the scrap, she found a smudged scribble. It said M Tanner, and the date. Tears came. "Oh, God, Michael."

"Hey, it's all right now." Tanner put his arms around Mary and squeezed her where she half-lay on the bunk "Put it back in the hole."

She did so and they left the cabin. "Someday that scrap may be a useful piece of evidence."

Tanner and Mary searched through the other cabins and other spaces on the yacht, including the bridge. They found nothing to indicate what sort of activities might have been taking place aboard. The ship's log was missing.

Three hours later they were back at their hotel, having reported to Hilda that Tanner was sure *Maid Marian* was the craft on which he'd been imprisoned. Hilda had no new developments to report. Barnes and his crew were still missing although believed to have left Tortola.

"What's the basis for that?" said Tanner.

"More street talk," said Hilda. "But several sources from Tommy and from your detective agree. By the way I've just been talking to Washington. Your new passports, expedited by our eager to please Secret Service, will arrive tomorrow night in Charlotte Amalie."

Mary's smile at the news was an easy-to-decipher message. "My, would you believe it? We just might get in a day of relaxation."

Tanner placed a call to the police department to report to Detective Smythe that he was now sure *Maid Marian* was the right craft.

"Let's rent a car and go across to Cane Garden Bay," he suggested. "We'll make a day of it. We can swim, eat, drink and I understand there are plenty of opportunities to sample life on the beach. Something we don't do enough of when we're living aboard."

31

By ten o'clock the following morning, Mary Whitney and Tanner had found a tiny blue Renault automobile for rent. All four windows were open and Mary was at the wheel, smiling widely. They were relaxed for the first time since Tanner had been kidnapped. The hotel kitchen had packed a picnic lunch and a day of fun lay before them.

Over the mountain to the north they wound their way along narrow roads through lush thick groves of trees and brilliant frangipani.

Eventually the road carried them down to a tiny settlement in Cane Garden Bay. The shore was a long gently curving stretch of white sand dotted with trees and people and a few small structures. The bay itself was spotted with more than a dozen anchored sail and power boats. Partway across the mountain they'd switched drivers so Mary could use her new digital camera while they were on the move.

"With a little luck we'll have a few pictures to show the folks back home."

Tanner braked and drew to a halt near a ramshackle building at the edge of the water that housed a restaurant and a bar. He stepped from the car muttering, "Here we are, carefree tourists in Eden on a gorgeous white tropical beach. Let me just check out the nearby idlers for anybody with a gun."

Early as it was, crowds of swimsuit clad young people surged along the sand and clustered at the open air serving counters. A raucous volley ball game was actively going on farther down the long white beach. In the harbor numerous dinghies scuttled back and forth between the beach and the anchored boats. Boaters, tourists and islanders populated the beach in a wild variety of colorful swim suits and casual cover-ups.

"I don't see any way to hide a weapon in most of those suits," Mary remarked, eyeing the scantily clad throngs. They walked onto the sand and felt the heat rising through their feet.

Minutes later Tanner noticed that Mary was staring out into the bay, largely ignoring the people on the beach. She turned her head and said wistfully, "that's where we should be. Out there on our sailboat, tidying up the foredeck, having snacks, a Pussers Painkiller in the cockpit after a hard day of sailing. Dammit anyway!"

Tanner took Mary's hand and drew her into an embrace. "It'll get better. We'll get through this and we'll come back another time. I promise."

Mary mumbled something he didn't catch.

"I mean, I'm thinking about those first idyllic days, remember? Swimming off the boat? That missing bikini?"

A small smile appeared on Mary's face and she whacked Tanner on the shoulder. "Yeah, yeah, sailor, you're always able to talk me out of my moods." Her smile widened. "Mostly."

"Next time I'll just let the soggy money float on by."

Mary laughed. "Sure you will."

"Then there was that lovely dinner and night at the Drunken Parrot. Remember that?"

"The what? The Drunken Parrot? That wasn't the name of the place! You're talking about Virgin Gorda, and Spanish Town, right?" Mary giggled and then the grin left her face. "You know, that was an odd thing, running into that policeman and his wife that way."

"Yeah, you're right. What was it he said?"

Tanner looked at the harbor and thought back to that warm night. "He just asked us to come by the department in Road Town the next day."

"Right. He said he had some things to tell us about the case."

"But then when we went we only saw him for a few minutes and he really didn't tell us much of anything. He asked a few questions that covered stuff we'd already told him, and then we left."

Mary stepped back a pace and stared up at her husband. "Exactly! We left and you were kidnapped."

Tanner frowned. "You know, you're right. Do you suppose asking us to come to see him in Road Town was just a means to get us there? Seems far-fetched, doesn't it? Coincidental?"

"Yes," Mary admitted. "But Archambault really didn't have anything important to tell us, did he, and if he's involved in the smuggling, that could mean he had something to do with the killing of McGwean and even Henry Jensen."

She paused and looked up at the hard blue sky. "Thinking back to that day, what would have happened if I hadn't decided to go to the bank? They would have captured both of us. I bet that was the original plan. I think meeting that morning with the lieutenant was just an excuse to get us to Road Town."

"You're probably right. Maybe all this chatter in the local press and on the radio about corruption in the government is more accurate than I first thought," said Tanner. "Even though she hasn't said so, Hilda's superiors must think there's something large enough going on here to warrant her being posted to the BVI, no matter they told her it's supposed to be a temporary assignment. You gotta admit there probably isn't a lot of international crime in this part of the world."

"Which is probably why the heads of this particular smuggling enterprise chose this area, don't you think? I mean, law enforcement here is mostly focused on keeping things smooth for the tourist trade. They wouldn't have to bribe very many cops, even if they paid off the whole force."

"Well, why not? Tourism is the main business, and I agree with you," said Tanner. "The choice of a high tourist traffic area with lots of boats here and in transit to South America or the Lesser Antilles and no real reason for heavy duty crime makes sense. These islands are a logical choice for a transit route."

"Sounds like a quote from a seminar speech of some kind."

Tanner nodded. "Last year, that seminar I attended put on by the Kings County prosecutor's office. I think he was referring to the Inside Passage, not the Sir Francis Drake Channel. Enough of this. How about we have a drink at that little beach bar over there and forget this topic for a while."

"Like for a month or two," agreed Mary.

* * *

The steel drum band was going into a third or fourth chorus of a very long and complicated salsa piece. Mary had forgotten exactly how many choruses. She'd forgotten how many rum drinks she'd had as well. Mary knew she was acting uncharacteristically, but the tropical night, the casual beach bar and the spiraling down of her tension over Michael's kidnapping and recovery, the loss of their charter, and the looming danger of the murders, all seemed to have loosened her natural restraints. The ground was shifting under her feet. The day had been calm, fragmented, relaxed and devoid of unusual activities.

She felt a sort of lump in her gut that told her she'd have to take these feelings out and examine them in some detail before too long. But not now. Right now, she grinned and slung her arm around Tanner's shoulder. "It is late, my friend. I think we are not capable of driving back over the mountain to our hotel. I have had far more drinks than I usually do. What do you think?"

"I think I am not ready to do much thinking about anything. That's what I think. I suggest we find a nice soft sand dune on which to rest. I know I have absolutely no interest in trying to drive back over the mountain to Road Town," responded Tanner slowly. He'd had far less to drink than had his companion, but he still wasn't physically completely recovered from the ordeal of his kidnapping. His energy levels were at a low point.

The couple found unoccupied canvas deck chairs on the sand near one of the two beach bars that was still open. The snacks and drinks service to a small crowd of young people who appeared ready to stay on the beach the entire night continued. The lights from the place cast a soft glow over the surrounding sand.

"This reminds me of one of my spring break trips from college," said Mary.

Tanner didn't respond. In the years since the murder of his first wife Ann, and his subsequent descent into alcoholism, he had never allowed himself more than the occasional glass of wine with dinner. Today, since they had arrived in Cane Garden Bay, he had consumed more hard liquor than usual. Somehow, this trip over the mountain, the Caribbean atmosphere and his relief at being reunited with Mary had relaxed his internal safeguards, lessening his self-imposed restraints.

"I'm not capable of driving back tonight, at least not until I've had several hours of rest. A few hours here in this chair would help."

Mary nodded owlishly. "Ooookayyy, tiger. I b'lieve have a better solution."

"You do?"

"I do."

A short silence ensued while Mary struggled to her feet and tugged at Tanner's outstretched fingers. "C'mon, sailor. I have a place for us to go."

"You do?"

"Yes, I do. One of my, no one of our good friends on this island has a place right here in Cane Garden Bay."

"Really," grinned Tanner. "One of our good friends has a place here on Cane Garden Bay? Do I know the name of this friend?"

"You do, and it so happens that I asked him before we left Road Town, if he knew where we might rent a room." She smiled and waved her arms widely. "C'mon it's just up the beach here. I think."

"Just on the chance, right? The chance we might not want to make it back to our hotel. Such foresight. I'm impressed." Tanner smiled and grabbed her arms when Mary stumbled over loose sand on the beach. She giggled again.

"So who is this mysterious benefactor and where is the perk?"

Mary stopped and rooted around in the purse she had carried all day, coming up with a small flash light and a folded scrap of paper. She unfolded the paper and handed the flashlight to Tanner.

"Find the Tiki Beach bar, with the steel drum band. The cabin is directly up the hill overlooking the beach. It's painted red and has a blue roof. The door is yellow." Taped to the bottom of the note was a well-worn, old fashioned brass key. Mary peeled the key away from the paper and grinned up at Tanner.

"There's the bar." Tanner pointed down the beach toward a shelter where the sounds of steel drum rhythms banged out on several brightly painted oil drum covers, were easily heard. It was the same place where they had watched and marveled at the athleticism and talent of the steel band. He swiveled and pointed the other way across the expanse of the beach toward the hill. Several small cabins stepped their way along the shoulder of the mountain. "C'mon," Tanner said, pulling Mary by the hand. "In this light, we have to get closer to see the yellow door."

After a short walk they located the red cabin with the yellow door and discovered the key fit perfectly. Inside the neat and clean single room, they found a double bed, a counter with an ancient-looking gas ring, and behind a curtain, a tiny bathroom.

"All the comforts of home, and actually a little bigger than the cabin of *Passions Messenger*," said Tanner, latching the door and sliding open a window across the room from the bed. He breathed the rich scents of the frangipani and oleander flowers growing close around the back and sides of the place. When he turned back, Mary was sprawled across the bed, sound asleep.

32

"Jeez," groaned Mary, rolling over in bed. "Who hit me in the head?"

"Good morning, sunshine. Care for some tea? I did figure out the gas plate and I even found some ground coffee that appears to be reasonably fresh. We'll have to go out for tea,however."

"Yes, please, coffee is fine. Thank you and my absolute and total apologies for last night."

Tanner poured a second mug of coffee and carried it to the bed where Mary struggled up and leaned against the headboard. Tanner kissed her and handed her the steaming mug. "Nothing to apologize to me for." He paused and then grinned, "But I'm not so sure how that steel drum player feels."

Mary frowned and searched her memory, then, squinting at her husband through the steam, realized he was teasing her. "Well, he'll just have to live with it, whatever 'it' is."

"I have an idea. After you've cleaned up, I think we should go back to Road Town and raise some dust."

"Dust? Meaning?"

"I've been thinking about this whole thing this morning. We've been mostly reactive so far, don't you agree? Ever since we found those hundreds. Maybe we should start pushing people to see what we can shake loose. Fact is, I'm starting to get a little impatient with this whole 'be a polite American tourist and stay out of the way' attitude of some of the island authorities. Do you see what I mean?"

"I do," Mary nodded in time to the vigorous brushing she was giving to her luxurious hair. "I think you're right. I can start throwing my
weight around a little."

"Yup, and it turns out, we should remember, that my agency might
have a certain level of influence here owing to some previous contracts."

"Let's go get some breakfast on this fabulous beach and then go
back to Road Town." Mary stepped away from the mirror, grabbed her
purse and the couple strode purposefully through the cabin door.

* * *

Mary and Tanner walked the short distance down the gentle slope from
the cabin to the edge of the water. Nearby, a small beach cabana with a
hot grill sent the smell of banana and macadamia nut pancakes along the
gentle on-shore breeze. At the shore side counter they found two unoccupied stools next to a pair of teen-aged boys who were happily devour-
ing stacks of the fragrant cakes.

"These are wonderful," commented Mary, after her first bite. "I can
make these at home."

"I'll remind you," said Tanner through a mouthful. "Count on it."

Having satisfied their inner needs, as well as their desire for a little
R & R, Tanner and Mary headed back over the mountain to their hotel
in Road Town.

They checked their room carefully and found that the threads
and toothpicks they had set as telltales if the room had been entered,
were undisturbed. "I feel like we've gotten into some sort of spy caper
here," Mary said, picking a toothpick out of the crack in the bathroom
door jam.

"Not far from the truth," Tanner said. "I'm for the shower."

"Me second," said Mary. "You go while I write a note to our MI5
benefactor for the loan of his cabin. Then I'll call Hilda and we'll sit
down with her for a little review."

Ninety minutes later they sat in Agent Hilda Martin's office. Martin reported that the police had made no discernable progress in solving the murder of Agent McGwean, nor had they been able locate the people who everyone believed had kidnapped Tanner.

"Look," Tanner said testily. "We're due to fly out of here in a couple of days. Our sailing vacation has been totally disrupted. I've been kidnapped and now we've practically handed you the culprits by—" he stopped short, when Hilda abruptly raised a hand and frowned deeply, shaking her head at the same time.

Mary was standing and not watching the byplay. "I don't understand this. I'm looking out the window at one of Homer Jensen's employees sauntering down the street like any ordinary citizen. What's being done in the investigation into his death?" Alerted by a complete silence behind her, she turned around to see both Tanner and Hilda gesturing at her.

"I think we better stop this conversation before one of us says something we regret." Hilda's voice was smooth and neutral and at odds with the warning frown on her pretty face. She shook her head.

Mary made an inarticulate and most unladylike sound in her throat. "Right. This obviously isn't getting us anywhere. I'm going back to my room." She grabbed her purse and flung herself out of Hilda's office, slamming the door behind her.

Tanner rose and made to follow, wigwagging his fingers at Hilda, who remained seated. As soon as Tanner left, Agent Martin opened a bottom drawer and entered a code into a tiny battery-operated keypad. Her mouth twisted as she did so. This cloak and dagger stuff was more than she'd bargained for. The tiny low-powered signal the keypad transmitter sent would alert other Treasury agents that she was leaving the office to meet the troubled couple who was still under surveillance by at least two separate agencies of two countries.

* * *

Mary stood at the window of their hotel suite and examined the street below and the small building that housed Hilda Martin's office. She stood well back from the gauzy curtain to be sure she wasn't observed from the street or any of the windows that faced her.

"Hilda just left the building," she reported, "but she's going down the street. I thought you said she was coming over here."

"She will. I suppose she wants to know if she's being followed." Tanner was seated at the small table beside the bed, sorting through some raggedy notes from his pocket and pages torn from a notebook similar to one he habitually carried.

"Well," Mary said a moment later, "she is being followed. At least it looks that way to me. Of course, I'm no expert at these things."

"Man or woman?"

"Man. A middle-aged white guy, casually dressed, big sunglasses and no hat."

"Okay."

"Oh. I think I just saw somebody else sneaking around the back of the building where Hilda has her office."

"At the back of the building? That's interesting. Following, now sneaking, what's next, I wonder." Tanner moved up beside Mary and laid a hand on her shoulder. "How do we tell who's walking and who's sneaking?"

"I'm going to lose sight of Hilda unless I lean out the window."

"Don't do that. Let's just wait a few minutes."

Ten minutes later there was a soft knock on the door. Tanner checked through the peephole and then swung it open. Hilda Martin was there, smiling slightly.

"Come in, come in," said Mary over Tanner's shoulder. She started to go on but stopped at Tanner's wave. Martin winked and held up a sheet of paper on which she'd printed, CAREFUL YOUR ROOM IS BUGGED. "Let's go down to lunch," Martin said.

Mary and Tanner accepted and the trio left the room. In hushed tones as they strolled down the stairs to the hotel dining room, Hilda explained that they were removing only one of the listening devices in her office so they would have a channel to the counterfeiters to spread disinformation.

"Did you know you were followed after you left the office? And that I think I saw someone sneaking into your building from the back?"

"I thought someone was looking my way. That's why I took an indirect route here to the hotel. Maybe we got some pictures. Can you describe the man at the building? I assume it was a man because we don't know of any undercover women on the island right now."

Mary shook her head. "I'm sorry, but I just got a glimpse. He wasn't wearing a hat so I'm almost positive he's a white man. But he was balding, with just a fringe."

Hilda smiled and relaxed. "That must be Jedediah. Jed is one of our tech guys. He's going to sweep the building and tweak the jamming equipment he installed last month. Then he's going to sweep your room. Most of the stuff we're finding is old and looks beat-up so we're assuming they won't be surprised when some of it malfunctions."

Tanner bent his grave look on the agent. "This is getting very heavy again. I can't speak for Mary, of course, but I am tired of the game. I want to go back to my own games in Seattle."

Hilda and Mary nodded their understanding. "I agree with my husband, here," Mary put in. "We aren't spies or agents. This is not what we signed up for when we booked this charter. We came down here for a vacation that has been largely ruined by your finding those damn bills in the water." She pointed a long slender finger at Tanner and scowled as ferociously as she could manage.

Tanner said, "I've made reservations on the American flight leaving Charlotte Amalie in two days and I really intend for us to be on it. I'm sorry if that crimps your plans."

"I understand completely. Lunch is on me. No, I insist," said Martin when Tanner began to protest. "And something else. "I've had a couple of new reports on Gonzo Barnes. The gentleman and key members of his crew were observed departing Tortola late last night in a launch we know Barnes or one of his cronies owns. They left out of Sopers Hole and now we have a sighting of the same boat nearing St. Barts."

"Great, but I wish he was in jail," said Mary, as they all left for lunch.

"The Coast Guard is watching for him and we think he knows there's now an arrest warrant issued. He won't be back anytime soon."

Tanner smiled. "Good. I guess we can relax for the last couple of days before we leave. It's got to be tough on you, knowing there are possibly listeners monitoring your office."

"It's hard to remember what to say and what not to say. And with the corruption Smythe has uncovered in his own police department here, we're not sure who to trust. I've asked Washington for some additional help. I'm sure you realize this case has expanded way beyond my expertise."

Mary smiled and accepted the plate offered by the waiter on the covered dining veranda. "Thank you." Her gaze followed him as he seated Hilda Martin and then went off toward the kitchen. "I swear I've seen him somewhere before," she murmured.

"Very likely," acknowledged Hilda. "He's not an agent, if that's what you're thinking."

"And you know this how?" said Tanner.

Hilda just shrugged, a movement that could have meant anything.

"It must be tricky, moving agents back and forth across international boundaries."

Hilda smiled. "You have no idea, especially when the agents in question are undercover. But let's leave all that for the time being. I have a proposal."

Tanner and Mary turned their attention from their crisp white wine to the Secret Service agent seated across from them.

"You two have been great troupers and helped the department immeasurably in this business. I know you want to get home and out of all this. I agree. I know you had a grand time in Cane Garden Bay yesterday—"

"Why am I not surprised," Mary grumbled.

"But I thought we might try to have a real island vacation outing before you go. With Barnes and his friends out of the way, my British friends and I have made a little arrangement." She paused to sample her wine.

Mary said. "What do you have in mind?"

"You came here to sail so it seems to me you should have another opportunity to do just that. How about two nights around a whole day on the waters of Sir Francis Drake Channel? No worries, no work, essentially a crewed luxury charter. Just the three of us, and the captain and cook, of course. If you say yes, we'll meet the charter right here in a couple of hours, beginning early this evening. What do you say? It'll be fun. You can teach me to sail, we'll catch some rays and just bliss out on some really first-class food. I know the owners well, one of them is a great chef, and we'll provision with the best the islands have to offer."

Hilda's eyes sparkled as she thought about a peaceful day with two people of whom she had actually grown quite fond in a short time. "What's more, I guarantee we'll not talk one second about this case."

Tanner looked at Mary. He smiled broadly, feeling the tension of the past several days beginning to leak out of him, and said nothing.

"What's the boat?" Mary asked.

"It's called *Island Gull*. It's a fifty-foot Swan."

"Sloop? Single mast? Dark blue hull?

"Yes, but how did you know?"

"I've seen it in the harbor. I notice boats. That's a wonderful offer," Mary went on. "I can see my friend here is eager to accept." Mary laid a hand on Tanner's wrist. "I am too. It's a very generous offer and sounds lovely.

Hilda smiled with evident satisfaction. "Great. I'll let Clarice know right away. The plan is to have an early dinner in the harbor this evening and then sail out to an anchorage for the night. Their boat is over there on Wickham Cay. Why don't we meet at their slip in a couple of hours. Say four o'clock?"

33

Gordon Allborg and his wife Clarice, owners of the *Island Gull*, an elegant well-appointed Swan, turned out to be long-time residents of the British Virgin Islands. Allborg had been an investment banker in Toronto for many years and still kept his eye on the markets and the couple's portfolio.

"Modern technology has made it so easy to stay in touch. And we find the lifestyle here in the Caribbean much more conducive to a good life than even living in Toronto."

Mary and Clarice hit it off immediately. "I was fortunate. My grandfather and my uncles all thought I shouldn't be treated much differently from the boys in the family, just because I was a girl. So I learned to sail and to get around on the docks as a kid. I brought you a resume. You can see I've had a lot of experience sailing and my friend here is a top hand already. I can't think of anyone I'd rather have as my first mate."

Clarice nodded. "Tell you the truth, I'm not surprised," she remarked, after Mary explained the few changes she proposed. "Hilda explained a little about your experiences so far. I hope you'll come back one day and we can sail together for a much longer time than just overnight."

Meanwhile Tanner talked quietly with Allborg and Hilda Martin about some of the intricacies of the electronic equipment aboard. *Island Gull* sported some of the latest radar and sonar equipment as well as top-grade GPS and radio receivers. "I don't believe in short-changing my boats, especially when it comes to communications equipment. Besides, since we often offer crewed charters, safety is important. There's nothing tricky about any of this."

Tanner paid close attention and then he and Hilda went back over the key operations of the radio and the radar, along with the GPS settings, while Allborg listened.

"I'm impressed with your experience, the two of you," commented Clarice. "It'll be fun sailing for a day with people who are happy to participate in crewing. We love chartering, but sometimes it would be nice if our guests helped a little instead of expecting to be waited on all the time." She stepped into the galley from the navigation station. "If we pick up the pace a little we can have the galley provisioned and be on our way to a nice romantic anchorage for the night. I think we have time to get across the channel and anchor before dinner. Gordon?"

"Great idea," enthused Allborg. "Much better than being here in the marina. We're just waiting on one more delivery and then we can cast off and head across the channel."

Half an hour later, with more than an hour of daylight ahead of them, the five sailed *Island Gull* south across Drake's Channel toward an anchorage in Little Harbor at Peter Island.

In the middle of the seaway, Gordon turned the wheel over. Mary took command. Clarice and Tanner came aft from the foredeck and they all five gathered in the cockpit. Clarice said, "I have a little speech. I usually do this before we sail, but with the rush to get underway I forgot." She glanced around the little group.

"One of the things we like about our life here in the islands is how relaxed everything can be. It's so different from living up north up. We're all adults here and we should be able to talk frankly to one another. Being together on a sail boat, even one as large as this, brings us into closer contact than we may be used to. Personal space is at a premium. Gordon and I tend to dress minimally on these excursions and I sleep in the nude. If something disturbs us in the middle of the night and I have to run topside to help, I'm likely not to bother with clothes."

Gordon grinned and nodded vigorously. "Being this close can sometimes highlight bad habits unnoticed before. We just want all of us to have a nice relaxed time out here."

Clarice picked up the thread. "You all are encouraged to dress any way you're comfortable. There are no hidden messages of any kind. We don't run an alternate lifestyle cruise, but I tend to be something of a hedonist." Hilda raised her eyebrows at that. "There are a couple of charterers like that out here," Clarice said.

"I might just add," said Gordon, "that after a couple of hours of hot sailing, a naked swim around the boat is very relaxing."

"Been there, done that," quipped Tanner.

"So, all clear? Any questions? Good." Clarice clapped her hands and disappeared below.

Hilda also disappeared to her cabin for a few minutes. When she reappeared, she'd changed into a two-piece swimsuit of bright iridescent blue. Mary grinned at her and said, "Very not buttoned-down, Agent Martin. Nice. But where's your weapon?"

Hilda laughed. "It's safely tucked away in the safe in my house. Thankfully I'm not required to carry a weapon at all times."

Tanner appeared from the foredeck where he'd been tidying lines and stowing two hanging bumpers that had protected the hull from grinding on the wharf edge or when docked. He smiled and wiped an arm across his forehead. "I think the humidity is rising. We may have fog before morning, and a swim once we're anchored sounds excellent." He glanced at Mary and then speared Hilda Martin with a look.

"Okay, 'fess up, Agent Martin. I don't believe for a minute the United States Secret Service would ever make these kinds of arrangements for a couple of civilians who happened to be in the wrong place at the right time. What gives?"

Hilda grinned and spread her hands. "Okay, okay. I knew we wouldn't get away with that explanation. This is a private arrangement between me and a few others. Our way of thanking you for your help and a little compensation for a whole lot of intrusion and aggravation."

Mary smiled and said, "Ah, would one of those others possibly be the owner of that cute cabin on the other side of the island? One Tommy Corwin, perhaps?"

Tanner and Mary watched a lovely warm blush rise in Hilda's cheeks. "He was going to join us, but at the last minute he got called away," she murmured. Then she ducked her head and went forward toward the bow.

Mary glanced around and then bent below the boom to scan the sea ahead of the fast-running sloop. They were nearly alone in the dusk, the low dark shadow of Peter Island dead ahead now, rising from the horizon of the sea.

Tanner dropped below to the navigation station to check the instrumentation against the repeaters that Mary was watching from her position at the wheel of *Island Gull*. When he returned to the cockpit, Mary put a hand on his arm and nodded at the foredeck. "I think you better not go forward for a little while," she said.

He glanced forward to see Clarice and Hilda Martin, both clad only in bikini bottoms, standing side by side staring out at the darkening sea. Hilda had her feet firmly planted on the deck and was holding one of the steel stays lightly in her right hand, while from her left dangled the top to her suit. Her head was up and she seemed to be staring beyond visible limits high above the island ahead. She swayed gently with the movement of the boat. For long moments, as Peter Island grew on their horizon, no one said anything, all of the four busy with their own private thoughts.

Then Mary, after another scan around them, reached forward and flipped on the running lights. She saw Hilda flinch as if the change abruptly brought her back to the present from wherever she had gone in those few moments of meditation. "I need crew on the foredeck at the anchor windlass," she warned Hilda. The woman half-turned, donning her bra as she did so and waved.

"We've got it covered," called Clarice.

Tanner watched as Clarice instructed Hilda. She unshipped the anchor from its cradle. Both women then sat down beside the electric windlass control box.

With Gordon beside her, Mary neatly brought the big Swan into the small harbor and made a tight circle, checking out the situation. There was only one other boat in the anchorage. Gordon stood at the very point of the bow, peering into the water. With hand signals he guided Mary and together they threaded a short twisting path through coral heads and reefs to the inner cove, leaving a hundred yards of sea room on all sides. A sheltering arm of land cut the wind to a small breeze and the main sail flapped.

The big anchor went to the bottom with a rattle of chain through the bow chocks. "We'll let enough out so the anchor will have a horizontal drag," Clarice said to Hilda, manipulating the electric windlass. "You can feel the stretch from the anchor digging in." she placed Hilda's fingers on the anchor rode. Then she waved to Mary who reversed the engine prop and when the line tautened, dug the anchor flukes hard into the sandy bottom.

Clarice disengaged the windlass clutch and pulled a loop of anchor line out of the storage locker below their feet. "Here, run this length of line around that cleat by your feet and tie it off so there's slack at the windlass. It's a bit awkward with the middle of the rope because you don't have a free end. Some people just use the windlass brake but it puts strain on the motor and the gears. Cleats are meant to be used."

She watched as Hilda wrapped the anchor line on the cleat. The overhead work lights came on as the deep tropical night fell about them. Tanner grinned at Hilda and she and Clarice scurried back along the deck to the cockpit where Mary had shut down the engine and was just securing the wheel so the rudder would not swing back and forth while the boat lay quiet in the night.

As Clarice and Martin made their way to the cockpit, Gordon Allborg's voice rose from the galley. "Set up the cockpit table, please, dinner is ready."

Later, after an excellent meal of grilled sea bass and a huge green salad, Tanner volunteered to go below and find glasses and the brandy. Just as he turned back to the companion ladder with glasses, he heard a splash and a quiet laugh, followed by a second splash. He smiled to himself and draped two big beach towels over his shoulder, then climbed to the deck.

Hilda was standing by the space in the safety rail next to the boarding step at the stern. At her feet was a small puddle of clothes. "The captain and the mate are...umm...overboard," she giggled.

"I suspected as much when I heard the splashes. Will you join them?"

Martin shook her head shyly. "Not right now, thanks."

Tanner looked out into the dark water and located the pale form of Mary's face and body as she stroked back to the boat. Clarice hung by one hand to the boarding ladder at the stern.

"Heads up and watch out for barracuda," came a low cry. A naked Gordon Allborg flashed up the ladder from below and made a clean arching dive over the heads of the two women and disappeared into the warm dark sea. Splashing and quiet hilarity ensued for several minutes around the stern of *Island Gull*.

"Permission to come aboard?" Mary called.

"I dunno if we can allow naked hussies here," cracked Tanner. "What do you think, Seaman Martin?"

"Oh, we better make an exception, this time. Three exceptions, I guess."

Mary climbed up the step, bringing drops of sea water with her sluicing off her naked body. Tanner handed her the hose from the fresh water tank at the stern step and after she rinsed the salt water out of her hair, wrapped her in the big towel he'd brought up.

At Clarice's direction, Hilda brought up two big fluffy towel robes from the Captain's cabin, and handed them to Tanner. He heard a small splash and turned to discover that Seaman Martin had succumbed to the lure of the warm sea and was floating in the water, one hand holding the lowest rung of the boarding ladder.

"This is really lovely," she said, smiling up at the sky. The All-borgs came up the ladder and donned their robes while Tanner poured small brandies all around except for his tall glass of club soda. They sprawled in the cockpit so relaxed even conversation seemed too great an effort. Hilda Martin took the big beach towel from Mary and disappeared below with her discarded clothes.

A few minutes later she returned from her cabin where she'd donned shorts and a loose tee. Instead of accepting the small glass of brandy Mary offered, she sank to a cushion and said, "I found something odd. You better look at this."

Clarice switched on a tiny LED in the binnacle tower and peered at Hilda's extended palm. She was holding a small silver-colored object about the size and thickness of a battery for a cell phone. "What is it?" Mary asked.

"I'm not sure," Hilda responded, "but it might be a signaling device."

"Really," said Tanner, "were did you find it?"

"Feel the sticky surface? It fell out of a shoe." She picked up a tan deck shoe and displayed it.

"That's one of mine," said Tanner. "I shucked them right inside the cabin door earlier."

The five of them stared at each other in the small circle of light from the binnacle, light that winked off the small circle of silver in Hilda's hand.

"Where did it come from?" asked Mary.

"It must have been planted sometime today while we were out," mused Tanner, picking up the disk. "Damn! I thought we'd been careful to check the telltales on our door."

"Telltales can be replaced," said Hilda.

Mary poked the thing with one finger. "What do we do now?"

34

Clarice looked around at the dark bay, then back at the others. "We ought to haul anchor and get back to Road Town." There were solemn nods.

Gordon shook his head. "Remember how we got in here? Tricky even in daylight. We need good morning light to get out of here."

Hilda took the tiny disk from Tanner and stared at the innocent-looking thing in her palm. After a minute or two of silent contemplation, she flipped it over. "I don't want to destroy it, and I want to give it to our tech guys, but I want to kill the signal if it's still sending."

"What does it transmit?" Mary asked. "Surely not voice."

"No," agreed Hilda. "I think it's a low power locator, that's all. The signal does go farther across the water. Until the battery dies, I suppose it would reach a thousand or more yards in any direction."

Tanner frowned. "It must have been a backup to the transmitter somebody stuck on the hull of *Passions Messenger*." He looked at Gordon Aalberg. "Didn't you tell me you've done a lot of photography over the years here?"

"Sure. What's your point?"

"We've all switched to digital, but I was wondering if you have any plastic film canisters lying around?"

"I use them to keep track of buttons and odds and ends, so there'll be some in the drawers below."

Gordon looked thoughtful and said to Tanner, "look in the drawer below the sink and see what you find."

A few minutes later he reappeared holding a small plastic film roll canister often used to hold a single roll of 35mm film. In his other hand was a small fabric zippered pouch that was surprisingly heavy when he handed it to Agent Martin.

"Lead-lined?" she said, hefting the pouch in one hand.

"Yes. Photographers used to carry film in these to thwart scanners at airports that sometimes fogged their film, but with the increased security, it's become a hassle. Converting to digital photography removes the problem. I noticed this pouch when I was pawing through the drawer. It will at least reduce the signal range and with luck, block it altogether."

Hilda smiled at Tanner and dropped the tiny wafer into the bag. Tanner zipped it closed and folded it into a small parcel he then stowed in a port-side cubby-hole next to the wheel. Then he turned and stared out at the dark water. "Look. We don't know when it was planted," he said, "and we're sure that Barnes and his crew have left the island, probably for good, right?" He looked at Hilda, who nodded vigorously. "I say we just forget about it for tonight and tomorrow."

"Me too," drawled Mary. "I'm for ignoring that bug and continuing with our drinks and in a minute Gordon and I will serve up some serious dessert."

Mary smiled her approval at Tanner's tall glass of club soda as she went below.

Tanner realized the others had caught the look. "Before I met Mary I was married to a lovely woman who was murdered because we were sailing in the wrong place at the wrong time. She was my college sweetheart. I drank a good deal more in those days and a few people insisted the murder wouldn't have happened if I'd been more careful." He stopped and took a sip.

From below Mary's voice floated up the hatch. "They were wrong and he proved it."

"Were you sort of a swashbuckler back then?" Hilda's voice carried an amused lilt.

Tanner looked askance at her comment, then he smiled. "No, in fact, I was president of the Young Republicans on campus. I've never thought of myself as piratical. Swashbuckling? Nope, don't think so." He sighed. "Smugglers ran us down, sank the boat and Ann died. I tried to get the authorities to listen but I didn't get to first base." His voice turned bitter.

"I didn't think they investigated adequately and there was that suggestion I was personally responsible, that maybe I covered up a sloppy or dangerous circumstance. Well, I wasn't when it happened, but after, I became a drunk, or something close to it. Fortunately I got help from friends and partners before I totally disintegrated." He sighed, remembering.

"The whole thing left a bad taste and I guess my total trust in government agencies up to then eroded. Eventually I quit drinking and solved the case on my own. With substantial help from another quarter." Tanner smiled in the gloom and his voice turned lighter. "Along the way I met this smart, gorgeous and enormously talented woman, the one rattling around in the galley there, and we fell in love. And here we are. "

Hilda rose to her feet. "It's sure obvious the love she has for you, bub. I'm going to see what I can do to help." She pressed Tanner's shoulder and slipped below.

Serving sounds and the murmur of feminine voices floated up from below deck. Tanner let his eyes roam randomly around the cove where they were anchored. Only two other boats had joined them, both big luxurious-appearing ocean-going sailing vessels. They were in the outer section of the bay. The nearest appeared intent on maintaining a party mode. Two tenders were tethered in the water toward the stern and the sounds of music and shouts of laughter wafted faintly to *Island Gull*. He decided he was glad they hadn't anchored any closer.

The other boat appeared at a distance to be buttoned up and silent. No lights showed. Aalborg went below. Tanner noted that although it was now full dark with the sun a mere memory at the horizon, that boat had no masthead light to show it was at anchor. Thus reminded, he glanced aloft and discovered that their own anchor light was not yet illuminated. He examined the switches and labels. Not finding what he needed he called down the hatch.

"Ahoy, below. Would one of you step over to the nav station and switch on the masthead anchor light?"

"Aye, aye," came a lilting voice from below.

A moment later the masthead light flickered on. Gazing up, Tanner realized that there was thickening mist in the air. The two other boats at anchor were becoming indistinct and the faint glow of light from Road Town had disappeared altogether. "It's getting thick out here. Let's eat in the saloon." He stepped into the hatch and then stopped.

A faint rumble that grew in volume came to his ears. There was a powerful diesel engine nearby and it was approaching. Tanner hoped the operators were cautious if they came into the bay. He and Mary had seen hotdoggers get into trouble in low visibility situations. Unfortunately, that sometimes involved damage to other people's boats. The rumbling engine drew steadily nearer and then faded. Tanner dismissed the sound and headed below.

* * *

At two o'clock in the morning, a rare sea-born fog had settled in, blanketing the bay where *Island Gull* was anchored. Mary wasn't sure what had disturbed her. Tanner was sprawled half on his back beside her on the big bed in the owner's cabin. He snuffled quietly, somewhere between a gentle snore and loud breathing. There was no sound at all from the next cabin where Hilda Martin was presumably soundly asleep. She'd hardly made it through dessert, eyes drooping. Finally she admitted she was wiped out and disappeared to her cabin. Gordon and Clarice had gone to the captain's cabin a few minutes later and it had been quiet ever since.

So what had awakened her?

Mary lay on her back and listened to the silence, to blood pulsing in her ears, and stared up at the unseen overhead. There it was. An infinitesimal change in the rhythm of the boat. All boats lying at anchor are prey to wind and water, even in what appear to be dead calm conditions. An experienced sailor like Mary became attuned to the rhythms of any boat even though she had been aboard this one for only a few hours. Now she felt something different, alien, a subtle change of the conditions. Tanner snuffled again and rolled over. She smiled and reached out a hand to caress his hip. Little short of a loud bang would disturb her husband, who always slept soundly.

Sitting up, she slid her feet into her deck shoes and pulled on the long light-weight robe she'd found at a local shop. Quietly she eased open the door to their cabin and stole like a wraith into the saloon. The thick tropical night seemed undisturbed and she saw nothing through the windows of the saloon. Then there was the tiniest sound, a movement on the cabin roof above her head. The boat shifted again. Mary stopped, listening hard.

She realized instantly that whoever was on deck over her head was an intruder, not a drunk or someone boarding the wrong boat in the dark. Whoever was up there was sneaking about, trying to be as quiet as possible. She peered up through the main hatch. Against the dark sky she could just make out fingers picking at the edge of the screen.

"Michael! Hilda! Gordon! Boarders!" She shouted and then screamed at the top of her lungs, a long wordless rising scream that could have been mistaken for panicked fear. Mary grabbed for the knife rack and her fingers grasped the haft of the long razor-sharp chef's carving knife. When she yanked it from its scabbard, it made an evil whispering screech as if it were already searching for a warm target.

With the knife outthrust in front of her, Mary yelled again for her companions and lunged upward for the screen hatch cover. The blade slid through the screen like it was hardly there. Awakened by her screams, Tanner yelled a guttural response and banged out of the cabin behind

her. He almost collided with Gordon and Clarice, who burst simultaneously from their bed, throwing clothes over their nakedness.

There were startled yells from the foredeck as Mary erupted into
the cockpit. She screamed another challenge to the strangers on the deck
and whirled, slashed wildly at a dark figure crouched on the cabin roof
above the after hatch. It was no time for a verbal challenge. Whoever
they were, these were intruders, bent on evil. The figure cried out in pain
and fell back under Mary's determined onslaught.

Tanner appeared behind Mary in the cockpit with a boat hook in his
hands. He slipped to the starboard side and started cautiously forward,
seeking a target. Suddenly work lights, high in the spreader overhead,
bloomed. Light cascaded through the mists to reveal a frozen tableau of
four men grouped at the very bow. The man nearest the hatch clutched
his bleeding arm to his chest. The kitchen knife had ripped through his
sleeve and left a long bloody gouge in his arm. The other four, two waving machetes, started forward.

Suddenly, Hilda Martin appeared in the center of the cockpit, wearing a long Grateful Dead tee-shirt. She looked as calm as Mary and Tanner seemed frantic. Hilda faced the intruders and said in a commanding
voice, "Stop! I'm armed and I'm an excellent shot." She raised both
hands to shoulder height, revealing the black handgun in her grasp. She
stared down the strangers and carefully aimed the weapon at a spot between the men crouching on the foredeck.

They gave way instantly, aborting their advance and abandoning
ship. Four splashes as the men, including the wounded thug, went over
the side, were almost simultaneous. Allborg knelt at the rail, watching
and then flattened himself on the deck. "Kill those lights," he snapped.

Mary roused herself from staring at the blood drying on the blade of
the knife she still clutched. The knife dropped to the deck with a metallic
clatter. "Michael?" She called.

"I'm okay. "Kill the lights!"

Hilda Martin glanced at Mary and let out a long breath. Clarice
slipped below then and switched off the overhead work lights, plung-

ing the deck into the blackness of the moonless night. She clicked on a few low-powered red lights in the cabin and sank, shaking, into a seat. Minutes later, Tanner joined the others in the cabin. He was carrying the bloody carving knife which he set in the sink.

"They've gone," he said, studying Mary closely. "I tracked them quite a distance. After I cut loose the rubber dinghy they arrived on and shoved it away, it sounded like at least one or two of them found the boat and paddled away. Maybe the others drowned."

Mary's tremors ceased and she looked at Hilda. "I thought you said you left that in your safe."

"I lied," shrugged Hilda. "I almost never leave home without it."

"You were great. Saved our bacon," Mary said. "Are you really an expert marksman with that gun?"

"Pistol," Hilda murmured. "It's a nine millimeter Beretta. Not a gun." She looked down at her hands. "I qualified. We have to do that every year," not really answering the question.

"Awesome," murmured Mary.

35

Tanner stared at Mary for long seconds. "How are you doing?" he reached out and took her hands.

She grimaced and shook her head. "Honestly, I don't know. I never sliced anybody with a knife before." They lapsed into silence.

"I never shot anybody, either," Hilda murmured in a barely audible voice. "I never even shot at anybody. Just targets on the range." She roused herself then and scrabbled in the reefer for something to drink.

"They gave up pretty fast," said Tanner.

"Did you see the looks on their faces?" Gordon shook his head.

"I think that we're pretty lucky to be here on this boat with two such brave women," said Clarice. She and Gordon were sitting side by side, holding hands. "You guys were great."

"Armed, aggressive resistance caught them completely by surprise," Gordon resumed. "I don't think they were prepared for us. I bet they hoped to quietly butcher us and then steal whatever they could find, and slip away, no one the wiser for days. I didn't see any guns, except Hilda's."

"How did you know they were there?" asked Hilda.

"When I woke up, the movement of the boat just didn't feel right," Mary replied. "Then I realized whoever was up there wasn't in the cockpit, they were way forward. Who boards a boat from the bow? If you were just trying to get back aboard and down into bed, you'd stand in the cockpit to open the main hatch, right? There was just no chance this was a mistake, so I reacted."

"Now we'd better figure out how to protect ourselves for the next few hours until daylight," said Clarice.

"That's no problem," Mary responded. "I'm so jazzed I feel like it'll be a week before I come down enough to sleep." Hilda nodded her agreement. "So you grab some shut-eye if you can manage it. Hilda and I will take the first watch. But shouldn't we radio the law? Call the Coast Guard or something?"

"I'd prefer we not do that, if it's all right with you," said Hilda. "I recognized two of those brutes who came aboard. One was Gonzo Barnes, ex-captain of *Maid Marian*. The other was a guy I've seen at the Road Town Police Department. He's a jail attendant or something. He's one of the people we suspect of being involved with the smuggling ring."

"I thought you said Barnes and his gang were gone," said Tanner.

Hilda sighed, "I know. I'm sorry. I never would have suggested this excursion if we'd had any idea they were still around."

"I know. Sorry I snapped at you." Tanner sagged back onto the cushion.

"Cell phone," said Mary, getting up.

"I deliberately didn't bring mine," Hilda said, "and I think yours are not plugged in." Mary returned from their cabin holding out the dead instruments.

"Don't have ours with us," said Clarice in a tremulous voice.

Tanner turned his head and stared at Hilda. "Seems to me you have been watching half the population of the island," he said. "I think you owe us some explanation, yes?"

Hilda nodded. "You're right. The other side apparently believes you've known all along the whereabouts of the bale of money we recovered. I guess they don't know yet we located the crates and they think you have it or have moved it somewhere."

"That's preposterous," said Mary. "How could we have moved that container?"

"I know, I know. But people like that make strange assumptions. They moved it in, so they assume if you came here to hijack their goods, you're equipped to handle it. "Incidentally, there may be several more containers like the one we saw being retrieved.

"We believe that as soon as you reported finding the money and then your contact with McGwean, the smugglers assumed that it was an elaborate ploy to keep us from discovering that you two had stolen the cargo of counterfeit bills." Hilda blew out her breath.

Allborg grunted and said, "so that's what this has been about. It's been pretty much an open secret that the smuggling involved a few people in authority."

"We still aren't sure how far the corruption goes inside the police department. And elsewhere. If we make a radio call, we risk alerting the rest of the gang. They'll disappear or worse, come looking for us."

"As long as we're serving up confessions, I have some suspicions you might want to hear about." Tanner jumped to his feet and grabbed the big flashlight. He went up the companion ladder and made a circuit of the boat to be sure none of their adversaries had returned.

"I wondered about you," he said to Hilda, when he returned to the cabin. "Your prompt appearance on the scene after we went to the police and I was kidnapped seemed mighty convenient. Who else do you have on your list of suspects?"

"My being in the bank was sheer coincidence," Hilda's smile flickered. "We had just decided to talk to you and I saw you leaving the police department. You know about our suspicions regarding the local law. We're sure there are a number of civilians involved. Some of them work for the city. Others seem to have jobs with private companies that have interests around the island. It appears to be a pretty widespread network.

"Most of the island government is clean, of course." Hilda went on to name the individuals they were prepared to request arrest warrants for from British authorities.

When she finished, Tanner said, "There's a name missing." He glanced at Mary. "I'm prepared to bet that Lieutenant Archambault is in this up to his neck."

"Archambault?" said Gordon Allborg. "Are you sure?"

Mary nodded her head. "We had a meeting with that detective, Smythe. I just forgot to tell you. He told us they're looking for Archambault." She picked up the flashlight. "Our contacts with the lieutenant have been odd at times. He seemed to vacillate between intense interest and total lack of concern."

"That's right," Tanner chimed in. "Remember that encounter at the Prince William restaurant in Spanish Town?" He turned to Gordon and Clarice, "The lieutenant spotted us across the dining room and dragged his wife to our table to give us an emphatic message to see him the next morning in his office."

"And then, when we went in, it didn't amount to much at all." Mary turned around and flipped on the radio receiver in the nav station that was tuned to the general calling frequency used all over the islands to reach boaters when messages for them were received. Weather radio bulletins and other news were also broadcast on the same frequency. For a few moments there was only silence. Then the announcer read a weather bulletin that predicted fog but calm conditions for several hours.

"*Island Gull. Island Gull.* Please come in. Over." The voice was stern, authoritative and Clarice instinctively reached for the microphone.

"Wait!" said Hilda. "I don't know who that is but it's not the authorities. Not the Coast Guard. Not any of my people. The Coast Guard and my people all know where we are. They'd identify themselves if there was a need to reach us." The call was broadcast two more times while they listened amid growing concern.

Tanner pulled out a large-scale chart of the island and their anchorage and said, "Dark or not, I'm for getting out of here. Are you sure we can't leave now?" We can sail up the channel until it's light enough to see. A moving target will be harder to corral. Let's do it now and let's be quiet about it."

Clarice looked out a nearby porthole and shook her head." We can't risk it for at least another hour. And with the fog it could be even longer."

* * *

At four-thirty in the gray early morning, Mary climbed the ladder to the deck and unlashed the wheel. Gordon came topside and said, "Turn her around so we're right over the anchor pointing the way out."

Mary nodded. Tanner appeared in the cockpit beside her and place a reassuring hand on Mary's shoulder. Below, Clarice switched on the night-vision illumination and doused the regular lights in the cabin and over the navigation desk. The sky overhead was lighter with the coming dawn. Residual fog hung about the mast.

"Go forward with Gordon, Hilda. When you are ready just point the flash at the deck and blink it twice. If you have to stop for any reason give me a single dash."

"Got it," Hilda whispered.

"But always be sure you have a secure handhold once the anchor is out of the ground."

Hilda nodded and she and Aalborg scuttled forward to the bow.

From the middle distance, somewhere outside the entrance to the bay, the soft sound of a slow-running marine engine came to their listening ears.

"Good," murmured Tanner, shortening the painter to the dinghy. That engine will cover the sound of ours."

Mary grimaced unseen in the gloom. "Raise the main," she said quietly. Tanner cranked the windlass that hauled the bloused mainsail up the mast. At the halfway point she saw the double flash of white light from the forward deck that told her Gordon was retrieving the anchor. A moment later, a single flash sent a tiny clutch to her stomach. She waited. After what seems a long time a quick double flash came. Mary waited for several counts. Memory of the water depth told her just about when the anchor should break water. Tanner hauled on the mainsail halyard again and got a brief whistle which was Gordon's signal the anchor was aboard.

Watching her two companions at the bow, she saw Gordon take his big flashlight and lie down to hang out over the bow for the best position from which to scope out the dangerous coral that lay in their path.

36

Their slow tortuous path through the bay to reach open water had been excruciating. Once they'd brushed against a coral head that produced an awful scraping, rumbling sound. Mary, still at the wheel of *Island Gull* played with the throttle and eased the big sailboat back and forth through the narrow channel. Once beyond the embrace of the bay itself, the wind picked up and the boat gathered a little speed. The five gathered and held a brief tense conference in the cockpit

"We're almost out of the reef," said Clarice.

"We have to assume those guys will be back before too long," Allborg said.

With no running lights, lookouts were needed.

"You need to keep your eyes peeled for anything that looks like a boat or a rock or whatever," Mary admonished. "If you spot something tell me immediately."

"Try not to look right at it," Allborg said. "For some reason, you can see more detail if you stare to one side."

Mary positioned Tanner at midships on the starboard side with a pair of Navy-issue night glasses he'd found in the cabin. Clarice stood on the cushions of the port side cockpit staring anxiously into the gray night. Since Hilda had no experience at night sailing, Mary kept her close in the cockpit beside her on the other side. Twice Mary offered to turn the big wheel over to Allborg. Both times he declined. "You've got more experience at night sailing that we have," he said. "I'm comfortable with you at the helm."

Without the jib up, after she shut down the engine, their path through the dark water was sedate, but still filled with potential danger.

She swung the wheel to turn the boat across the channel and slightly downwind. It gave them stability and a quiet ride. There was nothing they could do to camouflage the bright blue hull and the white sail. For long moments no one spoke. It was as if their escape from the embrace of Peter Island had exhausted them.

An hour passed without incident. Dawn came. They began to relax, tuning in to the rhythms of the sea and the sailboat. Mary told them her plan. "You all need to know what I think. As long as I have the wheel, I believe it's risky to head straight for Road Town, but going there directly will take the least time to reach safety. I think we should turn now and head to Road Town. It's going on six, going to be full light in minutes, We'll have no trouble navigating into the harbor. There's been no sign of any other boat out here. No apparent pursuit. If they were watching for us, we must have given them the slip. I hope. We've been heading southeast since we left Peter Island. I want to head back, sail between Salt and Peter, keeping that rock off Peter on our port side. That will take us almost directly into the Road Town harbor." She looked to the owners for their reaction.

"Sounds like an excellent plan," agreed Allborg. Tanner nodded and gave Mary a thumbs up. Clarice turned immediately to the jib halyards and they shook out the sail.

The eastern sky was bright as they sailed back toward Tortola. As they neared the western side of Salt, the boom of roaring engines reached their ears. Light from a powerful searchlight on a long low cigarette boat slashed across the water and pinned them in its glare.

"That's not the Coast Guard," shouted Tanner.

Mary hauled the wheel over to run before the wind. As the power launch closed the distance, she looked at Peter Island dead ahead and made a lightning-fast decision.

"Hang on!" she cried. She cranked the wheel sharply to starboard and the sloop responded, swinging about, almost in its own length. With a shudder and a pop the main sail and boom slashed across the beam and they tore back, directly into the path of the oncoming power boat. A collision seemed imminent. This was apparently not something Gonzo Barnes and his crew had anticipated. At the last desperate second, the powerboat driver twitched the wheel, skidding to one side in the turbulent water, and narrowly avoiding the larger sailboat. The bow wave of the sloop crashed across the low coaming of the launch and poured over the four men visible in the cockpit. Shots rang out. The power boat turned about in a wide roaring circle to give chase. By now, *Island Gull* was back at full speed and slashing across the waves. Mary zigged to starboard and when the powerboat tried to follow, she turned hard to port as the launch came alongside, ramming the hull of the sailboat against the other craft, sending it lurching through the water. The man at the wheel fought to maintain his balance and control.

"Where's Hilda?" cried Tanner stumbling into the cockpit from his post at the mast.

"Dunno," said Mary, hauling the boat around one more time. "I think she went below."

Again, the power boat slammed alongside, this time from the stern and a man jumped, getting his hands around the safety rail that ran the perimeter of the boat. The stanchion bent outward from his weight. There was a shot, then another, and Mary glanced across the gap to see the windscreen on the powerboat shatter into pieces and disappear. A third shot and the man they recognized as Gonzo Barnes, screamed and threw up his hands, falling backward over the driver. With a lurch that dragged the man clinging to the rail off and into the sea, the powerboat executed a sharp uncontrolled left hand turn, almost swamping. Without slackening speed it sped off into the gathering waves. As long as they could see it, no one appeared to be at the controls.

Hilda Martin, her face set in grim lines, still clutching her pistol, climbed out of the forward hatch and crabbed her way aft to the cockpit.

Mary gave her a quick grin and a thumbs up. Tanner found a blanket and threw it around the agent's shoulders. Hilda laid the weapon in her lap and bowed her head for a long time as the sailboat returned to its original course, headed for Tortola and Road Town and safety.

* * *

Detective Emmett Smythe of the Road Town Police Force was waiting on the dock when they slid into their assigned slip. Gordon Allborg and Clarice, handled the mooring lines and were the first to reach the waiting detective. Smythe looked angry then upset and then seemed to calm down.

Mary skipped off the boat and went immediately to Clarice Allborg. "I am so so sorry about what happened out there. I'd never forgive myself if either of you was injured." She turned to Gordon, "you've got a really nimble boat there. She saved our behinds."

Clarice Allborg put her arms around Mary and held her close. "It's all right, my dear. We are just so happy we all made it back uninjured. That we're all safe. The boat is repairable."

"I cannot express how relieved I am to see you safe, and back in port," said the detective. "We learned only an hour ago that a crew member of Barnes had been seen in town. We tried to radio you but there was no response."

Mary nodded. "We were probably a little busy right then."

Emmett Smythe raised one hand saying, "I am sorry, Mrs. Tanner, but I do need all of you to make a report for me while the incident is still fresh in your minds. Please accompany me to the station." He was polite but firm.

Tanner and Mary sat on one side of the conference table with Hilda Martin. The Allborgs, interviewed separately, had gone back to their boat. Detective Emmett Smythe and a dour young man who was not introduced sat across from the trio. Smythe had an untidy file of papers in front of him. During the interview, which he recorded, he occasionally shuffled through the papers or made a note.

Tanner concluded, "then we sailed back and here we are."

Smythe looked keenly at Agent Martin and said, "I take it you have never shot anybody before?"

She nodded wordlessly.

"I can recommend a very good psychologist here in Road Town if you feel the need for some conversation."

"Thank you," she whispered.

"We are quite sure the tracking device on your charter was planted by one of Barnes' men. In fact, we believe we have the man himself and some of his illegal supplies. Apparently the tracking devices were to be used on the crates of money if they had to be jettisoned. Your surmises are quite correct, these people believed that you had somehow arranged to have the crates of cash secretly moved and were here in Road Town to arrange transshipment out of the islands. Thieves often think the worst of everybody they encounter. They simply could not accept that you were just innocent bystanders, at least in the beginning. Barnes was the man who went aboard your boat at the Bitter End to steal back the hundreds. One of the gang has confessed to seeing Mr. McGwean killed." He smiled bitterly. "Ian was a casual friend, given lately to too much drink, I am afraid. I already miss our occasional conversations.

"As to the button tracking device, we are quite well aware of the man who probably planted it on you, Mr. Tanner. Proving his involvement is another matter entirely. I hope you will not press the matter." This to Hilda Martin.

"Mr. and Mrs. Tanner, I am most sorry that your vacation has been so thoroughly disrupted and on behalf of all of us who live and work here in the British Virgin Islands, I hope you will come back one day. We have made arrangements to see you safely to Charlotte Amalie for your flight home."

Everybody stood and while Agent Hilda Martin left the interview room, Mary extended a hand to the detective. "Tell us about the search for Lieutenant Archambault and about the murder of Homer Jensen."

There was a moment's hesitation by Detective Smythe as he took her hand in his. He glanced at his silent companion and said softly, "We have not yet located the lieutenant or his wife. The untimely death of Mr. Jensen is being actively investigated. More I cannot say. I'm sure you understand."

After their interviews with the police, Mary, Tanner and Hilda Martin said goodby to *Island Gull* and to her owners, Clarice and Gordon Allborg. The three of them waited on the veranda of the hotel until it was time to take the water taxi to Charlotte Amalie.

"I can't tell you how much I appreciate all you've done for us, Hilda," said Tanner. He leaned forward so nearby vacationers wouldn't overhear. "This wasn't exactly what we'd hoped for on our first ever sailing trip to the British Virgins, but it's been...interesting."

Hilda nodded solemnly, still quiet after the violent and deadly confrontation they'd experienced on the Francis Drake channel.

"I wonder if they'll ever find Lieutenant Archambault and the rest of that crew," murmured Mary. Her concerned gaze stayed with Hilda Martin.

"I had a call while you were wrapping things up with the detective," she said. "Coast Guard found the launch adrift. One man was still aboard. He had a broken arm. The bodies of the others may turn up eventually." She sighed and pointed toward the city dock. "Here's the taxi."

The three walked silently to the dock where Mary turned and embraced Hilda. "When I saw Barnes standing beside the driver, a man I've recently talked to, I almost didn't pull the trigger," Hilda whispered.

"I'm sorry you had to do it," Mary responded. "But I'm glad you did."

"Safe journey," Hilda said. She released Mary and leaned to give Tanner a kiss on the cheek. Aboard the taxi, Tanner and Mary sat with their arms around each other and waved goodbye.

"I like Agent Martin," said Tanner. "Maybe she'll still be here the next time we come for a vacation."

"Maybe," smiled Mary.

A few hours later, Mary Whitney and Michael Tanner boarded an

American Airlines jetliner for Atlanta and home. Their seats were on the left side of the airplane heading north to the mainland. Mary leaned past Tanner to stare through the window at the brilliant sunset that stretched as far across the horizon as she could see.

"Look at that sunset, will you," she whispered, "that flaming red sky."

OTHER WORKS BY CARL BROOKINS

Short Stories
"Night Sail," *The Pinehurst Journal*, 1992.
"A Winter's Tale," *Silence of The Loons*, 2005.
"Hard Cheese," e-book, 2005.
"A Winter's Tale," e-book, 2005.
"A Fish Story," *Resort to Murder*, 2007.
"Daddy's Little Girl," 2011.
"The Day I Lost My Innocence," 2011.
"The Horse He Rode In On," *Fifteen Tales of Murder, Mayhem, and Malice: from the Land of Minnesota Nice*, 2012.

Novels

THE SAILING MYSTERY SERIES

Inner Passages, Top Publications, 2000.
A Superior Mystery, Top Publications, 2002.
Old Silver, Top Publications, 2005.
Devils Island, Echelon Publications, 2010.
Red Sky, e-Book, Brookins Books, 2011.

THE DETECTIVE SERIES

The Case of the Yellow Diamond, North Star Press of Saint Cloud, Mn, 2015.
The Case of the Deceiving Don, Five Star Mysteries Press, 2008.
The Case of the Greedy Lawyers, Nodin Press, 2008.
The Case of the Great Train Robbery, Brookins Books, 2011.
The Case of the Missing Case, e-Book, Brookins Books, 2012.
The Case of the Purloined Painting, North Star Press of Saint Cloud, 2013.

THE ACADEMIC SERIES

Bloody Halls, Echelon Press, 2008.
Reunion, Echelon Press, 2011.

www.ingramcontent.com/pod-product-compliance
Lightning Source LLC
Chambersburg PA
CBHW070925180626
46817CB00003B/1191